Drag Strip

Also by Nancy Bartholomew

The Miracle Strip

Drag Strip

— Nancy Bartholomew —

ST. MARTIN'S
MINOTAUR

NEW YORK

Library of Congress Cataloging-in-Publication Data

Bartholomew, Nancy.
    Drag Strip / Nancy Bartholomew. — 1st ed.
        p.   cm.
    ISBN 0-312-20295-4
    I. Title.
PS3552.A7645D72   1999
813'.54—dc21   99-22205
                                                    CIP

First Edition: October 1999
10 9 8 7 6 5 4 3 2 1

Always, for Adam, Ben, and John—
where would I be without your love?

and

For Chi-Chi—my beloved aunt and mentor,
my safe harbor.

Acknowledgments

My heartfelt thanks goes out to my editor, Kelley Ragland. I am fortunate indeed to have such a dedicated and talented force in my corner. I would be remiss if I failed to mention the extraordinary efforts of my hardworking publicists: Naomi Mendelsohn and Katie Monaghan. They came through for me time after time.

I would like to acknowledge the invaluable assistance of my critique group: Nancy Gates, Wendy Greene, Chris Farran, Charlotte Perkins, Ellen Hunter, Diane L. Berry, and Rene Gilleo.

Thanks to the members of the Panama City Police Department, in particular Sergeant Joe E. Hall. Thanks also to Corporal Stan Lawhorne of the Greensboro Police Department for spending countless hours driving me around southeast Greensboro, explaining police procedure. My thanks also to Clay Harvey, author and noted gun expert, for his support and advice in both areas.

This book was researched and written with support from the Central Piedmont Regional Artists Hub and the North Carolina Arts Council.

I would be lost without the support I have found from the mystery reading and writing community. Sisters in Crime, the

Atlanta chapter, gave me my start. Mystery Writers of America, in particular the South Florida chapter, pushed me further along. There are so many, many wonderful writers out there always willing to help out a fellow author and to lend a hand whenever possible.

Then there are those wonderful independent bookstore owners who held signings, fed me, encouraged me, and endorsed my efforts to their customers. Thank you!

I am forever indebted to my loyal family of first readers: Suzi and Larry, Nancy and Jeff, Mom, Betsy, Chuck and Edie.

I am a working mother, as all mothers are, and I would never have finished this book without the caring support of my friends. For all the moms who took my boys for an afternoon, or said, "You go, girl," I am eternally grateful. My very best friend from childhood, Betsy, called all of our old friends and organized a reunion, reminding me that she'd always known I would one day write a book. Thanks for believing in me; you don't know how much I value your friendship.

Last, but never least, I thank my family. My parents were always there in a pinch, promoting and publicizing when they weren't rescuing us all. My husband listened to each word, every day, as it was written. My boys ate noodles, wore wrinkled clothes at best, and were late for almost everything except soccer. The house remains a shambles. The dog is still untrained. But we are all together, dirty and happy, piled up on my bed eating Chinese takeout from little white cardboard containers. Thank you for enabling me to chase my dream.

Drag Strip

One

John Nailor and Vincent Gambuzzo are trying to drive me crazy. If they were working together on this project, I'm sure I'd be in a straitjacket somewhere, gulping down Prozac cocktails. As it is, I'm still one up on both of them, but they're gaining on me.

John Nailor is a detective with the Panama City Police Department, and up until he kissed this little brown-headed woman, I thought he was pretty interested in me. It wasn't like we were dating. We had shared an encounter of a personal and dangerous nature and I thought that in the near future we would evolve into something a bit more horizontal. But when he looked over at me before he kissed her, I knew I'd gotten it all wrong.

I guess he's not really my type anyway. He's too clean-cut. His hair is straight and brown, and he wears suits, with crisp oxford-cloth shirts and ties. He's not even quite as tall as me when I wear my five-inch stilettos, but still, there's something about him that makes me forget that I prefer a biker with a panhead Harley. Maybe it's his eyes. When I stare at him, he never backs down. That is, until he kissed that woman right in front of me. He looked away then.

Vincent Gambuzzo, on the other hand, drives me crazy for an entirely different reason. He's my boss. He figures it's his job to make my life a living hell. The Tiffany, where I work, is his little kingdom. He figures if he micromanages his exotic dancers, especially me, his headliner, then his club will one day be as well-known as the Gold Club in Atlanta. I say what Vincent knows about managing talent could be stuck on the head of a pin and you'd still have room left over.

Take, for example, tonight. I'm out on the runway doing my tribute to Dorothy and *The Wizard of Oz* when Vincent comes barreling right down front with some young guy in a black satin jacket. Vincent can never do anything small. He weighs about three hundred pounds, all of which he squeezes into a black suit and black silk collarless shirt. He talks loud and he wears black wraparound sunglasses 24/7, even with it dark as ink in the club.

"Hey, Rita," he shouts, "bring Mr. Rhodes here a gin and tonic. And bring me my usual."

Did he not have any respect for a working artist? Judy Garland is crooning "Somewhere Over the Rainbow," I'm reaching behind my back to undo my red sequin bra, and guys are down front panting. He completely blew the moment.

Vincent didn't even notice. He was too busy arranging for Mr. Big Shot's comfort. For somebody who's always intimating that he's mob connected and therefore fearless, he sure was kissing up to this Mr. Rhodes. It was sickening, but then, I know Vincent is no more connected to the mob than my third-grade teacher, Sister Mary Rose. So he needs all the big-shot connections he can get. Of course, that still doesn't justify why he saw fit to drag me into the whole thing. If Vincent Gambuzzo hadn't dragged me into his little plan for Mickey Rhodes and the Dead Lakes Motor Speedway, then I wouldn't have seen John Nailor kissing that bimbo and I certainly wouldn't have gotten myself in such big-time trouble.

Vincent waited until I was down to my pasties and my red sequin shoes to point me out to his visitor. He leaned across the table and bellowed: "Now you'll want her for sure. That's what you get when you use the Tiffany talent."

I'm thinking whatever scheme Vincent Gambuzzo is trying to promote, Sierra Lavotini will avoid like the black plague. I don't do lap dances and I don't have nothing but a hands-off relationship with the clientele. Vincent had to be out of his mind, and the dirty look I shot him told him so.

Vincent laughed. "She's a feisty one, that Sierra, but she draws a crowd."

I'm thinking to have a little talk with Gambuzzo after his friend leaves, maybe remind him that Sierra Lavotini is perhaps connected to the "Big Moose" Lavotini syndicate out of Cape May, New Jersey. That usually kept Vincent in his place. He didn't need to find out that I was in no way related to Mr. Moose.

When I clicked my heels three times for the finale and started saying "There's no place like home" to my crowd of admirers, Vincent started talking again. I'm sure he ruined my tips by a good fifty percent.

"Sure," he was saying. "Pick any two girls you want. I'll have them up to the Speedway for opening night. It's no problem."

I snapped my garter, trying to get Vincent's attention, but he ignored me. If he thought I was going up to some racetrack and stand around while greasy-fingered motorheads rubbed their hands all over my ass, well, he was mistaken.

Of course, if the money was right, I might consider it.

Two

*R*uby Diamond was born to strip. I knew it from the moment she walked into the Tiffany. You can tell a natural at a glance. It's the way she moves. Ruby's walk was a caress. She was comfortable with herself and vulnerable, all at once. When she got up on stage to audition, the men in the club stopped to watch, and not because her figure was outstanding, which it was. They stopped because something in them reached out to her.

Ruby walked out on stage and the music started, but she didn't move for a full thirty seconds. She just stood there, looking out like she was searching past the bright lights for something or someone. She stood there, biting her lower lip gently, wearing nothing but an FSU T-shirt and a bikini. She had long brown hair, coiled into a sleek French twist, and large liquid brown eyes. For one moment, every man in the place imagined that Ruby was a virgin and she was going to offer herself to only him.

They moved, like a herd, down to the front of the stage, their faces changing into soft, comforting older-but-wiser lovers. She seemed to look at each man, a smile playing softly across her face, and then she began to move. She held those men in the palm of her hand, and before she'd even lost her T-shirt, her garter was full of bills.

The men didn't whistle and call out like they do the ones who strip to get naked. They whispered encouragement. They smiled like newlywed husbands on their honeymoon night. They were entranced. Ruby, in her soft, open way, was seeming to give herself up to them, but I was watching her eyes and I knew the truth. Ruby was a pro, just like me. She was new and her act lacked refinement, but she was pro material nonetheless.

Later, after Vincent hired her, I gave her the backstage tour. That's when I got the scoop, just like I do with all the new girls.

"So what do you think?" I asked. I swept my arm around the locker room, including the long makeup bar with its wall-to-wall mirror and the rusty metal lockers.

Ruby was glowing. "It's great. Just great." In the light of the dressing room I could see she was no more than nineteen, about the age I was when I started.

"First job?" I asked.

She turned to me, her eyes gleaming with the knowledge she'd just conquered the room.

"Yeah," she breathed. "Yeah. But I won a wet T-shirt contest on the beach last month." As if that counted for something.

I knew the look. She'd just discovered that there was something she could do really well. She could make men want her, and for that, she could make a lot of money. I felt the same way my first time. Most of the time I still feel that way. There's nothing like standing at the edge of the runway, towering over a crowd of men, and realizing they're yours. You own them.

"I just moved here from Wewahitchka," she said abruptly. "I got my own place and everything, but my roommate, she took off on me. I didn't know how I was gonna make the rent. Then I saw the audition sign, and it was just like my psychic said: 'Don't turn down any opportunities; this is your lucky cycle.'"

6

Ruby was running on adrenaline now, driven to give me every detail of her short life.

"I don't know if I can really do this," she said honestly. "I mean, Mr. Gambuzzo said we were supposed to have themes and choreography and, well, I can dance and I took lessons from Miss Loraine at the Wewa Dance Studio, but this is different." Her voice slowed and she seemed overtaken by the enormity of her situation. She looked at me as if she were seeing me for the first time.

"What in the world am I gonna do?" she asked. Her legs seemed to give out under her and she sank into one of the chairs by the makeup bar. "Aw, man," she sighed.

"Ruby, get a grip," I said. "You're new. You're green. And you got talent. Without talent, technique ain't nothing but T-and-A working a pole. Vincent is a windbag, and nobody expects you to be a pro right off. You'll learn the moves from the rest of us. Pretty soon it'll come natural, from inside somewhere."

"Like when you know something but nobody ever taught you and so you start thinking you must've done it in a past life?"

No, I thought, nothing like that. "Past life?" I shrugged. "Whatever. Alls I know is, when I stepped onstage my first time, I felt just like you did. At first you're scared, but when you see their faces, and you see that money sliding into your garter, you get this rush that's better than anything you ever did before. That's when you know you're a dancer. If you don't fight it, it'll come and take you over. Then you're on a big stage making big bucks, and don't nobody own you. Not ever."

Ruby's eyes were silver dollars. "Yeah," she said, sighing, "that's it exactly. That's what I want."

From that moment on, Ruby attached herself to me like a young puppy. When I came to the club to practice, she was there. When she worked out her first routine, I helper her. A lot of the girls ignored her or, worse, snubbed her. But that's life when you work this business. There's a lot of jealousy. I figure it this way: If you can dance, if you've got it, can't nobody take it away, and can't nobody ruin your stuff. The no-talents will move on or be moved out, so there's no sense in sweating it if they take an attitude. It's the real dancers who look out for each other. We're a family of loners and outcasts. We have to stick together to survive.

Ruby was good, but she was young and inexperienced. What I knew took years to learn; not that I'm old, but twenty-eight is light-years ahead of nineteen. I could do the vulnerable virgin for days, but I could do Aphrodite's night of a thousand pleasures, too. You don't learn that stuff at nineteen.

When Mickey Rhodes picked Ruby Diamond to appear at the Dead Lakes Motor Speedway along with me, I couldn't have been happier. My protégée was going to make her first publicity appearance. She didn't know enough to realize how fast those things can get old.

"Why did he pick me?" she kept asking. "Why not Marla, or Yvonne? They're bigger acts than me." We were lying on the floor of my living room, exhausted from working on a new routine, when I decided to finally answer her.

"Ruby, Vincent and Mickey Rhodes are looking to do a business deal. The Tiffany sponsors the opening race and one of the drivers. In return for Vincent laying out a small amount of cash, the Tiffany gets a lot of publicity. You and me are just the pawns in this little game. It's not an honor or a privilege to get picked out by Mr. Rhodes. It is more or less a pain in the ass compounded by the fact that we ain't making enough extra jack for submitting ourselves to God knows what kind of physical and mental harassment by redneck racetrack fans."

There was a moment of silence while Ruby considered

this. Then she laughed. "Oh, go on," she said. "Sierra, don't you know nothing about racing? Mr. Gambuzzo is sponsoring Roy Dell Parks. I went to high school with his little brother. Roy Dell Parks is gonna be the next Richard Petty."

She was serious. I turned and looked out the bay window, biting the inside of my lip so I wouldn't laugh and hurt her feelings. Ruby Diamond actually thought some three-quarter-mile dirt track driver was a threat to the Indy 500. I didn't know anything about racing, but I sure as heck knew one thing: The big racers didn't come out of little bitty racetracks in North Florida.

Ruby rolled over and sat up, looking at me with her big brown eyes. I suddenly had the feeling we were on dangerous territory.

"Sierra, I grew up in Wewa. Those people out at the race-track, I went to school with them. A lot of them talked bad about me behind my back, and you know why?" Ruby wasn't waiting for an answer. "Because I was adopted out of foster care when I was three. That was the only reason. Well, that and because I used to make believe I was reincarnated."

"Reincarnated?"

"Yeah," she said, her tone a bit defensive. "Reincarnated. You know, like I had a past life as somebody else. Madame Jeanette thinks I was Mata Hari."

I was biting the inside of my lip hard now, and I would've laughed if my hairless chihuahua, Fluffy, hadn't picked that moment to come into the room and distract us. Fluffy skidded into the room, sliding to a halt on the wooden floor by Ruby's side. It was a credit to Ruby that Fluffy accepted and liked her. Fluffy doesn't like just anyone. In fact, I have considered myself such a bad judge of character, particularly men, that I usually subject them to the Fluffy Test. If Fluffy doesn't like you, I don't date you.

I'd only seen Fluffy make an error once; that was when she took to John Nailor right off. Even I could've told her that was a mistake. Of course, Fluffy didn't see John Nailor plant one on that bimbo at the Dead Lakes Motor Speedway.

Three

*M*ost folks consider Panama City to be a small town, despite its reputation as the Redneck Riviera. We get people flying in here all the time from L.A., but around here, that just means Lower Alabama. We are a village made famous by a strip of white sand beach and MTV. Most people drive right past the real town in their rush to stake a claim on the sugary sands, and that suits the locals just fine. Better the tourists should not know about the huge Victorians that line St. Andrews Bay. Better they should stay away from Uncle Ernie's or Joe's. Leave the good living to those of us who can appreciate it.

I don't think the people of Wewahitchka feel like that about their town. When your biggest local attraction is a three-quarter-mile dirt track, you've got problems from a Chamber of Commerce perspective. Having dancers from the big metropolis of Panama City was not their cup of tea either. I could tell we were unwanted right away. When I pulled up to the pit gate in my '88 black Camaro, there was a small crowd already waiting. Their signs read: NUDITY IS EVERYONE'S PROBLEM and GOD SO LOVED THE WORLD THAT HE CLOTHED ADAM AND EVE.

They were blue-hairs, mainly, who carried the placards, but there was a sprinkling of dark-haired, fresh-scrubbed Christian righters. The younger ones looked mean, in particular a man with a bull horn and black-rimmed glasses. I'd heard about protests, but usually they happened outside of clubs. Surely they didn't think Ruby and I were going to get naked here? Ruby sank down in the passenger seat as we approached the gate.

"Oh Gawd," she moaned softly, "that's Brother Everitt, from my mama's church."

I looked over at her. She sat slouched down in the seat, a scarf around her head and huge dark glasses covering the top half of her face.

"Didn't you figure this might happen?" I asked. I stared out the window at the tiny crowd of protesters. The women were wearing pastel polyester, their eyes focused rigidly in front of them, ignoring the cars backed up behind us in line, seemingly oblivious to the incredibly loud sound of engines being pushed to their limits.

"Well, I'd hoped not. I mean, Brother Everitt is bad to do stuff like this, but I just thought with the racetrack being technically outside the Wewa city limits, and closer to Panama City than anywhere, he wouldn't come." She sighed again, and her hand went nervously up to touch her hair. She was wearing a Dolly Parton blond wig.

"So that's why you wore a wig?"

A small grin played across her face. "Yep. Pretty slick, huh?"

No, not really, I thought. "Yeah, kid, slick," I answered. "Now put them idiots out of your head and get ready to work your ass off. These gigs aren't for your lightweight."

Ruby straightened up in her seat and took a deep, cleansing breath, just like I taught her.

"Feel your inner child," I said as we pulled into the pit entrance. "Be at peace with yourself." It might have worked had we not come face-to-face with Roy Dell Parks, the self-proclaimed King of Dirt.

I had gunned the accelerator of my Camaro and was just starting to cross the track to get to the pit area, when out of nowhere a dusty yellow Vega, vintage 1972, appeared, barreling across the straightaway, seemingly out of control.

"Sierra, look out!" Ruby screamed. "Oh Gawd, Roy Dell's spun out!"

There was no time to slam the Camaro into reverse. Instead I braced myself, anticipating the shuddering thud that would jar every bone in my body. At the last second before impact, I saw a wild-eyed man with a bushy red beard and hair frantically fighting to turn the wheel of his battered yellow Vega. It was no use. Roy Dell Parks careened off the front right side of my car, throwing us backward into the line of waiting vehicles.

For a moment I was too stunned to move. The impact had shaken me, but other than that, the only damage seemed to have affected my precious '88 Iroc Camaro. Once I realized that a piece-of-shit Vega had demolished the front right side of my car, I was out of the door, heading for Roy Dell Parks and vengeance.

Roy Dell had managed to extricate himself from his car, which to my amazement seemed to have suffered no damage, and was directing his pit crew and the others who'd raced onto the track to offer assistance.

He saw me coming and headed toward me, his hand outstretched as if to shake mine.

"Roy Dell Parks, ma'am," he said. "That Vega'll run like a scalded dog, won't she?"

That's when I decked him. I pulled my arm back as far as I could and sent it steaming forward, hoping to punch right through his solicitous face and into the middle of the track.

It was pure pleasure to connect with his big fat lips. Roy

Dell Parks was a bleeder. His mouth gushed blood, his eyes rolled up backward in his head, and ever so slowly he pitched forward as his knees buckled under him.

This brought about an instant reaction from his supporters. Half of them rushed to Roy Dell where he lay on the dirt track, and half just watched, trading looks of amazement for grins of admiration. I guess they didn't see many women punch men in their neighborhood. Where I come from in North Philly, growing up with four brothers, learning to deliver a punch was as much a way of life as going to Catholic school. I just happened to have paid more attention during the defense part of my education.

Ruby was standing by my side, her Dolly Parton wig slightly askew and her eyes wide.

"Good God Almighty," she said, "they're gonna kill us."

"Kill us?" I said. "Because some self-proclaimed king of racing hit my car?"

As if on cue, a scrawny man with thick muscled forearms and a wealth of tattoos stood up and headed in my direction. In the distance I could see two sheriff's deputies walking quickly toward us.

"What in the hell kind of thing to do was that?" the scrawny man asked. Others were falling in behind him, and the mood seemed to be heading toward a good old-fashioned lynching. Ruby jumped behind me, and I was thinking about how fast I could make it back to the car and grab my tire iron, when Roy Dell Parks rejoined the living.

"Now, Frank," he said weakly, "let me handle this. Can't you see the little lady was acting out of shock?" He chuckled as he stood up and swayed ever so slightly. "And a hell of a shock it must've been, too, if that punch was any judge."

Frank looked at me and snarled, just like Fluffy does when she disapproves of someone. Roy Dell walked slowly in between the two of us and once again stuck out his hand.

"Roy Dell Parks, ma'am, King of Dirt."

I looked at his outstretched hand for a second, then ignored it.

"Sierra Lavotini," I said, "the Queen of I Really Don't Give a Shit."

Roy Dell laughed, then winced and touched his lip.

"Don't be mad, ma'am," he said. "It really wasn't nothing I could control. One of my boys must've left a bolt off the steering column." He held up a hand as if to forestall any further comments from me. "I know, you're worried about your vehicle, but ma'am, honest, ain't nothing to it. Hell, the boys here'll take that car over to the pit and have it right as rain before the night's out."

Despite myself, I could feel my anger easing.

"Thanks, Roy Dell," Ruby said, taking over. "I know Sierra'd feel a lot better if you took care of her car. You know, Sierra's car means the world to her."

Roy Dell seemed to see Ruby for the first time. His eyes widened and he wiped his beefy hand on the front of his coveralls before extending it toward her.

"And who might you be, darlin'?"

Ruby blushed and placed her hand in his. "Ruby Lee Diamond," she murmured softly. "It sure is a pleasure to meet you."

I was gonna be sick. There was enough love juice and chemistry oozing out between the two of them to gag any self-respecting person. Roy Dell still hadn't let go of Ruby's hand, and she hadn't taken her eyes off of him. If Mickey Rhodes and his entourage hadn't joined us, accompanied by the sheriff's deputies, we might have stood there all night waiting for the blessed consummation of Roy Dell and Ruby's newfound romance.

"Ladies," said Mickey, "I am so sorry for this mishap." His pudgy little face was wrinkled with concern. "Of course, the track will absorb any cost incurred by Mr. Parks's negligence."

This snapped Roy Dell Parks back into the here and now. He whirled around to face the track owner, his face turning scarlet.

"Let's us just get one thing clear," he said, his voice dropping by two octaves and assuming a menace I hadn't thought possible. "This was an unavoidable accident. Weren't nothing to it but a loose bolt, and Miss Sierra and Miss Ruby know that. I'll be fixing this Camaro up better than new, and ain't none of your money needed."

Mickey puffed up like a rooster, and I was thinking that Roy Dell could fix my car for me, but there was no call to be turning down the track's money. After all, I could be the victim of delayed whiplash. One could never be too careful.

"Ouch," I moaned, grabbing the back of my neck.

"Sierra, what is it?" Ruby asked, rushing to my side. The little crowd had fallen silent, their total attention turned to me.

"Ow, I don't know," I said, massaging the back of my neck tenderly. "I just felt this sharp pain."

Mickey Rhodes's face paled as he smelled his liability burning. "Hey, Meatloaf, call them ambulance attendants over here. Looks like we might have a casualty."

A thick, tall man broke loose from the crowd and moved off at a trot toward the pit, and I stared off after him. From where we stood, at the top of the slanted dirt track, I could look down on the pit area and up over at the grandstands. Even though no cars were on the track, the sound coming from the pit where crews revved car engines was strong enough to feel as if it hit me square in the chest, pounding away like a bass drum.

"I'll be all right, I think," I said. Ruby hovered by my side, her wig now completely twisted.

"Miss Lavotini, I don't want to take any chances on you

being injured," Mickey said. "We'll get you checked out and your car towed over to Roy Dell's crew."

There was no way I was letting some motorhead drive my baby. I'd worked too hard to obtain that car, and I wasn't taking any more chances.

"Nope," I said, "no way. I'll drive the car myself."

The EMTs arrived, accompanied by the man Mickey Rhodes had called Meatloaf.

"Miss Lavotini may have a neck injury," Mickey explained. I grimaced and allowed them to tilt my head this way and that.

"Ow, fellas, take it easy," I said. "You could do more harm than good here."

We were sailing along just fine with them prodding and me wincing, when I caught a flash of familiar movement on the edge of the pit where a crowd of onlookers had gathered. For just a moment, I thought I saw a man who looked a lot like John Nailor. I snapped my neck to the left suddenly and almost forgot to moan while I scanned the crowd. The man stood just on the back fringe of the crowd staring, if I was not mistaken, at me. If it wasn't John Nailor, then it was his spitting double. Only thing was, I couldn't imagine a man like him at a dirt track. It just didn't match up.

My stomach did that little flip it always does when I'm around him, the true test that my unconscious recognized him, even if my eyes were a little slow.

"You know," I said, pushing the prying hands away from my neck, "I think I'll be fine. Moving my head back and forth seems to have fixed the problem. Let's get moving."

Mickey Rhodes looked relieved. In fact, if I was any judge of human character, I was guessing there was going to be a very hefty tip from him at the end of the evening. Fluffy'd be chomping on gourmet dog food this week.

"Come on, Ruby, let's get to work." I said. Ruby smiled

happily and hopped back into my car. If John Nailor was at the track, then it could only be for one reason: He'd come to see me.

"Follow us," Roy Dell called, jumping into his battered Vega. Driving slowly, he led us to the pit entrance and down a narrow dirt lane. There were cars everywhere, hoods open, with men hanging half into the mouth of the car, tinkering. Big panel vans sat behind some of the cars, with wrought-iron railings around their roofs and aluminum lawn chairs perched up on top. Small children played in the dirt, pushing little cars and trucks around. But there was no sign of John Nailor.

The track photographer rushed us as soon as I parked my battered baby. He was a short oval of a man, with a belt line that hit him just below the armpits, white socks, black sneakers, and a bald head. He looked like a brown shiny egg, and the closer he came, the more I realized that he smelled much worse than a rotten egg.

"Ladies," he said, but it sounded more like "lathies," due to a profound lisp. "I am Harold VonCopage. We're behind schedule. Follow me."

Harold quickly led us over to a small wooden platform, where he apparently intended to photograph us with every driver and crew member at the Dead Lakes Motor Speedway. I don't know how he intended to do this because I couldn't even see. Thick clouds of red-clay track dust whirled around us and car exhaust fumes made my eyes water. However, as soon as Ruby and I climbed the steps, men began appearing, lining up at the bottom of the platform as Harold had instructed.

"Are you ready?" Harold asked, an eyebrow arching as if daring us not to be. I looked over at Ruby, who was slathering on blood-red lipstick and hitching up the bra of her little Dutch girl costume. She nodded to Harold. I made an attempt to brush off the dust from my French maid's outfit. It was pointless.

"Just a sec," I called, more to irritate Harold than anything else, and pulled a compact from my purse. My long blond hair was piled high on my head, making me look even taller than my six-foot height in five-inch stilettos. It would be a rusty-red color by the end of the night. I licked my lips slowly and heard the men in the front of the line moan. I wanted to bend over and shift my cleavage even farther north, but this was a family event. My 38DDs probably wouldn't be appreciated by everyone.

I stowed the mirror, looked over at Ruby, and nodded. Then I stretched out my arms to the first man in line.

"Come to Mama, big boy," I crooned, and the night began.

We'd been standing and posing for about an hour when the smile faded from Ruby's lips.

"Sierra," she hissed between photo ops, "why didn't you tell me they pinched? My derriere is going to be black and blue, and my costume's gonna look worse. Honey, they didn't even wipe their hands off first!"

I smiled. "Welcome to the life, kid. You're building yourself a consumer base. They'll walk off with your picture, and within a week, half of them'll be in to see you. Think of your bruised ass as an investment in your financial future."

Ruby looked dubious, but she put on a big smile when the next driver climbed the steps. Throughout the evening I'd look over at her and she never lost that smile, although once or twice I saw her grab a man's hand and pinch the fleshy part between his thumb and forefinger, just like she'd seen me do. But she kept her smile, and the men smiled right back.

Roy Dell Parks was the worst. He kept finding reasons to wander over and talk to her, and Ruby didn't seem to mind him at all. She smiled and spoke softly to him. I couldn't figure what she saw in the big guy.

It was getting late in the evening when I spotted John Nailor for certain. There'd been God knows how many races, all announced over a loudspeaker that was too distorted to understand, and everyone was gearing up for the main event of the evening. Roy Dell Parks and about twenty others were getting set to go fifty laps around the track for the big money purse of the evening. In another half hour the race would take place, and then Ruby and I could leave. I was counting the moments when I looked up and saw John staring at me.

I opened my mouth to call out to him when I realized there was something very wrong with the picture. John, the same guy who'd come into the club on numerous occasions and not all of them professional, the same guy who'd driven me home after some bozo coshed me on the head, was standing not twenty yards away from me with his arm around some tiny brunette.

I should make it clear, here, that John Nailor and I were smoldering somewhere between chemical reaction and friendship with intent to distribute the affection into the physical realm at some point in time.

As such, I recognize the fact that I had no possessive claim on the son of a bitch, but the sparks that had passed between us on a number of occasions led me to believe we meant a lot to each other.

He was watching me not the same way he always did when we first met, from a distance, with an impassive expression on his face, as if I didn't faze him, but I knew different. I'd seen that same look on his face the first time we met, when he was investigating a murder and thought my girlfriend and I had something to do with it. Every time he came to talk to me, he'd look like that, but he kept coming back, even when he didn't have to.

So my mouth dropped open, and my eyes got wide, and I froze, staring at him. He looked at me with those dark eyes of his. Then his companion saw him looking and started to pull at his arm, as if she intended to bring him up to the stage to have his picture taken. He looked down at her, then back at me for just a flash, and that's when he turned away, leaned down, and kissed her.

He kissed her just the way I'd always imagined he'd kiss me one day: hard and like he meant it, like he played for keeps. Then he grabbed her arm and spun her around and they walked off. He was walking rough, and she looked a little surprised but was clearly enjoying this new side to his behavior. I could've told her I'd seen it all before, but I was busy having my picture taken by a smelly egg and my ass pinched by yet another psycho dirt racer.

You'd think by now I wouldn't let stuff like that get to me. It's not as if that was the first time some guy did wrong by me. Far from it. It's just that the kind and quality of man I usually associate with can be expected to be mean. John Nailor was about the last man I thought would deliberately hurt me, and I decided on the spot that I had to know why.

"Break," called Harold. "Big race is in fifteen minutes. We'll take one last round with the winner, and then you girls can go on home."

Ruby was looking wistfully after Roy Dell Parks, who seemed to be beckoning her toward his car. Mickey Rhodes was heading in our direction. He was leading Vincent Gambuzzo and some guys in suits. More publicity, and I was in no mood for it. I wanted to look John Nailor in the face, up close and personal, and see if he was as brave eye to eye as he'd been a few seconds ago.

"I'm outta here," I said, heading for the steps.

"Sierra, where are you going?" Ruby called, but I didn't answer. I kept walking off in the direction I'd seen John head with that perky little bimbo. If he could have picked the almost total opposite of me, he couldn't have done better. She was short, terminally short. I bet in heels she didn't come up over five feet four inches. And she was flat-chested. That is a problem I'll never have to worry about. Her hair was dark and mine was macaroni blond—natural, not bottle—courtesy of my northern Italian ancestors. And she looked like one little puff would blow her away, a real lightweight in your most Junior League sort of way.

I was searching for them and cursing myself. What was wrong with me that I'd let myself get so worked up over a guy? It was just not like me. No, I take it back, it was just like me, but the me of my North Philly days. Since I'd moved to Panama City two years ago, I hadn't made a fool of myself over anybody. In fact, I hadn't even dated anyone—hadn't wanted to, really.

I walked past the drivers and the pit crews, barely noticing the catcalls and the whistles. The smell of coffee and greasy hamburgers from the snack shack reminded me that I hadn't eaten since lunchtime. My stomach finally won over where my brain had not succeeded. It was a much saner idea to eat a burger, drink a cup of coffee, and reflect upon my loss of control with John.

I stepped up to the dirty white shack and let the girl working the counter shove a wax-paper-wrapped hamburger into my hand.

"They all got chili and coleslaw on 'em, hon," she said. "That'll be three dollars with the coffee." If my French maid costume seemed out of place at the track, she never noticed. Her eyes were glued to the track, where the last semifinal race had just ended.

"Aw, hell," she said, turning to a young teenaged girl who was wrapping hot dogs. "Meatloaf done lost to Frank. There'll be hell to pay at our house tonight. He'll come home drunk,

I guess." The girl nodded, never looking up from the dogs. "Son of a bitch," the cashier muttered.

I turned away with my food and wandered out behind the shack. The inner circle of the pit was reserved for parking. It was dark and the ground was a combination of gravel, red clay, and sparse grass.

"All I need is to trip in these heels," I muttered. I almost bumped into a cluster of three picnic tables and decided the safest thing for me to do would be to sit down and eat while my eyes adjusted.

The loudspeaker began to blare over the constant sound of engines being pushed to their maximum rpms. From what I could catch, the starting lineup for the last race was being announced. I didn't pay much attention. I just wanted the entire evening to come to an end so I could go home to Fluffy and the comfort of my double-wide.

As my eyes adjusted, I could see a trash bin about thirty feet away, and now and then I could discern shapes moving past, heading to or from the parking lot. Someone tossed a bottle and it hit the side of the Dumpster, clanging noisily above the dull roar of the pit.

I started to feel sorry for myself. I was sitting alone at a picnic table eating and thinking: What am I doing here? Why wasn't I home, curled up with a book? True, Vincent had bribed me with money to be here, but was it worth it to come all the way to Wewahitchka, just so I could have my fantasy shattered? I didn't think so.

I got up and started walking toward the Dumpster so I could pitch the rest of my hamburger and get back to the platform. I figured I might as well watch the race and talk to Ruby; that was better than stalking John and his new love interest.

"Son of a bitch," I muttered, thinking of the cashier at the snack shack. "They're all alike."

Someone giggled. It sounded like it came from the other side of the Dumpster.

"Why, I don't know what to say," a woman's voice said. It was Ruby. I started to say something, but hung back instead. If she wanted to ruin her evening by fooling around with Roy Dell, who was I to interrupt her? She'd learn soon enough that they're all alike. Or maybe she knew something I didn't. I doubted that.

I had turned to leave when I heard her again.

"I couldn't, really," she said, and I heard a different tone come into her voice, an edge. If that brain-damaged redneck thought he could mess with Ruby, he would be in for a surprise.

I whirled around and started back, only to hear her giggle again. I froze, uncertain about interrupting. A man's voice rumbled and I couldn't make out what he said. The loud-speaker had blurted out something, drowning out their conversation. I started to walk away again.

"Look here," the man said.

Another giggle from Ruby and then the horrible, unmistakable sound of bone snapping. I sprang forward, lurching to cover the distance to the other side of the Dumpster. As I rounded the corner there was a brief painful flash as I collided with something or someone. The last thing I remember as I slid into darkness was the word "No!" echoing soundlessly inside my head.

Four

I heard quick little movements, a scraping of foot against gravel, the shifting of weight from one leg to the other, and the small gasps of exertion that come with effort. I felt myself stir, involuntarily, before my brain could remember that I was in danger and must move with caution. Adrenaline poured into my body, making my heart race. All at once I was aware that I was not alone. A man turned to face me from where he'd been kneeling, looking at something. Even in the darkness I recognized him.

John pushed off his knees and stood, quickly closing the distance between us.

"Don't move. Just lie still a minute. Let me check you out."

I opened my eyes wide in the darkness and started to sit up. Something stung the corner of my left eye and I brought up a hand to wipe it away.

"Damn it, I said lie still!" John hissed. "You've cut the side of your face on the Dumpster. Let me see about it."

I brushed his hand away impatiently and sat up. Jumbled images and sounds came to me in a rush. John kissing the brunette. The sounds of Ruby's laughter. Then suddenly, the remembered snap of bone against bone. I gave him a hard shove, rocking him back onto his heels, and rose up. A crumpled heap lay just beyond us, half hidden by John's purposeful obstruction.

"Ruby!" I cried, scrambling to get to her, knowing even as I moved that she was dead. John grabbed at my arm.

"Sierra, don't. Stop and listen to me."

I lashed out at him, panicked. He reached over and grabbed both my arms, forcing me to look him in the eyes.

"How did this happen, Sierra?" he asked. I stared back at him, remembered running toward the Dumpster, colliding with someone, and then seeing John bending over the body. Ruby had been with a man. Could it have been John? I mean, I'd thought I knew him, but that was before I'd seen him kiss that woman. Who was this man anyway?

That's when I started screaming. It was loud. Loud enough, I hoped, to bring whoever was nearby to help. John's expression changed from one of concern to outright alarm and, if I wasn't mistaken, exasperation.

"Shit, I wish you hadn't done that," he said. "The whole park'll be here in a second." What the hell did he think should happen? Ruby was dead and I wasn't sure he hadn't done it. I felt short-circuited and out of viable responses. He was standing and looking down at me.

"I'm sorry, Sierra," he said softly. "There's nothing I can do for you now." As I watched in amazement, John Nailor turned and ran off into the darkness, leaving me there with Ruby's lifeless body. I could hear footsteps approaching, a few people were running in our direction.

"I heard a woman's voice screaming," a man was saying, "over this way."

"Help!" I screamed. "Police!"

Five

The Panama City Police Department is housed on the same road as the Sanitary Department. I guess that's appropriate since they both deal with the city's garbage. The police department is the first building you come to, and you'd miss it if you weren't looking. It's a squat, one-story building the same color as the sand in the road that runs alongside it.

I had the dubious privilege of entering through the back door tonight, the one reserved for officers and citizens brought in for one reason or another. The officers escorting me led me into the rabbit warren of hallways and cubicles that divide the overcrowded department into units and down the hall to an office no bigger than my tiny walk-in closet at home. I would've left by now, but it seemed that I was being held as an unwilling guest of the city.

They'd made it clear at the crime scene that I was considered hostile and uncooperative. I can't see how they'd think that. Whatever it was that I'd said or done to upset the officers at the racetrack had won me an all-expenses-paid trip downtown in the back of a police sedan complete with a plastic shield and no door handles.

It was closing on two A.M., and I was tired. Tired and numb, but with an awareness that somewhere just beneath the surface sat a time bomb of emotion that would spill over soon. I just hoped I could make it home to the safety of my trailer before I lost it completely.

Sooner or later, Vincent Gambuzzo would send Ernie Schwartz, the company attorney, down to advocate for my release. A dancer getting arrested was viewed as an occupational hazard, and Ernie's services were just part of the benefit package Vincent extended to all of his employees. I'm sure it griped Vincent that he couldn't just pay somebody off, and maybe he could have if he'd only had connections. But as it was, he was forced to do it by the book. Poor Vincent, all he wanted in life was to be viewed as a legitimate threat, a real wise-guy, not the son of a fifth-rate bookie/used-car dealer.

The door swung open and a tall, thin, attractive man walked into the room.

"Miss Lavotini?" he asked in a deep Southern drawl. His voice was husky with interrupted sleep or a cold, I couldn't tell, and he had a thick mustache. "I'm Detective Wheeling."

He had to be the detective in charge. He exuded the same manner they all did, self-assured but always on guard, watching the suspect's every word and movement, waiting for the fatal flaw in their otherwise seamless stories. I was suspected of something, what I didn't know, but he was watching me like a cat. I waited for him to start, but it seemed we had to go through a song and dance first. It was called "making the suspect uncomfortable."

He sat down in the chair across from me and started paying attention to a clipboard that held several sheets of official-looking papers. He whipped out a pen, made a few marks on the sheets, and now and then scribbled a few words. The only sound in the tiny room was the rustling of paper and the ticking of the clock on the wall.

"Miss Lavotini," he said at last, "it seems you are no stranger to this office."

I shrugged and stared at him for a moment, waiting until he looked up and we made eye contact.

"If by that you are referring to the fact that last year I found a couple of dead bodies and happened, like the good citizen that I am, to call them in, then yes, you could say I'm familiar with this office."

He didn't break eye contact right away, just stared at me with hazel-green eyes. At one time, probably when he was a little kid, his hair had been red, but now it was faded to auburn brown with a touch of gray.

"Tell me what happened tonight," he said. He reached for a small tape recorder and started to switch it on. "You don't mind, do you?" he asked. "Makes it easier for me. I can listen and not worry about writing it all down." He smiled and it was supposed to reassure me. "Then we'll just type it up and have you sign it."

I shrugged. What did it matter? He took that for an assent and switched the recorder on.

"May first, 1997. Statement of Sierra Lavotini taken by Detective Jeff Wheeling. Go ahead, Miss Lavotini."

So I started talking. I hadn't even reached the part where I found Ruby before a disheveled Ernie Schwartz came bursting into the room. It wasn't that he'd been summoned from his bed; I'd never seen Ernie when he didn't look disheveled. It seemed to be his state of being. He was short, pudgy, and wore Coke-bottle-thick glasses that hid a beautiful pair of bright blue eyes.

You couldn't tell by looking at Ernie that he was anything but a passive little bookworm, but I knew better. I had seen the inner Ernie Schwartz drunk and playing the ukulele like a professional while standing on my kitchen counter. It had been three A.M. on the Fourth of July; and I should mention that Ernie had been naked as a jaybird and singing at the top of his lungs.

Ernie also loved chihuahuas. He told me this when I asked him to draw up a will for me and name himself as my little Fluffy's guardian. He did it all for free, and I don't think it had a thing to do with me promising I would never tell anyone about him singing the Oscar Meyer wiener song in his birthday suit. But I digress. The Ernie Schwartz who arrived at Panama City's Police Department was all business.

"Dummy up," he said to me in a monotone. To Detective Wheeling he said, "My client is tired. I'm sure she's told you all she can tonight. She needs to go home and sleep. This has been a traumatic evening."

Detective Wheeling stared up at Ernie, apparently sizing him up and trying to decide how much of a threat he posed to his interview.

"Just five more minutes, Mr. Schwartz, and we'll have this all taken care of."

"No, Detective Wheeling, my client is tired. We'll talk in the morning." Ernie placed his hand on my shoulder and squeezed, indicating that I should stand.

"Ernie, I'll do it," I said sighing. "If it'll help find Ruby's killer, I can answer a few more questions."

Detective Wheeling didn't wait for an invitation. He got right to the point.

"There are some disturbing elements in the statement you gave my officer at the speedway, Miss Lavotini, and I thought we'd clear those up before the investigation goes much further."

"What could be more disturbing, Detective Wheeling, than me saying I'd just heard my friend get her neck broken?"

Detective Wheeling leaned back and ran his hand through his wavy hair. "It disturbs me that you put one of our officers at the murder scene."

"Yeah, well, why isn't he here? Why don't you ask him what happened?"

"I did, Miss Lavotini. I went to his home, woke him up, and asked him where he'd been all evening. And do you know what he told me?" I didn't move. "He told me he'd been right there, watching the Marlins and drinking beer. It's his night off, you see."

I wanted to say something, but I couldn't.

"He said he hadn't been to the racetrack, that he didn't like races, and that he couldn't imagine why you'd tell us such a preposterous story." Detective Wheeling leaned forward, turned both hands palm up, and shrugged his shoulders. His wedding band made a small click as it hit the table. "Now, why did you tell us a thing like that?"

I could feel tears welling up in the back of my throat, closing it off and choking me. What in the hell was going on?

"Well, he was there," I said.

Detective Wheeling sighed. "Miss Lavotini, as I understand it, you took quite a blow on the head when you ran into that Dumpster. Maybe you saw someone who looked like Detective Nailor. Maybe you were disoriented. It was dark. Your friend was dead, lying right in front of you. Maybe you confused the person you saw with a more friendly face. Maybe you just wished it was Detective Nailor." He was talking like he would to a child. "Or maybe you were afraid of what the police would say if you once again turned up a dead body."

"Detective Wheeling, I was not confused or afraid, and I know what I saw. Maybe you just wish I hadn't seen Detective Nailor, but I did, so deal with it. My friend is dead and Detective Nailor was there." I stared right back at him, daring him to try to contradict me again, but before he could, a young female officer entered the room and handed him a piece of paper. Detective Wheeling stared at it, his face an unreadable police mask.

"Did you recognize the other man's voice?" he asked, never looking up from the paper. The officer shifted her stance by the door, leaning closer as if to hear my answer.

"No."

"Would you recognize the voice if you heard it again?" This time he looked at me, waiting for my answer.

"I don't know," I said. "Maybe."

"Did it sound like anyone you know?" he asked.

"I don't know. It could have, but I don't think so. I'd have to hear it again to know."

I pressed my hands to my temples, thinking. I was tired and confused. Images and voices ran together.

Ernie stepped behind my chair and pressed both of his beefy hands down firmly on my shoulders.

"On that note, folks," he said, "I think we'll call it an evening. If you want to speak with us again, just phone my office and we'll be happy to schedule a time."

Wheeling nodded curtly and stood up.

"We'll be in touch," he said.

"I'll wait for your call," Ernie answered.

Ernie wasn't wasting any time in getting me out of the police station. He kept a hand securely anchored to the small of my back, pushing me gently forward, through the maze of hallways that led to the outside and freedom.

We pushed through the glass double doors and out into the warm evening air. Ernie was still in his warrior mode, pumped up with attorney adrenaline. He didn't say a word until he had me ensconced in his pride and joy: a '67 Mustang, original paint job, seat covers, and radio, completely authentic and unrestored.

"What in the hell is going on, Sierra?" he asked, pulling out of the parking lot and onto the main drag. "I've never seen Vincent so upset. Do I know this Ruby?"

I shook my head, futilely pushing my hair back out of my face.

"She's new. I don't think you've been in since Vincent hired her."

Ernie stopped for a red light and turned to stare at me through his thick glasses.

"Is there anything about this situation, any little thing at all, Sierra, that I ought to know?"

The light changed to green, but Ernie didn't look away.

"Ern, honest, I told them guys all there was to know. I heard her with someone, I don't know who. Then I heard it go wrong. By the time I reached her, she was dead. And, Ernie, I swear to God, it could have been Nailor. I don't know what's going on, but he was there."

"Shit! Sierra, that isn't good. That's not good at all. You know that's why they're all over you."

Ernie was driving again, winding his way down Bayou, heading out of town toward the Lively Oaks Trailer Park and home.

"How'd you hear her with all the noise at the track?" he asked suddenly.

"Damn, Ernie, what is this? You sound like a cop. All right. It was between races. I was no more than fifteen feet from the Dumpster when I heard them talking. Is there a problem?"

Ernie didn't look at me, just stared straight ahead and focused on his driving.

"I don't know, Sierra," he said finally. "I just don't like the way it feels. You're placing a cop at a murder scene and he's denying it. Vincent said the police were asking a lot of questions about you."

"Oh, that's just Vincent," I said, "always needing something to worry about. I'm clean."

Ernie seemed to accept this because he didn't follow up with any more questions. He pulled onto my parking pad and cut the engine.

"Sierra, I don't know you too well."

I laughed. "Not like I know you, Ernie."

"Whatever. I just want to give you a piece of advice: Stay out of the cops' hair on this one. They don't do things here like they did in Philly. Panama City's a small town; it takes care of its own. Don't try to tell them how to do their job and don't play cute with them. Call me if you have any further contact."

"Don't worry, I'll call you. And, Ernie?"

"Yeah?" There was a hopeful tone to his voice, as if he was hoping I might actually invite him in to show my gratitude. I was grateful, but not that grateful. The Oscar Meyer wiener tune started running through my head and the vision of Ernie naked jumped into my mind.

"Thanks, Ern. I'll call you." For a second his shoulders slumped, but then he grinned and threw the Mustang into reverse.

"That's what I'm here for, Sierra," he said, "to keep the wolves away from your door."

I wasn't really listening; my mind was on getting inside and falling into bed. Somehow the pieces would fall together, but not tonight. I stuck my key in the lock and pushed the kitchen door open. I hit the light switch and nothing happened.

"Shit!" The light had blown again, and I'd just put in a new bulb. That's the problem with mobile homes—built cheaper than shit and always unpredictable.

I closed the door behind me and stepped cautiously into the kitchen. My luck I'd trip over Fluffy's dish. I took another step and froze, the hairs on the back of my neck standing up. Someone was in the trailer.

From behind me I felt rather than heard a brief rush of air as someone closed the distance between us, grabbing me and placing a strong hand over my mouth.

"Don't move. Just relax and lean back against me. If you move you'll get hurt."

I struggled a little bit, just to make sure, but the grip he had me in made it excruciatingly painful.

"See?" he said. "Now relax."

I acted relaxed, but I was planning my next move. Where was Fluffy? What had he done to my dog? We were moving slowly into the living room.

"I'm going to let you go and take my hand away from your mouth," he said. "Don't scream. You promise not to scream?"

I nodded yes. I wasn't going to scream. I was going to kill his ass.

Six

I like my trailer. It's nothing like the hole I lived in when I was in Upper Darby. The El doesn't rumble by, shaking the windows and screeching to a halt just outside my back door. It's clean here, and aside from my psychotic neighbor, Raydean, the neighborhood is safer than Philly. So, when I considered killing John Nailor, I had to take into account the fact that this action would do considerable damage to my living room and probably ruin my image around the neighborhood.

He had led me through the darkened living room, across the bare floors, and over to the one piece of furniture I allow in the room: my prized down-filled sofa. He sank into the cushions slowly, taking me with him and settling back so that I was pulled tight against him. It was going to be difficult to kill him without messing up the denim finish on the sofa, but perhaps I could have it re-covered.

"I know what you're thinking," he whispered softly, "and it's pointless." He eased up on my wrists, and when I didn't move, he slowly took his hands away. I felt him slide his arms back by his side and his body relaxed for a moment; that's when I took my shot.

Just as quickly, he moved, grabbing my wrists and pinning my arms in a crisscross against my chest.

"Ow! That hurts!"

"I told you not to move. It's your fault if it hurts." He smelled of leather and the faint musk of his cologne. Despite myself, I felt my body respond to him. Damn him.

"Let me go!"

"I don't think that's a good idea," he said, tightening his grip. Fluffy chose this moment to make her presence known. She tapped her way noisily across the floor, stopping to stretch and yawn. Her tail started going ninety miles an hour when she saw us, and she pranced across the floor and jumped against John's leg.

"Hello, Fluffy." Fluffy licked his leg and John laughed softly. He was enjoying this.

"Bite him, Fluffy!" Fluffy licked my leg. Always good in a crisis, that's Fluffy.

"I can't stay long. I just wanted to know if you were all right."

"All right? You son of a bitch! Why did you run off like that? Why did you tell them you weren't there? What's going on? Why didn't you help Ruby?" I was firing the questions off as fast as I could. I wanted answers, and they'd better be the right answers.

"I couldn't help Ruby, Sierra. She was dead when I found her. I was following you when I saw you start running toward the Dumpster. By the time I reached you, it was too late to help Ruby and you were lying on the ground. I didn't know what had happened."

"Then why did you leave?" My head was pulled tight against his chest, making it impossible for me to look him in the eyes to read the truth. I could feel his heart pounding and the heat of his body enveloping me. What was going on here?

"Sierra, when I came around the back of the Dumpster, I practically fell over you. You were out cold but starting to come around. Before I could do anything else, I saw Ruby. I had to check and make sure she was dead, but I knew really, before I even reached her."

Tears stung my eyes as I relived that moment. All the feelings I'd stuffed inside threatened to burst out like a dam and swallow me whole. I was trying to keep it inside, but my body shuddered involuntarily, and he felt it. His hands slid up from my wrists to my arms, holding me. Slowly he rocked, ever so slightly, his breath coming softly against my ear.

"Shhh," he whispered. "Let it go." He held me like that as I struggled for control, fighting the urge to give in and cry for Ruby and for how helpless and frightened I'd felt, knowing that there was nothing I could do to help my friend. Maybe if I'd moved sooner, or faster.

"Why didn't you stay?" I asked at last.

"I couldn't." The image of John with the tiny brunette suddenly flashed into my consciousness and I remembered it all. John standing at the edge of the crowd, looking into my eyes, certain that I was watching, before he turned and kissed her. That was all it took. I took advantage of his loosened grip to break free and face him.

"I'll bet you couldn't stay. You had to get back to your girlfriend. God forbid you should help out a friend with a piece of certain ass waiting for you!"

I'd stung him. I could see it reflected in his eyes, the momentary pained look quickly replaced by another. What was it? A soft, sorrowful look. Compassion? Pity? Well I didn't need that.

"Sierra, I can't." He broke off and just stared at me.

"I'll bet you can't," I said with a sneer. I was lashing out at a man I'd trusted with my life a few short weeks ago, and now I wouldn't give him the benefit of the doubt. I knew this, and yet I couldn't help myself.

"Sierra, I really need you to trust me right now," he said. I could tell from the stiffness of his body that he was working hard to stay in control. "I know what you saw hurt you."

"No, I'm not hurt. Why should I be hurt? Because you didn't stay and help out? Because you made me out to be a liar to the police? Or maybe because you didn't turn out to be who I thought you were?"

His hands tightened on my arms, gripping me so tightly that it was all I could do not to cry out in pain.

"I won't let anything happen to you, Sierra. You've got to believe that." He stood up, pulling me with him. "I can't stay and I can't explain to you what's going on. We could both be in a lot of trouble if I was seen with you right now."

The mobile home was still in complete darkness and I was suddenly afraid. What was going on here? John was walking toward the door, gripping my hand in his. He stopped short, turning as he reached the door and pulling me into him. His arms slid around my waist and moved firmly up my back, gripping my shoulders and then pushing me ever so slightly away from him and up against the kitchen wall.

My heart was pounding and my stomach flipped over and over as his hands moved up my neck, gently exploring my face, as if memorizing my features in the dark.

"Sierra," he said, his voice a husky whisper. It was then that he kissed me. Everything inside my head shut down and my body responded. My hands pushed against his chest, feeling their way up until my arms wrapped around his neck. I let my body mold against him, blending with the warmth of his body.

This was not the kiss I'd seen him give the girl at the racetrack. There was no force, no showmanship. He was gentle but insistent, trying to convince me with his body of what my mind wanted to deny. It was a first kiss. The kind of kiss that signals a beginning, not just the means to an end. He was taking his time and forcing me to enjoy the moment. This John Nailor was the same man I'd come to know. Whatever had happened at the racetrack, whatever he'd done this evening, had to be filed away for later. The man who held me was the one I trusted.

Then he was gone without speaking, quietly opening my kitchen door and slipping away into the night. I listened, standing still and barely breathing, until somewhere in the distance I heard a car start up and I knew he was gone again.

Seven

*I*n the gray light of morning I knew better. I lay awake in my bed, Fluffy beside me, and let all the doubts and emotions come bubbling to the surface. I'd let John Nailor sweet-talk me into forgetting that he'd left me at the murder scene and lied to the police. To top it off, I'd let him kiss me and had pretended that it meant more than the kiss he'd laid on the bimbo at the racetrack. That wasn't the worst of the situation; not by far. If I really wanted to face reality, then I had to look at the bottom-line truth. It was my fault that Ruby Lee Diamond was dead. I had taken her under my wing, taught her the moves, and then turned her loose. Now she was dead.

I had failed to protect my friend and she had died. Therefore it was up to me to make it right by her, as right as things could ever be now. Maybe someone else would've left it to the cops, but not a Lavotini. First off, the cops don't give a good shit about a dead dancer. They figure one riffraff type got whacked by another riffraff. The score, to them, looks even. Second, when you hurt a friend of a Lavotini, you wound a Lavotini. We take care of our own. It's our way. That's why I like dancers; they think like I do about family. You become a dancer, you become part of a family of underdogs. We hang tight and tough. So whoever killed Ruby was asking for me to take them on, to avenge her death, to right a hideous cosmic wrong. It was my duty, now, to find Ruby's killer.

I staggered into the kitchen, fed Fluffy almost without thinking, and hit the switch on the coffeepot. I am not a morning person. I move through the routine in a fog and only become truly awake sometime after my third cup of coffee. I opened the kitchen door and retrieved the paper, unfolded it, and began to read while the coffee was brewing.

Right off the bat I had two problems. The coffeepot wasn't brewing because I'd failed to set it up the night before. I hadn't set it up because I'd run out of coffee the day before, intending to pick some up on my way home from the racetrack. The second problem lay in the headlines and the picture that lay above the fold on page one: DANCER KILLED AT DEAD LAKES SPEEDWAY. FRIEND IDENTIFIES SUSPECT.

I read on, wondering who Ruby's friend was who could identify the killer, only to realize that things were moving from bad to worse. The paper, citing an unidentified police source, stated that "Sierra Lavotini, a coworker and friend of Miss Diamond's, told police that she would cooperate fully with their investigation and could identify the suspect by his distinctive voice."

"Great, Fluff," I said. "Now, why would Detective Wheeling say a thing like that?" Fluffy didn't answer; instead she nosed at her food dish and seemed disgusted.

"Better chow tomorrow, I promise," I said and turned back to the article. The police were talking to "several people seen with Miss Diamond earlier in the evening" and "declined to comment further." Well, fine, put my name out there as the person most likely to identify the suspect and let me hang in the wind. I was starting to boil.

"Pardon me if I don't stay and keep you company while you eat, Fluff. I've gotta have coffee or die." Fluffy didn't seem interested. "I'll be at Raydean's if you need me," I said. Fluffy smiled her chihuahua grin and kept on eating.

My across-the-street neighbor, Raydean, would have coffee. It would come at a price, but she would have it and be glad to offer it to me. That is, if she was in her right mind and the aliens weren't dropping in on her. Raydean is not exactly your typical retiree living on a fixed income. You can tell this at a glance just by approaching her house. It is the only trailer in the park that the fearless trailer-park children are afraid to approach.

The trailer itself is innocuous enough, but the yard surrounding it is a maze of birdbaths and statuary, tropical plants and cacti, all carefully rigged with booby traps designed to ensnare and torment the unsuspecting visitor. The few people she allows near enough to enter her compound know to avoid the third segment of her walkway, to duck as they approach the steps, and to knock at the door three short raps instead of ringing the doorbell, because it is electrified. And all of us know, at all costs, that we must never make reference to the Flemish, because if Raydean has not been to the mental health center to get her monthly shot of Prolixin, then she will be certain that the Flemish are alien beings plotting the takeover of the world.

Most of us do not find out about Raydean the easy way. We wake up to the sounds of yelling and gunshot and believe that we are indeed under siege, only to find that it is Raydean and she is off her medication. However, the rest of the month, when Raydean is calm, you will never meet a nicer, more giving woman. Many's the time Raydean has intervened for the better in my life. You just need to be able to work around the peculiar with Raydean.

I walked across the road in my purple chenille bathrobe and feathered high-heeled bedroom slippers, carefully avoiding the third segment of pavement and ducking as I started up the trailer steps. The curtains in Raydean's bay window twitched as she moved from her lookout post to the kitchen door.

"Who's there?" she called in a husky voice. She knew full well who it was, but it always paid to be careful in Raydean's world.

"I come in peace," I answered, saying the phrase Raydean had carefully instructed me to repeat.

"How will I know?" she asked cryptically, waiting for the next phrase in our crazed ritual.

"I have only love in my heart," I answered. You lie, I thought, but it was Raydean's rules or no coffee.

Slowly Raydean undid the multitude of locks that stood between her and alien takeover. At last the door cracked and Raydean's wrinkled face broke into a grin.

"Well, it is you!" she said. The door was thrown open and Raydean stood back, waiting for me to walk in, paying no attention to the fact that it was almost noon and I was still in my bathrobe. She stood in her faded pink housedress, with her gray hair in bright pink curlers and her knee-high hose rolled carefully down around her ankles.

"Going somewhere?" I asked, pointing to the curlers.

"Safety precaution," she said and moved toward the kitchen. "Want some coffee? I just brewed a pot." Raydean was addicted to caffeine and Moon Pies.

"Thanks. That'd be nice."

Raydean moved across the room toward the coffeepot, stopping to move her shotgun from its place on the kitchen table to a spot near the counter. Raydean was well armed. She kept at least one gun in sight in every room and I suspected there were many more I didn't know about.

Raydean poured the coffee and headed back toward the table.

"You had an intruder last evening," she said, calmly placing the mug in front of me. "He entered your home at one twenty-seven A.M. and exited at two-fifteen A.M."

"Why didn't you warn me?" I asked. John Nailor was lucky to be alive.

Raydean giggled. "I was pondering that when I noticed it was that cute boy you introduced me to when I was over at your house playing cards. I figured he was a welcome intruder."

"He was not!"

Raydean fixed her bird eyes on my face and looked sad. "Have I done wrong?" she said, her voice childlike. I had hurt her feelings.

"No, Raydean, I'm sorry. It's all right. I'm just confused."

"I know what that's like," she muttered.

"There was trouble at the racetrack last night," I said. With Raydean I never like to venture too far into an explanation. I'm never sure what will set her off.

"Trouble in paradise," she sighed. "Ain't it just the way?" She was shaking her head and staring at the chair beside her. The morning paper lay there, so Raydean probably knew all about it.

"Did you read about it?" I asked.

"Honey, I don't have to read the paper to know racing's bad news. Got a nephew who's made a fool of himself over that stuff. Calls himself the King of Dirt." Raydean looked disgusted and I felt a chill go up to the back of my spine. "His wife's said if he don't quit fooling around with cars and women, she's gonna leave." Raydean smiled. "Of course, if you ask me and his mama, that'd be for the best. His wife's a slut and he'd be well rid of her."

"I ran into him last night," I began.

Raydean looked at me and laughed. "Don't surprise me at all. A half-naked woman on a racetrack? Roy Dell'd sniff you out like a coon dog. But don't worry," she said, catching my frown, "he's harmless."

I was all set to debate harmless, but from across the street,

I could hear Fluffy barking. Raydean hopped up and ran to her spot by the window, shotgun in hand.

"All right," she snapped, "I'm warning you. You got company and he don't look familiar." Raydean stiffened. "Don't be fooled by the facial hair," she said, "they got transmitters encapsulated in almost anything. Technology is a dangerous thing in the wrong hands."

It was getting close to Prolixin time, I could tell. I couldn't figure out what she meant until I wandered up and peaked through the bay window curtains. Detective Wheeling was standing on my back stoop, repeatedly ringing my doorbell.

What happened next was not exactly my fault. Could I have stopped it? The case could be made either way. I went out onto Raydean's stoop, still holding the mug of coffee she'd given me, and yelled. Detective Wheeling turned around, saw me, and quickly headed in my direction.

"Wait," I said, "I'll be right over." But he either didn't hear me or didn't think I meant what I said, because he kept coming. Fluffy had emerged from her doggie door and was following him, yipping at his heels and causing him to walk in a broken-step weave.

I started down the stairs and hit the walkway at the same time he stepped onto Raydean's booby-trapped section of lawn. Fluffy, who knew what would happen next, turned around and ran for the safety of her own yard. Detective Wheeling was not quite so fortunate. The sprinkler system turned on and completely drenched him.

This was perhaps the new low point in my relationship with the police department. Not so much because my neighbor's sprinkler system had watered Detective Wheeling down, but because I saw the situation as funny and started to laugh.

I cut a wide path around him and continued on my way to my trailer.

"If you want to dry off," I said, looking back over my shoulder, "I've got a towel."

He had two alternatives. He could leave and drive off sopping wet, or he could come inside. I could feel him warring with himself. He was mad as hell, but he was the type who hates to mess up a vehicle. I hadn't opened the kitchen door when I felt him start up the stairs behind me.

"So I thought my attorney told you to call him if you wanted to talk to me," I said after I handed him a towel and let him perch on one of my barstools. Wheeling's short hair stood in tufts around his head, giving him a sort of punk look.

"I wanted to explain to you about the article in the paper. I thought you might see it and—"

"And what?" I interrupted. "Think you planted it so you could flush out a suspect? Leave the dancer high and dry, 'cause after all, I'm just low-rent?"

Wheeling flushed. "We can talk or you can cuss me out and I'll leave. What's it going to be?"

"Say what you came to say."

Wheeling hunched his shoulders like he had a stiff neck. "First off, I didn't talk to the press. We don't do that here. I issue statements after the fact, not in the process of an investigation."

"So what are you saying? That no one in the police department said anything to the press and that they fabricated a story?"

Wheeling ran his fingers through his hair, making it look even more wild. The gesture made him seem somehow much younger, almost boyish, and frustrated.

"I'd like to say no one in the department talked, but you and I both know that I can't do that. I'm busting my ass trying to find out who, if anyone, talked, but I'm also working on finding your friend's killer."

"So how many people knew I was a witness?" It was hopeless, I knew. In Panama City, everyone knew everything in a matter of moments.

Wheeling shifted on the barstool. "Well, the officers at the scene know you were there, but they didn't know you could identify the killer."

"I didn't say I could. I said maybe."

"Well, then I knew and Detective Nailor knew."

"What? How the hell did he know?"

Wheeling looked at me, his eyes unwavering. "He's the other homicide detective. We work our cases together, unless one of us is already on a case. In Panama City, that's rare. We only have six or eight homicides a year." He was burning me with the facts while I was still stuck on Nailor possibly being the only other person who knew the details of my statement. I was going to have to do a little investigating of my own. Nailor kept popping up, first at the racetrack, then in my trailer, and now investigating Ruby's murder. What was the man up to?

A glint of red outside the bay window caught my eye, drawing my attention to the street. A cardinal-red Porsche was slowly passing the trailer, the windows tinted a smoky gray, with a vanity plate that I knew by heart: MR.TNA Vincent Gambuzzo was circling the block, noting the government tags on the standard-issue beige Taurus, and deciding to keep a low profile until the heat was gone.

"Listen," I said, turning my attention back to Detective Wheeling, "it really don't make no never mind to me how you want to explain this. I'm just asking that you be a little forthcoming with some police protection."

Wheeling started to say something, but I cut him off. "I know, you can't be placing a cop on my doorstep twenty-four hours a day, and maybe that's because of who I am and who the victim was, and maybe it's because you're short-handed. Whatever. I'm just asking for a profile. A high profile. Send a marked cruiser past my house every hour or so." I was walking toward my door, holding it open and making like Wheeling should quit acting like a big baby Huey and take a cue.

He wandered out into the bright sunlight of another steamy Panama City afternoon with Fluffy once again at his feet, trying her best to trip him up. His car hadn't been gone thirty seconds when Vincent Gambuzzo pulled into Wheeling's spot on the parking pad and gunned the engine of the tinny-sounding sports car. Whatever version of a Porsche it was, it wasn't the big-ticket, top-of-the-line model. His car was the best he or any other midlevel wannabe could afford.

Vincent de-wedged himself from the driver's seat and lumbered over to my steps, panting from exertion and the heat of wearing a black suit in the friggin' tropical nineties.

"About goddamn time that cop took off," he said, heaving himself up the steps. "Any longer and I'd have run out of gas. Then them damn juvenile delinquents that live in this dump woulda made off with my tires. Jesus, Mother Mary, and the saints, it's hot!" With that, Vincent Gambuzzo entered my trailer.

He looked around, almost visibly sniffing the air, trying to figure out with his nose what had been up and who'd been saying what to whom. Then, without asking, he strode over to the refrigerator and pulled open the door, standing there as the cool air hit him in the face.

"What? You don't got nothing in here, Sierra. Friggin' mineral water! Fruit friggin' salad! What is this shit?"

"I knew you were coming, so I hid the good stuff," I said. "Are you here to eat or talk?" With Vincent, there was no separating the two.

"Aha, there it is." Vincent had finally stooped low enough to find the cannelloni and the leftover ziti.

"Help yourself," I said, but the sarcasm was wasted.

After he'd popped a plate in the microwave, Vincent got down to business.

"I been in the trade a long time, Sierra, and I ain't never lost a dancer." He paused and shook his head slowly back and forth. I knew what he was saying wasn't exactly the truth. Vincent hadn't been in the exotic emporium business more than the five years he'd been in Panama City, because I'd done my homework and I knew the facts. Vincent had worked for his father in Miami before he'd made the move to the Panhandle. His father was a small-time bookie and used-car dealer. The Tiffany was Vincent's attempt to make it on his own, but he didn't want any of us to know how little he knew about the business. To challenge Vincent was to ask for him to swell up with machismo bravado and make a fool of himself and perhaps do something rash at the expense of face-saving. I didn't want that, so I stayed silent.

"She was beautiful, Sierra," he sighed. He pulled his piping-hot plate from the microwave and gingerly carried it to the kitchen table. "Nobody should die that young." He sighed again and began to eat. "Them cops," he said, his voice choked with ziti and emotion, "they ain't gonna take this seriously. Not like us, eh, Sierra?"

I was starting to have a funny feeling in the pit of my stomach. Vincent was heading somewhere, and I didn't think I was going to like it.

"Yeah, Vincent," I replied cautiously, "this isn't good."

"Them cops, they're gonna blow this off, being as how she was a dancer and such. It's gonna get the wrong sort of publicity in the papers. They'll say she was a young girl, lured into the dangerous world of exotic dancing. You know where it'll go from there, don't you?"

I nodded, but I had no idea where he was heading.

"They'll start saying it was bound to happen. That dance clubs are full of the criminal element, and before you know it, they'll be putting a black eye on the whole profession." Vincent was fired up now, his chin covered with red sauce, the muscle on the side of his jaw twitching the way it always did when he was agitated. "Next thing you know, Ruby's memory will be trashed and the Tiffany will be at the bottom of the barrel with them other trash-heap strip joints. Now, Sierra, we can't have that, can we?" Vincent's voice was at a roar, bringing Fluffy bounding into the kitchen growling.

"Vincent," I started, but got no further. He had pulled off his dark glasses, a sure sign we were in for a long diatribe.

"It ain't right, Sierra. You know it ain't right!"

"No, Vincent, it ain't right," I agreed.

"Then we gotta act, and we gotta act now."

Vincent stopped shoveling food into his mouth and set his plate down on the floor for Fluffy. She glanced warily at him, and then decided to throw caution to the wind and commence chowing down on ziti. Vincent and Fluffy had a tenuous truce that consisted of a system of bribes. Vincent supplied the food and Fluffy agreed not to bite him.

"We take a two-pronged approach," he said, rising from his chair and striding back toward the refrigerator. "First an appropriate PDA."

"What?" He was losing me. He'd moved away from the refrigerator to go poking into my cabinet; he was hunting for sweets.

"Public display of affection," he said. "We all loved Ruby. Her public needs a chance to mourn, and I don't mean at no funeral, although I think we should be visible there, too. I mean, the club ought to do something out of respect. Dedicate an evening to her, or wear black armbands like they do in the military."

"Maybe cover our pasties in black, like the cops cover their shields." Once again my sarcasm was lost on Vincent, who'd discovered my chocolate stash.

"Yeah, something like that. Tasteful." He popped a handful of chocolate chips into his mouth. "Something that says we're grieving while at the same time pointing out that dancers got hearts and a standard that others should look up to. See what I'm saying?"

I saw only too well. Vincent was concerned with the bottom line. Don't get me wrong, I think he had feelings for Ruby, but Vincent's true love was the Tiffany.

"Then we come to part two," he continued. Vincent's voice had dropped an octave, and he carefully put the chocolate back into the pantry before turning to face me. There was a terrible look in his eyes, one I'd never seen before, a frozen, arctic glare.

"Part two is we find the bastard who did this and we dust his ass." Vincent paused for a second, letting his words hang in the air. I felt a chill and pulled my purple chenille robe tighter. "You know them cops can't find the guy like we can. Anyway, we got a message to send. The Tiffany, i.e., Vincent Gambuzzo, don't let nobody fuck with its dancers and get away with it."

So far, he hadn't said anything I disagreed with. I was just troubled by the use of the word "we," as if I were somehow a part of Vincent's retribution.

"So I'm thinking you should make a call, and I'll make a call, and then we'll just see whose people can get the job done first."

"Vincent," I said, "I don't mean to act stupid here, but what are you talking about? What call?"

Vincent gave me a frosty, don't-be-coy-with-me look and put his dark glasses back on.

"Sierra," he said, his voice a warning, "you know who I mean. Call the Moose and let him know you need a favor. You're family. This is pigeon shit to a guy like that."

Sister Mary Margaret told us there was always a payback when you lied. She drummed it into our heads every day of our long Catholic-school education. Somehow I'd always thought she meant God would pay you back, not Vincent Gambuzzo. Here I was, about to reap the consequences of having told my boss that he couldn't mess with me on account of I was connected to a syndicate so big that if Vincent even dared to make me so much as uncomfortable, his entire club would cease to exist. Up until this moment, the implied connection had always done the trick and kept Vincent off my back. Now it was about to blow up in my face.

"Vincent," I said, "I don't know about calling Moose. This is a local matter. I'm sure your people would be more appropriate. Besides, they're local."

Vincent shook his head. He was bluffing. He didn't have any "people," local or otherwise. No, we were down to the moment of truth. If I didn't produce the Moose, then I would be chopped liver around the Tiffany.

"All right, Vincent, I'll make the call. But I'm not making any promises. Panama City is out of their jurisdiction. And while it's a huge matter to me, Moose may not see it that way."

Vincent picked up the phone and shoved it toward me. "Call him."

I stared at the phone and back at Vincent, my heart pounding and my face slowly turning red. Then I laughed.

"Vincent, I am not going to call him with you standing here. First off, we talk in Italian, and second, if he so much gets a whiff of someone, not a family member, within earshot, he would have my ass. Besides, you don't just dial direct. I gotta dial a number, leave a coded message, and then wait. It could take hours."

Vincent's jaw was twitching and he didn't pull the phone away. "Dial," he said.

I grabbed the phone like I was pissed. "Turn away," I demanded. "I don't want you to look."

Vincent sighed heavily and turned back to the pantry and my chocolate stash. I knew he was listening to me punch in the members, so I did the only thing I knew to do given my situation. I called my mother.

"Hello?" Ma always answers the phone like she's expecting the cops or a funeral home to be calling, and I guess given that Pop and three of my brothers are firemen and my baby brother's a cop, that's a fair expectation. Still, it's disconcerting to hear the panic in her voice.

"This is Sierra," I said.

"Oh, Sierra." She sighed with relief. She inhaled as if she was about to ask the 480 questions she always asks, but I cut her off at the pass.

"I need to get a message to Moose," I said. I glanced over at Vincent. He'd turned and was paying close attention.

"Moose? Who in God's name is Moose?" my mother cried. "Sierra, what's the matter with you? Who's Moose? Should I know?"

"No," I said, "that's fine. If it's not until tomorrow, well, I understand."

Ma was getting frantic now. "Let me call your father to the phone." There was a squishy noise as she pressed her palm over the phone, then the sound of her muffled shouting. "Frank! Frank! It's Sierra. I think she wants to talk to you."

"Thanks so much," I said quickly. "I'll wait to hear from you tomorrow." I hung up and looked over at Vincent, then let my finger slide up to click off the ringer. In about two minutes my parents would be dialing my home like it was the winning lottery number wanting to know what in the hell was going on. Vincent was smiling.

"That's a good girl," he said. "Now we're gonna see some action."

"Be careful what you wish for, Vincent," I said. "You may be in for more action than you were planning on."

Vincent nodded like he knew all about it. "These are desperate times, Sierra," he said. "I will make myself and the club available to whatever Moose Lavotini needs. You tell him I'm grateful and that Vincent Gambuzzo knows how to repay a favor."

Vincent got up and hustled toward the door, puffed up with the importance and self-satisfaction of knowing he'd brought in the mob to avenge a moral outrage. I closed the door behind him and wandered over to the full-length mirror in the living room.

"Hello," I said gruffly into the glass, lowering my voice as deep as I could. I grabbed the barre. "I'm 'Big Moose' Lavotini, at your service. Now, about that favor you need . . ."

Eight

*W*here I come from, in the suburbs of Northeast Philly, when somebody dies from the neighborhood, we all attend the funeral or drop by the funeral parlor. It's a sign of respect and, sometimes, more often than we'd like to admit, curiosity. When I arrived at work the second day after Ruby's death, I was heartened to find out that dancers operate on the same level of personal principle. Either that or Vincent Gambuzzo was a public-relations whiz kid.

"Sierra," he called as I came rolling in through the back entrance. "It's about friggin' time. I gotta talk to you before you go on." I looked at my watch. It was only seven o'clock. I was early.

"Vincent, I'm not late," I said impatiently. As I got closer I could see the jaw twitching. Vincent was in a state.

"Did you reach him?" he asked.

"Vincent," I hissed, looking around in mock paranoia. "Don't be running your mouth here. I told you I'd take care of it, and I did."

Vincent nodded. "Now listen, that's not all. I got some extras here tonight. Some of the other clubs sent over representatives. You know," he said, trying to prompt me, "for the tribute. The PDA."

"What? They did what?"

Vincent puffed up like a rooster. "Yeah, I was talking to some of the guys, and they were all offering their condolences. When I told them about the tribute and asked if they wanted a part in it, they were all right on board. They sent their best girls."

I had to give the guy credit. This was a public-relations coup. The best talent in town, from every club, all packing in the Tiffany. There wouldn't be a man in the area who'd miss this. The strippers with hearts of gold and the G-strings to match.

"I want you to coordinate things for the evening. Get the girls lined up. Tell them what you want and how long they have onstage. Set the tone, Sierra."

"Vincent, you are friggin' unbelievable." On the one hand, I wanted to slap him for exploiting Ruby's memory to his advantage. On the other hand, it was going to save the Tiffany from becoming "the place where that murdered girl worked" and turn it into "that club that cared so much about that poor murdered girl." It was brilliant and disgusting all at once. And damn it, it was up to me to turn it into the real tribute I knew it should be.

"So you're saying I get free reign here to do it like I want?"

"Anything you say, Sierra."

"Good," I said, turning and heading for the dressing room door. "Then stay the fuck away from us until I tell you different. I don't want you messing it up."

Vincent was fuming, but he was also remembering that he owed me now and he really couldn't afford to piss me off.

"You got two hours, Sierra," he growled. "Have your ass out onstage at nine o'clock and don't keep us waiting."

I didn't dignify it with a response. I had two hours to put on a really fine memorial tribute and that was what I intended to do.

Nine

A fine mist of smoke blew gently across the stage of the Tiffany Gentleman's Club at precisely nine P.M. I'd made Ralph, the stage manager, change our customary red backdrop curtain for a black velvet one, and at 9:01 the curtain slowly parted to reveal me standing center stage, dressed in a black velvet sheath, my blond hair piled high upon my head.

It was a packed house, thanks to Vincent's full-page ad in the local paper. The cover charge had been jacked up out of sight, with ten dollars out of each admission going to the local women's shelter, another Gambuzzo finesse. When I stepped slowly out to the front of the runway, the crowd fell silent.

"Gentlemen," I said, "welcome to the Tiffany. We have gathered here tonight to pay tribute to one of our own, a young dancer who I'm sure most of you have seen on this stage. A woman of extraordinary talent, who shared her gift freely with those who could most appreciate it."

There was an anticipatory stir among the men.

"Tonight, those of us who share Ruby's love of dance have assembled to pay our respects and to honor her life essence. We hope that by bringing joy to you we can remind ourselves that, while Ruby's song is over, her melody lingers on.

"Owen," I called suddenly to the bartender, "pour everyone a shot of Wild Turkey." This was clearly not in Vincent's good-hearted scenario, and the dirty look he sent me confirmed it, but what did I care? A few of the restless shouted out, "All right," but I signaled for silence.

"Gentlemen, if you would refrain from drinking, for a moment, I would like to propose a toast." Incredibly, they did. They stood silent, waiting as the topless barmaids handed out shots, thanking them respectfully, and not once hooting or attempting to pinch fleshy bottoms.

When everyone in the house had a glass, I raised my own.

"Here's to the road we all must go down. Here's to the gift that brought her to town. Here's to a life cut short in its prime. Let's honor our friend, 'cause, boys, it's showtime!" With this, I yanked at the slender Velcro strip that held my dress on, letting it fall to the floor, revealing my black sequined G-string and tiny black pasties. A large fake ruby glittered in my navel. I poured the shot back, letting the fiery liquid slide down the back of my throat.

"All right, girls!" I yelled. "Let's give them what they came for!"

The curtain slowly pulled back again, this time revealing twenty-five of the best exotic dancers that Panama City, Florida, had to offer, all dressed in tiny black G-strings and minuscule black pasties, all with red rubies glittering in their navels.

The girls paraded forward, took a turn around the pole, which had been decorated for the occasion in black, then strutted out down the length of the runway, blowing kisses and giving the boys a little taste of the evening to come. The men went wild. Bills littered the air and the stage like confetti. This would be a night for Panama City to remember.

Ruby would have been thrilled. She would've joined right in and danced her heart out. For a moment I thought of her, lying lifeless on the ground, and wanted to run away, but I couldn't. I was a pro and the others were looking to me to pull us through the tough times. That's what families do. They stick together through the rough patches, no matter what the cost and no matter how much it hurts.

I knew my job tonight. I was the mother and the referee to a bunch of the best and most highly strung dancers that the Florida Panhandle had to offer. There was no time for my own feelings, not with twenty-five others to manage. So I kept them moving. I teamed them up in pairs or threesomes. I kept them busy changing costumes, helping with props and circulating the room doing table dances, and I laid down the law.

"There will be no lap dancing. There will be no competition for the customer. This is a tribute, not a slugfest."

No one had a problem with this, not even the girls from some of the less formal clubs. The only dancer I had to ride was Marla, and that was no surprise. Marla fancies herself my competition for headliner, and so if I told her it was raining outside, she'd be the first to assure me how wrong I was.

"I don't see why I can't do a fly-over," she said, pouting.

"Marla, it would mean rigging the stage with extra stuff, and we don't have the time."

Marla had one big act. She called it her salute to our flying men in uniform. She dressed like a B-52 bomber, all silver sequins, complete with wings and wires so she could fly out over the runway, grabbing her tits and yelling, "Bombs away, boys!" It took a lot of wires to heft Marla and her 52DD "bombs" up over the stage, and this was just not the time.

"Well, Ruby would've loved it," she said, glowering.

"Ruby would've laughed her ass off like she always did," I answered.

"You're just jealous!"

"Marla," I said, "I really don't have time for this. We each get five minutes. I put you on third, so if I were you, I'd get my ass in gear and get ready because you're on in five minutes." I walked off from that one, but she managed to mix it up with the guest artists and need interference from me at least five more times that night. It was worse than watching a toddler.

The real trouble came toward midnight. Tonya the Barbarian was full tilt into her big number. It involved a fake-fur cavegirl outfit, a club with rubber spikes, and a lot of grunting. It was a primitive workout at best, with the club utilized in ways no true cavegirl ever imagined, but it drew a fascinated audience. It was the same kind of crowd who goes for women mud-wrestling topless.

Tonya was sort of rolling on the floor of the runway, much to the delight of the contingent of race car drivers who had elected to attend representing the Dead Lakes Motor Speedway.

"After all," Roy Dell had explained, "it happened on our turf. We felt like we ought to be here as a show of respect." He'd brought along Meatloaf and Frank and some of the other drivers and pit crew members. All in all a good turnout. Even Mickey Rhodes had shown up, but he chose to spend most of his time huddled at the bar, conferring with Vincent.

Roy Dell and Meatloaf were most enamored of Tonya's G-string, which seemed to be made of chamois cloth and chicken bones. They were risking the wrath of Bruno the bouncer by leaning as close over the edge of the runway as they possibly could to insert rolled-up bills into Tonya's tiny leopard-skin garter when a loud disturbance broke out.

It started at the back of the room, near the door, and rumbled like a tidal wave toward the front of the house. Watching from just off stage, I saw men being shoved aside like spent paper towels and heard a dull roar, but because of the crowd I couldn't tell for sure what was happening.

Things seemed to move in slow motion for a moment as I saw Roy Dell's facial expression change from a drooling leer to abject terror. Tonya was too absorbed in her act to clock that she was in danger of becoming a victim, and the only thing that may have saved her was Bruno taking a flying leap that landed him across the edge of the runway, effectively spinning Tonya back up the slippery runway and away from the action.

"Roy Dell Parks!" a deep throaty voice called. "I done warned you for the last time." The sea of bodies parted as a thick, beefy arm reached out and grabbed Roy Dell by the lapels of his bright yellow shirt.

"Now, honey," Roy Dell began, but his voice was quickly squeezed to a squeak.

I had a good view now. Men were scattering like Ping-Pong balls. A tall, bleached blonde wearing a red and white vertically striped shirt, with the name LULU embroidered in red across the top half of the back and DERBETTES stitched across the middle, reached for a beer bottle. With one hand clutching Roy Dell by the shirt collar, she neatly tapped the beer bottle against the edge of the runway, thus giving her a perfect weapon for fending off an enraged and determined Bruno.

Although she never made eye contact with Bruno or Fast Eddie, the backup bouncer, she seemed to sense their presence.

"Don't none of y'all bother us," she shouted. "This is a domestic situation brought about and aggravated by y'all's disregard for the sanctity of my marriage." She took a step backward, dragging Roy Dell with her. "Sex has done reared its ugly head and made an addict out of my husband. He is a fool for race cars and now he's a fool for women. It was only a matter of time."

"Lulu, honey," Roy Dell squeaked.

"Shut up, you worm!" Lulu continued to walk backward, the beer bottle waving in her left hand and Roy Dell gasping for breath in her right. "If you was half the man you think you are, you wouldn't be running around looking for inflation."

"You go, girl!" Tonya yelled, apparently forgetting that with Roy Dell went a sizable portion of the evening's tips.

Meatloaf and Frank looked at each other and shrugged. Meatloaf snickered. The other racers stood, open-mouthed, as did the rest of the men. Bruno followed Lulu, getting as close as he could but aware of the flashing beer bottle. Vincent seemed to be the only one with any sense about him. He anticipated Lulu's departure and pushed the double entry doors wide open so she'd have a clear path of departure.

"You think I don't know about you making a fool of your-self over that dead girl the other night?" she asked Roy Dell. "You think that creature found you attractive? Do you actually think I like sitting in the pit and looking across and seeing you sweet-talking some girl young enough to be your daughter?" She didn't expect an answer from Roy Dell. "Then you come here to publicly humiliate me?" She snorted. "Them days are over, Roy Dell." By now they had reached the doorway, but unfortunately, so had Detective John Nailor.

I saw him approach slowly, like he was out for nothing more than a stroll. Lulu was so wrapped up in her speech to Roy Dell and in guarding her front, that she never thought to look behind her. With one fluid movement, Nailor reached up, relieved Lulu of the beer bottle, and kept walking right past her.

"Y'all have a pleasant evening now, y'hear?" he said.

Lulu and Roy Dell continued on their way out to the parking lot, and the entire audience at the Tiffany stared at John for a long moment, then instantly lost interest as the music cranked back up and Tonya the Barbarian began to wriggle on her belly like a reptile.

I stood and watched John from my position at the edge of the backstage curtain. He appeared to have popped in for a quick drink, like he was only John Q. Public, but I knew better. Everything John did was for a reason.

Vincent Gambuzzo was apparently thinking the exact same thing I was, because he began to circle John's table, his face growing increasingly red as his jaw twitched angrily. I knew what was coming. It happened every time John Nailor entered the Tiffany. Vincent would puff up like a blowfish and Nailor would merely watch. One of these times Vincent was going to really make a fool out of himself, and then where would we all be?

As usual, it was up to me to see that cooler heads prevailed. I nodded to Ralph, the stage manager, signaling the girl I wanted to go on next, and headed out to play den mother.

"Detective," Vincent was saying as I approached the table, "you're bad for business." John was staring at him like he was a specimen in an aquarium.

"Gambuzzo, I'm a paying customer," he said, gesturing toward his Coke. "I'm just here to enjoy the evening."

"Nailor, you know and I know—" Vincent began as I stepped up to the table.

"Table dance, Detective?" I said, placing my stilettoed foot firmly up on the table in between the two men and giving John Nailor a good glimpse of the goods that made the Tiffany famous.

He didn't move a facial muscle, but he let his eyes do the talking, running them up the length of my leg like silk stockings.

"Don't mind if I do," he said slowly. Then he reached forward and slipped a twenty-dollar bill in my garter.

This was a first. Usually he'd settle for a smart remark and then leave, but not tonight. Vincent, mollified only slightly by the display of money, sniffed and moved back a few steps.

"Well, I guess there's nothing wrong with a paying customer," he groused, "but I got my eye on you two." With that he wandered back to his spot at the end of the bar, leaving us alone.

"What are you doing here?" I said. "I thought you didn't want to be seen around me." John eyed me slowly, lingering over the pasties and the giant ruby in my navel.

"Start dancing," he said softly, but with a firm no-nonsense tone.

I looked over my shoulder. Vincent's jaw was pumping. I began to move to the music. John leaned back in his seat, hands clasped behind his head, watching me like any other customer. But he wasn't any other customer. The memory of our kiss, shared in the darkness of my kitchen, came coursing through my body, and I felt suddenly vulnerable.

"Look at me," he said, "and step closer."

All right, I thought, if he wants the full treatment, then that's what he'll get. I looked him right in the eye and produced the best moves I had to offer. I brought my hands up to cup my breasts, then let my fingers drift down below my waist. John watched, a soft smile playing across his face.

"Is this how you like it, Detective?" I said softly, then let my fingers dip below the edge of my sequined G-string. I was waiting for him to break, to look away, to back down, but he didn't.

"I'm liking this just fine," he said, sliding forward in his chair. In his hand he held another bill, but it was wrapped around a thin white piece of paper. He waved the bill in front of me, beckoning me to come closer. I ran my hands down my thighs and wiggled so close I could smell his cologne. With an easy, practiced movement, he shoved the card and the bill in the front of my G-string. My stomach turned over as his fingers brushed my skin.

"In case you need to reach me," he said, "that has my pager number on it." He smiled, but the smile didn't reach his eyes.

"What makes you think I'll need you?" I asked. I placed my hands on either side of his chair and leaned over him, my breasts a few inches from his face. "Maybe it'll be the other way around." Nailor's hands moved involuntarily, reaching for me, then dropped back to his lap. He closed his eyes for a moment, as if willing himself to stay in control.

"I read the paper," he said, opening his eyes. "I don't know what's going on, but somebody doesn't like you. You need to watch your back."

"I wouldn't worry about me, Detective," I said. "I'm used to handling trouble." I pushed back from his chair and stood right in front of him, staring as hard as I could into his eyes. "Maybe you're the one playing with fire." My heart was pounding and I could feel my face turning red.

"Be careful what you ask for, honey," he said. "You just might get more than you bargained for." He pushed his chair back and stood up. Neither one of us moved. We were as close as we had been in my trailer. I could feel the heat between us and it took my breath away. He reached a hand out and touched me lightly under the chin.

"It's time to quit playing games, Sierra," he said. "You're moving into a whole new league."

I wasn't sure if we were talking about Ruby's death or me and him. Either way, I wasn't running away. I stood and watched him as he tossed back the last of his Coke and walked out the door.

Vincent was staring at me, his jaw twitching and his fingers drumming nervously on the bar. He knew something was up, whether it was the body language between John and myself, or just the fact that one of Panama City's detectives had come into the bar on an alleged social call. Vincent had that much going for him; he could smell a problem long before it ever materialized.

Ten

Ruby Diamond's memorial had been a huge success. The girls made money, the women's shelter made money, and Vincent made money. I don't think I allowed myself to feel the hollow emptiness left by Ruby's death until I'd packed my dance bag and settled back behind the wheel of my Camaro. Then the vision of Ruby wearing her ridiculous Dolly Parton wig and standing next to my dented car surfaced, as did a million other flashes of memory. Ruby dancing, biting her lower lip in that sweet, vulnerable way she had. Ruby lying on the floor of my living room, laughing and reaching over to scratch Fluffy.

I started up the car and pushed a tape into the cassette player. I was crying and trying to fit the tape into the damn player while I also shifted into first and attempted to pull out into the four A.M. traffic of Thomas Drive. I floored it and chirped the tires out of the driveway and halfway down the block before I made the turn onto the shortcut to the Hathaway Bridge and home.

I don't know what I thought about exactly. I know my mind wandered back to a lot of the dancers I'd known. I had no idea what had happened to most of them. In this business, friendships tend to be superficial and last only as long as you stay with the club. One night you look up, and you find somebody new sitting beside you at the makeup bench. You don't ask questions about the girl who used to sit where the new girl is now putting on her makeup. Maybe she got fired. Maybe she did too many drugs or got arrested. You don't ask because sometimes it's easier not to know.

I'd only made a couple of long-lasting friends in the whole eight years I'd been dancing. Ruby was gonna become number three, and what happened to her is the reason that I usually stay walled off from the others.

I was driving fast, catching all the green lights and coasting in and out of the few cars on the road. I had the T-tops off and my hair loose. For once, I didn't give a shit about anything but me, the night air, and the ride. The Camaro seemed to sense my mood and balked at the rough way I handled her. She was mushy on the curves and slow to respond, but I was too involved with my own feelings to care. I must've been doing sixty when I hit the entrance to the Hathaway Bridge and began the climb up the tall span.

The cool air at the top of the bridge, hit my face like a blast of cold water, shocking me back into the present. The car seemed to shake and shimmy more than it usually did on the concrete bridge. I have a fear of heights, especially heights over water. I can't drive over Hathaway without noticing every little shake and shimmy. Now I was having trouble keeping the car from pulling to the left. Probably out of alignment again, I hoped, but I was only fooling myself.

"Slow down," I cautioned myself as I started up the slope of bridge that led into Panama City. The state patrol station lay at the foot of the bridge and all I needed was a ticket to cap off the evening.

As I approached the top of the bridge, I realized that there was something drastically wrong with the car. The entire front end shook like a blender gone out of control, and it was all I could do to hang on to the wheel. I couldn't see the water below me through the inky darkness, but I knew it was there, a hundred feet down. My palms began to sweat. The Camaro lurched sharply, pulling me into the middle of the span and into the path of oncoming traffic.

I couldn't touch the horn to warn the other drivers, because I was fighting to keep from plowing across three lanes of traffic and through the guardrail. There was a popping noise, and then the car seemed to drop to the left and spin. I closed my eyes, not wanting to see what would happen next. Horns blared, brakes squealed, and I braced myself. The wheel shook out of my hands and I covered my face.

The car banged up against something, then shuddered quickly to a stop. Slowly I uncovered my eyes. Straight ahead, I could see nothing but darkness with tiny lights in the distance. The wind blew salt air off the bay and into my face. I had come to a rest against the low concrete guardrail, a thick strip of concrete and steel that didn't seem to be an adequate protection from the water below.

Bright lights from traffic in both directions lit up the top of the bridge, making it impossible to see anything but the immediate area around the car. I was less than three feet from the grille of a monster truck.

"Damn!" The driver of the truck, a frizzy-haired blonde in tight jeans and cowboy boots, was climbing down from the cab and starting to run toward me. "Damn, Shazamm! I nearly ran your ass over!" she cried. "Lookit there!" She was pointing to my left front fender.

I slowly stepped out of the car, my entire body shaking as if I were cold. My left front wheel was gone, completely gone, and the axle had ground to a halt in the thick concrete of the bridge span.

Other cars were pulling up and stopped by my car, which spanned the center lanes of the Hathaway Bridge. Doors were opening and slamming and I could hear but not see people beginning to approach.

"Sugar," the blonde said, "if I was you, I'd sue the asshole what put that tire on! You could've been *kilt*!"

From the base of the bridge I heard the high-pitched whine of a state trooper's siren as it started out of the patrol station and began climbing the span to reach us. I thought about Roy Dell Parks and his pit crew's assurances that my car had been fixed up good as new, and I swore that the first thing I'd do after I got myself and my car off the bridge was kick Roy Dell's ass.

Eleven

I lay in bed the next morning surveying the day's options. Fluffy lay beside me, her head upon the satin pillow that I'd bought especially for her and had embroidered with a pink satin *F*. I knew what I wanted to do, given the opportunity. I wanted to hunt down sorry Roy Dell Parks. I wanted to see the look on his scruffy face when I appeared at the track, or wherever he kept himself during the daytime, and pulled my fist back one more time. Of course, today that wouldn't be an option. Ruby Lee Diamond's funeral was to be held in her tiny hometown of Wewahitchka and I had to be there.

"Fluff," I said, staring into her huge brown eyes, "no disrespect to the dead, but I'm not exactly a funeral person, see what I'm saying?" Fluffy yawned and blinked. Clearly she felt entitled to more beauty sleep.

"Ruby's gone, Fluff. A funeral ain't gonna make it better. But maybe I'll find out something that'll help me catch her killer." Fluffy stretched, her tiny paws just reaching the edge of my shoulder. I reached over and scratched her neck below her chin. From the kitchen, the sounds of the automatic coffeepot swinging into action could be heard. The day was starting.

"You know," I said, stepping out of bed and searching for

my feather-trimmed bedroom slippers, "these Southern funerals can be kinda unpredictable." Fluffy was stretching on the end of the bed now, preparing to hop down and make a beeline for the doggie door. Fluffy's not much for morning conversation.

"Well, I'm just hoping they don't go having an altar call or start slipping snakes into the congregation." Fluffy left on that note.

"Well, I don't know about you," I called after her, "but I don't have a thing to wear." The slam of the doggie door answered me. "Fine for you," I called after her, "but I get first dibs on the shower!" I was talking to myself again, the story of my freaking life. I headed for the coffeepot. If I was going to be in Wewa by two, I'd have to get a move on. It was almost noon.

I had one other problem. As of four A.M., I was without transportation. The Camaro sat over at Bud's 24 Hour Service and Repair, awaiting a new wheel, and wouldn't be ready until late afternoon. I walked over to the bedroom window and looked out across the street to Raydean's trailer. There was only one option and I knew from experience that it would be a costly one. Raydean's 1962 black-and-white Plymouth Fury sat in her detached garage, neatly covered with a bright blue tarp for extra protection. Raydean's husband had bought the former police cruiser at an auction and treated it like the child they'd never had.

"Why, shoot yes, you can use the Plymouth to get to Ruby's funeral," Raydean said when I called. "I was just dreading making the drive alone. You can ride us both out there."

I knew better than to argue her out of it. She long ago explained to me that where her Plymouth went, she went. But still I tried.

"Raydean, you don't need to get all tuckered out going to

Ruby's funeral. It's going to be ninety in the shade today, and that heat's not good for you."

"Nope," she said firmly, "if Roy Dell went and fell out over this gal, well, I reckon I oughta go see what all the fussing was about. Besides, she was a friend of yours, and you'll need some moral support. These are trying times, honey."

I sighed and gave up. "All right, I'll be over in about a half an hour. Thanks, Raydean." Raydean slammed down the phone, apparently too caught up in the upcoming events to fool with the social nicety of saying good-bye.

I don't have many church outfits in my closet. It's not that I've turned my back on my Catholic upbringing. I prefer to think that the Church has turned its back on me. I haven't given up on God. I think She and I see eye to eye on a lot of issues. Organized religion and all the attendant hypocrisy is what I object to most. Ruby would be judged a sinner by a jury of her peers; I was just certain of that. They'd sit in their pews and call it mourning, but I knew it was smug self-satisfaction that would bring them to her funeral. I was only going because Ruby couldn't speak for herself any longer, and someone ought to be there to stand up for all that was pure and holy in her.

I was thinking about that, and how I'd probably be thrown out of the By Christ United in His Word Holiness Church, as I started down the stairs outside my trailer. Raydean was already waiting, the cover hastily torn off the Fury and the doors wide open. She was either airing the hot car out or shooing aliens.

"Let's get a move on," Raydean said, scrambling into the passenger seat. She pulled down the passenger side visor and adjusted what can only be described as an oversized Easter bonnet. Very slowly she pulled out a four-inch hat pin, carefully reinserting it in the exact same location.

"If you don't get a move on, they'll start without us. Didn't your mama ever teach you it weren't proper to enter a tabernacle of the Lord's sanctuary after the choir has done assembled for the pastor's good word? Put the pedal to the metal, sugar. We're gonna miss all the good stuff!"

Raydean actually turned out to be helpful. She knew Wewahitchka and led me straight to the church, a small cinderblock rectangle just on the edge of town. It was one of those drive-in-and-park-on-the-grass-up-to-the-front-door kind of churches, with a small white sign with black letters that looked to be poorly hand-painted. My heart sank further as I saw Brother Everitt's name at the bottom of the sign. We were in for a long sermon about the wages of sin and I was in no mood to hear it.

I hated to take Raydean's mint-condition Plymouth bounding over the rutted churchyard, but there was no other way to do it. People had filled up the front of the grass and gravel area, leaving us only the dusty red-clay pitted back area.

"Now, this is what I call a turnout!" Raydean declared with satisfaction. "We're gonna raise the roof here!" Raydean grabbed the top of her hat and directed her gaze skyward. "Be afraid, alien evildoers! Be very afraid!"

An elderly pair of women, making their way slowly across the dusty lot, stopped as Raydean shrieked her instructions skyward.

"Amen to that, sister," one murmured.

"Right on!" the other proclaimed. She wore wild orange beads and seemed to be a kindred spirit to Raydean.

As we approached the front door of the tiny church, a figure in a black robe emerged from the side of the building, rushing toward the door. Brother Everitt, his short black hair slicked back with pomade, was sweeping up the steps, an impatient scowl on his face and a Bible in his hand.

"Get your tail in gear, girl," Raydean said as we started up the steps after him. "The brother's fixing to give the call to worship."

We ran up the stairs, bursting into the sanctuary and coming to an abrupt halt as Raydean surveyed the congregation for a choice seat. Then, straightening her bonnet and adjusting her thick purse on her arm, she was off again, sailing down the red-carpeted aisle like a steamship.

I feared she was heading for the front row, but she stopped on a dime a third of the way up.

"This'll do fine," she whispered, clambering over the two elderly women from the parking lot in her attempt to get situated. "We won't miss a thing from here."

I sat down and took a moment to get my bearings. There were maybe eighty people packed into the minuscule building, all looking back over their shoulders as newcomers entered, darting a furtive wave, a quick smile, and whispered greetings. It seemed more like a social gathering than a funeral. St. Mary's wouldn't have tolerated such a display. Where I come from, church is a penance. You don't chat, you suffer.

The By Christ United in His Word Holiness Church was lacking in a few of the things we Catholics consider essential. There were no icons, for one thing. A color portrait of Jesus, hanging centered above the pulpit, seemed to be the only acknowledgment of the religious heavy hitters. There was no altar, no gold crosses or candles, and furthermore, there was no incense.

The interior was very plain. Paneled fake-wood walls with no stained-glass windows, just red colored glass. This was a bargain-basement house of worship. There wasn't even a real organ, just keyboards and a piano, with a big-haired fat lady thumbing through a sheaf of music. The nuns would've had a heyday with this place.

The fat lady glanced toward the rear of the church, stiffened, and brought her pudgy fingers down hard on the keyboard. Music began to play and the congregation rose to its feet. "The Old Rugged Cross" rang out through the room as Brother Everitt began his slow procession down the center aisle, followed by a couple who had to be Ruby's parents.

Ruby's mom was short and trim, with dark hair coiled neatly into a bun. She wore a navy-blue dress and hung on to her husband's arm, her face swollen with tears. Ruby's father looked as if he were barely able to stand, let alone support his grieving wife. His face was pale, his eyes dark black circles of pain, and he seemed almost unable to lift one foot and place it in front of the other.

I felt Raydean's strong arm slip around my waist and realized, as she pressed a handkerchief into my hand, that I had started crying. Around us, voices were singing. People's expressions seemed unaffected by the reality of why we were all in this church on a Thursday morning. My friend, her parents' child, had died and would never again be seen on the face of this planet. The grief suddenly stabbed like a knife into my chest. Raydean's comforting presence seemed to be the only anchor in an ocean of unexpected pain.

The hymn ended, Ruby's parents were seated in the front pew, and Brother Everitt began to pray. Raydean patted my hand.

"Brothers and sisters, God has called our little sister home," he began. Everitt had a high nasal whine that permeated the room. It was made worse by the sound system that had been installed on the podium. It was totally unnecessary and only served to give Everitt's voice a tinny, screechy quality.

"God reached, I say he reached forth from his throne of holiness and swept our sister out of the jaws of evil and temptation." There was a chorus of amens from the congregation.

I started looking around in an attempt to ignore him. Ruby's parents were softly crying in the front pew. Everyone else seemed obediently focused on the good brother's message about the wages of sin. They stared at him, mouths slightly open, hands stilled in their laps, and eyes following his every move. Several women sniffed, bringing handkerchiefs to their faces, but only one other person seemed completely overcome.

In the back row a small man sat with tears rolling down his wrinkled farmer cheeks. His shoulders were so hunched with grief that his neck seemed to have disappeared. He wore an olive-green plaid jacket, new in the sixties, and a narrow dark tie that stood out like a pen-streak against the white of his shirt. His gray hair rose up in tufts that blended with the wiry gray hairs of his beard.

"Raydean," I whispered, tugging at her arm. "Who's that? Do you know him?"

Raydean turned in her seat, shoved her heavily flowered bonnet back on her head, and squinted through her trifocals.

"No idea," she whispered, "but he's a looker, ain't he?" I turned to Raydean to make sure she was looking at the right man. She appeared to be staring in his general direction, but I realized she was focused on the door. Detective Wheeling had slipped into the back of the church and was quietly surveying the congregation. Our eyes met for an instant before I could turn away.

"If you ask me," Raydean whispered, "I'd say that other feller of yours is the prize, but that'un might give you a good run."

"I didn't mean him, Raydean," I hissed back. "The old guy crying on the back row."

Raydean looked over her shoulder again. From the corner of my eye I saw her wink at Detective Wheeling, then look away.

"Well," she said slowly as we rose to sing a hymn, "I'd still stick with the boyfriend you got. That feller's a mite old for you." She glanced back over her shoulder again. "He's more my speed, sugar. But you ought not be dwelling on the hormonal in the house of the Lord, honey." I gave up. Raydean lived in a parallel universe.

The congregation was belting out "Shall We Gather at the River." Brother Everitt had moved from the pulpit down to the front row, where he placed his hand upon Ruby's mother's head and appeared to be praying. Ruby's mother swayed slowly, and as I watched, she collapsed into her husband's arms. Brother Everitt eyed her for a moment, then abruptly whirled around and walked back to face the congregation as the hymn came to a close.

"Brothers and sisters," he said, "after the interment, the Diamonds have asked me to tell you that they will receive callers at their residence on Mebane Road. Let us pray." He stretched out his arms, threw his head back, and began to speak.

I couldn't listen. I closed my eyes and bent my head, but I wasn't listening. I was saying my own prayers, talking to Herself about Ruby and her family, and what a gift she had been in my life. I didn't want to hear Brother Everitt's message of guilt and shame. "And, God," I added silently, "if you need some help getting the ass—um, animal, that killed her, just put me to work, all right?"

Raydean elbowed me and I opened my eyes. The congregation was standing as Ruby's casket was carried slowly down the aisle. Her parents and other family members followed, then the rest of the congregation filed out of the pews and headed for the door.

"Honey, ain't no point in us going out to the cemetery. That wouldn't be a good thing for you." Raydean's voice was soft and she gripped my elbow gently with her gloved hand. "Let's us wander up to the drugstore and have a Coke, then we'll go out to her parents' and pay our respects."

"Sounds like a plan," I said, and started wandering toward the back of the church. I was hoping to avoid Detective

Wheeling, but that wasn't going to be possible. He had planted himself in our path and was staring me down.

"Let's talk," he said softly.

"Let's not, Detective, and say we did." I started to push past him, but Raydean missed the cue.

"Honey, you look thirsty," she said to him. Raydean came up to about his collarbone, but her hat was tall enough to brush the tip of his nose. "Why don't you just come on with us over to the drugstore and have a Coke. That's what we're gonna do. My sweet friend is just a bit overcome, you know. I figure it's best to refresh ourselves before we set out to pay our respects."

As I watched, Detective Wheeling's face switched from a look of consternation to a broad smile, all of which was directed over the top of Raydean's hat toward me.

"Why, ladies, that would be just the thing. Why don't I drive?" He swept his arm through Raydean's and placed a guiding hand on the small of my back. There was no other option but to allow myself to be led out the door, past Brother Everitt, and on to the Wewahitchka General Drugstore.

Raydean was thrilled, I could tell. She practically pushed me out of the way in her effort to climb into the front seat, and once enthroned, she began a rapid-fire conversation with Detective Wheeling.

"Smart thinking, boy," she began cryptically.

"How's that, ma'am?" he drawled.

"The way you screen out interference. You got your scanner, your car phone, and your radio all clumped up together and they're all turned on." She was right. The radio was pumping out a Reba McEntire song while the scanner squawked a sequence of numbers. "You keep out the interstellar galactic interference that way. It's best in case them Flemish decide to invade. Wouldn't do to be caught with our pants down, now would it?"

Wheeling's neck reddened and he laughed nervously. Maybe the good old boy had bitten off more than he could chew. I sat back in my seat and started enjoying the ride. We were at most a block from the downtown area.

"You and Miss Lavotini been friends long?" he asked, expertly whipping into a space that had materialized right in front of the drugstore.

"Shoot, boy, I been knowing Sierra since she moved into the trailer park two years ago. Weren't for her, I'd a been dead many times over. Them Flemish don't cotton to chihuahuas." Wheeling looked puzzled but didn't say a word. Raydean was half out of the car and headed for the soda counter before Wheeling could open his door.

We took stools on either side of Raydean, who by now was calmly sipping a tall soda. I was in a time warp. The soda counter was marble, the stools wrought iron, and the mirror behind the counter was turning gray with age. Even the counter boy seemed to be a throwback to another era. He was ancient, maybe in his nineties, and wore a peaked white paper cap.

Detective Wheeling ordered a soda and then whistled softly under his breath. Raydean looked over at him and smiled.

"You know, Sierra liked another boy at the funeral, but I told her you were the better item." Wheeling smiled slowly. "Of course," she added, "that was afore I saw that little gold band on your finger." She looked over at me. "You'd best keep the one you got," she said.

I felt my face flush and I started praying in earnest that she wouldn't mention Nailor's name.

"Hush, Raydean," I whispered.

"Sierra's shy," Raydean said loudly. "She's got her a nice young fella. Course, I can't say nothing for the calling hours he keeps." I kicked Raydean's ankle. "Youch!" she squeaked, her hand darting down to rub her sore ankle. "What you do that for?"

"I think we should be getting back," I said. Wheeling was smiling to himself, like he held all the cards and knew I was about to fold. "We don't want to be too late getting to Ruby's house."

Raydean took a huge suck at her straw, inhaling half of her Coke with one inhale. Detective Wheeling didn't move.

"Aw, ladies," he said slowly, "now there's no need to rush off. Heck, they just left out for the cemetery. They won't get back over to the house for another forty minutes. Miss Raydean, you just settle back and relax."

Raydean smiled and batted her eyes at him. "Don't mind if I do," she sniffed. Wheeling took another pull at his soda.

"A woman as pretty as Sierra," he began slowly, "I'll bet she's got all kind of fellas wanting to be her beau. He must be right special." My heart was beating out of my chest.

"I don't see as how that's really any of your business," I said.

"Aw, now, honey, there ain't no call to be rude," Raydean said. "And I'm sure he is nice," she said, turning to Wheeling. "He's a po-lice. I find po-lices usually to be on the wrong side of me, but this one's a sweet fella. Plays a mean hand of poker, too."

"Raydean," I warned. "I have many male friends, and yes, Detective, some of them are members of your profession. You see," I said, turning to Raydean, "Detective Wheeling is a member of the police force." I spoke slowly and deliberately, hoping Raydean would catch on and know to button her lip. "He's one of *them*."

Raydean stiffened at the mention of "them." "Them" meant only one thing to her. "Them," she said slowly, turning to stare at Wheeling, while at the same time pushing herself closer to me. "Uh-huh," she said. "Them, eh?"

Wheeling smiled disarmingly. "We're not really so bad," he said.

Raydean's eyes widened. "Not so bad?" she screeched, earning the attention of the ninety-five-year-old counter boy. "Bursting into people's homes in the middle of the night? Using force to control the minds and lives of innocent people? Ultimately working for world dominion? That's not bad?" She reached gingerly up to the counter for her purse and pulled it quickly toward her.

"Now, Miss Raydean," Wheeling said, sensing something was drastically wrong and mistaking it for common police phobia. "We're here to protect and to serve. Innocent folks have nothing to fear from us. We want to make the world a better, safer place."

"How many are there of you?" she asked.

"In Panama City? Oh, I'd say no more than five hundred, counting the county and the beach force."

Raydean jumped off her stool and headed for the door. "Come on, Sierra, we gotta clear outta here. Beach force! Who'd have thought they'd come by water!"

I stood up and prepared to follow the rapidly departing Raydean. Detective Wheeling grabbed my arm in an attempt to restrain me.

"What is it with her?" he asked. "What did I say?"

I grinned. "Well, Detective," I said, "you've somehow managed to convince Miss Raydean that you are an alien life form. I wonder how she ever got such an idea?" Wheeling followed me out the door. Raydean was walking briskly down the sidewalk toward the church, obviously not intending to ride in what was now a suspected alien vehicle. "Nice try, Detective," I said. "Maybe you'll have better luck interrogating some of my other friends and acquaintances. However, were I you, and not an alien, I would be talking to Roy Dell Parks, or any number of other swarmy assholes that were pawing

Ruby Diamond that night. I would not be sipping sodas and frightening harmless little old ladies in a wasted effort to find out more about me."

I whirled around and headed down the street after Raydean. Wheeling wasn't finished with me. He wasn't the type to let anyone have the last word.

"Miss Lavotini," he said, matching his stride to mine, "believe it or not, I'm trying to help." I stopped in my tracks, preparing to give him some choice advice on how to do his job, but the look on his face stopped me. He had the same earnest little-boy expression I had seen that first night in the police station. I'm a sucker for guys who look like that, and so I stopped just long enough for him to get a word in edgewise.

"Look, put yourself in my place," he said. "If you were trying to find the killer, you'd talk to everyone, track down every possible lead, gather as much information as possible, no matter how trivial or useless it seemed, wouldn't you?" Raydean was now a small speck in the distance, turning into the church parking lot, her bonnet a pastel dot of color in the red-clay parking lot. I looked back at Wheeling, staring into his clear eyes and hating myself for seeing his point.

"Of course," I answered. "So why aren't you out at the racetrack?"

"Because I wanted to come to the funeral," he answered. "I wanted to see who was here. And because you know things you haven't told me."

My guard was up again. "The hell I do," I said angrily.

"You do," he said evenly. "In every witness's mind there are fragments, bits that they may not consciously be aware of, that float around. They may be important bits or they may just be fluff, but you have them. One of those pieces might just hold the key to what happened or who did this. It's my job to keep talking, keep asking the right questions. You can see that, can't you?"

I nodded. Wheeling was wearing a dark blue suit, a pale blue shirt, and a subdued gray tie. For a moment I found myself liking him, even wondering about what he'd be like if he wasn't married. Stop it, I warned myself, don't let your guard down.

"The fact remains," he was saying, "you placed another detective in my squad at the scene. I've got to wonder about that. That doesn't mean I automatically discount what you said. It just means I've got to find out about that." Damn, I knew better than to lower my guard. "Was Raydean talking about Detective Nailor in there?"

"No," I answered, looking him straight in the eye. "Raydean's like that. She gets confused. I mean, she met Detective Nailor last summer when he was investigating a murder. Maybe that's what she meant." I could feel my neck flush and I felt just like I used to feel in Catholic school when Sister Claude Marie would demand my homework and I would lie about it.

"Sierra," he said, "it's not like I suspect you of anything. I'm just trying to get at the facts here. It makes no difference to me if you and John have a personal relationship."

I heard Raydean's car before I saw it. The unmistakable sound of a 1962 Plymouth Fury traveling fast with a small hole in its muffler made Detective Wheeling look up. Raydean was headed for the drugstore, no doubt to rescue me from the clutches of an alien evildoer. I could make out her face, set with a determined expression, her bonnet hanging lopsided over her forehead, covering one eye. She was coming in and she was coming in fast. Only one thing stood between her, the curb, and me: Detective Wheeling's unmarked brown Taurus sedan.

Wheeling realized this at the same moment that I did and jumped out into the street in a vain attempt to ward off her approach. He waved his arms wildly, yelling for her to cut the wheel, but Raydean either didn't hear him or chose not to listen. There was a small, high-pitched scraping noise as the front fender of Raydean's Plymouth tapped into the Taurus and then rubbed a thin even scrape all the way down the side of the car.

Raydean may have noticed this, because she then attempted to correct her error by backing up. This only served to neatly crease the entire left side of his car.

"Oh my God, would you look at that?" he moaned.

I looked. "Detective, I'm thinking a little rubbing compound and you'll be good to go." Wheeling glowered at me.

"Rubbing compound? There's a dent an inch deep on the side of my car." Raydean honked the horn impatiently. Apparently she saw nothing wrong and intended for us to put as much distance as possible between herself and this alien.

"Well, then," I said, "do you want me to get her to—"

"No, hell, no. Just go on. There's no use in me trying to get anything straight with her. Just go on. I'll take care of it."

"Thanks, Detective," I said softly. "I owe you one."

"One?" he said, a hint of a smile escaping as he looked at Raydean. "You owe me, all right, but one won't get it. How about we call a truce and you agree to sit down and talk to me. One on one, no crazy neighbors or attorneys."

"All right. One on one. Your office. Tomorrow morning."

Wheeling nodded, his attention turned back to his bruised Taurus. "Go on, get out of here. I'll see you tomorrow morning."

Raydean gunned the engine to let me know that time was wasting. I didn't want to linger, lest the detective change his mind and decide to make our lives more difficult. I ran around to the passenger side of Raydean's car and climbed in.

Raydean slammed the car into reverse and pulled out into the street without checking the rearview mirror. A car's brakes screeched and a horn sounded, but neither of us looked back.

"I'm thinking the boy was telling you that I'm certifiable," Raydean said calmly, once the car was rolling down the street.

"You did a damn fine job yourself," I answered.

"Some days you get the bear, some days the bear gets you," she answered cryptically.

Twelve

*R*uby Lee Diamond's parents lived on the edge of Wewahitchka in a small white frame house that sat behind a chain-link fence on a manicured stamp of crayon-green grass. Cars lined either side of the road, having been pulled over into the grass that ran to the street's edge. More people were pulling up as we arrived, parking and then making their way to the door with somber expressions and casserole dishes.

"I didn't think . . ." I said.

"Well, I did," Raydean replied, reaching over her shoulder into the backseat for a square foil-lined baking pan. "Always keep a spare in the freezer, just in case." I had no idea what was in the pan, and didn't really want to ask. Knowing Raydean, baked alligator was not out of the realm of possibility.

We walked up to the house and drifted inside, swallowed up by the covey of friends and relations, all come to comfort Ruby's parents. Brother Everitt was nowhere to be seen, and I was glad because I was in the mood to tell someone off and he'd have been my first target. Raydean, who's never met a stranger, wandered into the kitchen to deposit her casserole, leaving me to fend for myself.

The house was larger on the inside than it appeared from the outside, but still the house was packed with what appeared to be the entire population of tiny Wewahitchka. Ruby's parents sat on a sofa in the living room and an informal receiving line had been started. The dining room table was quickly being covered with food as women in hastily donned aprons ran back and forth from the kitchen.

"It's Sierra, isn't it?" a low voice said. I looked up to see Meatloaf standing next to me, distinctly uncomfortable in his too-tight polyester pants and short-sleeved white shirt.

"And you'd be Meatloaf," I answered. He smiled tentatively and extended a hand that, even though scrubbed, still looked gray with car grime. "Did you bring the rest of the boys, or are you doing this on your own?" Somehow I didn't think Meatloaf would brave a funeral alone. I tried to look around behind him, but he took up too much space for me to get a clear view.

"Nah, them others is here. I just saw you standing all alone, looking like a flower, and I thought, well, I wanted to say hello." His face was scarlet. Who'd have thought a big guy like that would be shy around a woman?

"There you are. Come on." I looked behind Meatloaf and saw his buddy Frank, who hadn't bothered to clean up much. He wore dark blue mechanic's pants, steel-toed work boots, and a pale blue shirt with short sleeves that showcased his tattoos. His one concession to formality was a too-short clip-on paisley tie.

Frank glowered at me, probably still remembering how I'd clocked his idol, the great Roy Dell Parks.

"Come on," he repeated impatiently. "Mr. Rhodes said we'd best git on." I looked around again and this time saw Mickey Rhodes standing in the corner, a Panama straw hat in his hand and a somber expression on his face.

"Where's Roy Dell?" I asked, suddenly remembering my damaged Camaro.

"Aw, he's outside in Mr. Rhodes's Caddy. He was so tore

up at the graveside, he couldn't face coming in," said Meatloaf. Frank snarled something about Meatloaf needing to shut up.

"Well, I need to see him about something, so let's step outside." I started walking out the door with Roy Dell's boys behind me. Mickey Rhodes made an attempt at a polite greeting, but I had one thing on my mind: retribution. Roy Dell and I had business to settle concerning a certain lug nut.

I heard Frank behind me. "I don't like the look on her face," he was saying. "She looks just like she did the last time." Meatloaf giggled nervously.

Mickey Rhodes's Cadillac was easy to spot. It gleamed white in the sunlight of the early afternoon. White exterior, fire-engine-red interior, and a magnetic sign on the driver's side door that advertised the Dead Lakes Motor Speedway. Hunched down in the backseat, his head lowered miserably, sat Roy Dell Parks.

I whipped open the back door, climbed inside, slammed the door shut, and quickly hit the lock. Outside, as the steamy heat of northwest Florida made everything look shimmery, I watched Frank and Meatloaf start to get frantic. Their boss was alone in the backseat of a car with a madwoman.

Roy Dell, for his part in things, looked up and clearly thought he saw salvation. His face lit up like a lost child's.

"Sierra, honey," he said. Then, as if remembering Ruby, he cut his eyes downward and let a tear slide down his cheek. "It's a terrible thing," he said, shaking his head.

"Roy Dell, shut your mouth." He looked shocked. "You and your sorry-assed pit crew left the lug nuts loose on my car and I nearly died last night. The way I see it, your ass is mine over this."

Roy Dell frowned. "Sierra, me and the boys didn't have nothing to do with your lug nuts."

"Don't run that crap with me," I said. "You were the only

people in a position to work on my car, and I'm telling you my left front tire fell off on top of Hathaway Bridge. Now maybe it was an accident, or maybe it was payback for what I don't know, but I'm telling you, I'm on to you."

Roy Dell looked even more puzzled. "Now, Sierra, I won't say me or Mr. Rhodes was there every second watching them work, but I know my boys and I stand by their work."

"Oh, and Frank, too?" I asked. I looked out the window and saw Frank rushing Mickey up to the car, talking and gesturing wildly with his hands.

"Frank don't work for me," Roy Dell said. "He's a driver. I taught him everything he knows. But I can tell you this, that boy wouldn't harm a hair on your blond head." I looked out the window at Frank's skull-and-crossbones tattoo and laughed.

"Yeah, right. You know, I'm thinking here, Roy Dell, that maybe you're not being on the straight with me. You see, the way I'm forced to think now, I'm thinking maybe you're lying. I don't know why the cops aren't crawling your butt, Roy Dell, 'cause you were the last one with her."

I wasn't watching Roy Dell. I'll have to admit I was staring past him out the window at Frank and Meatloaf, who were now dragging a reluctant Mickey Rhodes over to unlock the car, so I was unprepared for the power of Roy Dell's reaction. He reached over and grabbed me with such force that my teeth snapped.

"You don't know what you're talking about, do you?" he growled. "If I was you and I wanted to keep my pretty face and ass in business, I'd shut my mouth and keep it shut. If somebody wanted to communicate with you, honey, they'd need to go upside your head with a two-by-four and couldn't nobody blame them. Now, quit looking for trouble, 'cause I'm ready to tell you, trouble will find you every time."

At that moment, Mickey Rhodes unlocked the car door. "What's going on?" he asked.

"Nothing!" Roy Dell and I snapped in unison. We glared at each other and I pulled my arm out of his grasp.

"You're one to talk," I hissed, then threw open the door and jumped out. Roy Dell Parks, the King of Dirt, had a side to his personality that I bet his adoring fans knew nothing about. How much of Roy Dell had Ruby seen? What if things had turned ugly when Ruby wouldn't move along as quickly as he wished?

I straightened the collar on my blouse and moved past the gaping men, back into the house. I walked slowly, like I was out for nothing but a stroll, but inside I felt like Jell-O. The crowd had thinned a bit and the receiving line was down to a few people as the majority had made for the dining room. Raydean was deep in conversation with the two elderly ladies from the church. It seemed to me that the best thing I could do would be to pay my respects to Ruby's parents and get the hell out of Wewahitchka.

Ruby's mother took my hand in hers and tried to smile. "Sugar, I've heard so much about you," she said softly. I could feel the tears welling up in my eyes and there wasn't a thing I could do to stop them.

"I should've watched her more closely," I began, choking on the words that had lain hidden in my heart. "It's my fault."

"No, now, honey, that's not so," Mr. Diamond said, leaning close to his wife.

"She was so happy, Sierra," Mrs. Diamond said. "I can't say that we supported her at first, but eventually I made peace with her decision to dance."

Mr. Diamond nodded and patted his wife's knee. "I'll get you some water," he said, rising from the sofa.

Mrs. Diamond watched him walk slowly off toward the kitchen, then gestured to the coffee table, where three full glasses of water sat untouched.

"He can't bear to talk about it," she said in a half whisper, "but I just have to, you know?"

I nodded, not trusting myself to speak. Mrs. Diamond's hands twisted a shredded tissue, leaving strings of white against the dark navy of her dress.

"She was my baby, my only one," she said as tears once again fell into her lap, splashing on the wrinkled hands. "Some would think it would be different, you know, because we adopted her when she was three. But it wasn't any different than if I'd given birth to her."

I leaned down and placed my hand over hers, and she gestured for me to sit in the spot where her husband had been. "I'm so very sorry," I murmured, feeling so inadequate.

"You know, Ruby felt the same way about me," she said, her fingers restlessly tracing a pattern in the material of her dress. "I kept waiting for the day when she'd ask who her real mother was, but, you know," she said, turning toward me, looking deep into my eyes, "she never did." I looked away, remembering Ruby's sad face as she told me about being taunted for being from foster care.

"I could've told her," Mrs. Diamond said, "but I didn't. Maybe I was afraid, but I'd like to think Ruby didn't want to know. It was over and done with, and she belonged to us." Mrs. Diamond wasn't really talking to me; she may as well have been addressing the water glasses on the coffee table. She just needed to talk.

"Wewahitchka's a small town," she continued. "Everybody knows everybody's business. I pretty much figured out who Ruby came from. You know, I almost called her this morning. I would've said, 'Hello, Iris? You probably don't know me, and might not even care, but our baby's dead and I thought you might want to know.' I didn't do it, of course. She probably wants to forget, or she might've acted like I'd got the wrong number, or some such of a thing. And, you know, I just don't believe I could've stood it."

"Who was her birth mother, Mrs. Diamond?"

Ruby's mother looked up at me as if she'd been a million miles away. "What, dear?"

"Her birth mother. What was her name?"

"Oh." Mrs. Diamond smiled softly. "I really don't want to cause any pain to her by speaking her name. She's gone on, made a good living for herself, grooming dogs or some such of a thing. It's best just to keep our hearts on Ruby."

Mr. Diamond walked up with the fourth glass of water. I stood up, then stooped down and crouched by Mrs. Diamond's side.

"Your angel could dance," I said. "She is dancing. Dancing for joy where no one and nothing can ever hurt her again." Then I reached up and wrapped my arms around the little woman. We stayed like that for a long moment, and then I released her as the next trio of mourners—Meatloaf, Frank, and a somber Mickey Rhodes—stepped forward to take my place.

Mrs. Diamond uttered a short gasp and I looked back to see that she'd knocked over the fresh glass of water.

"It's all right," Mickey said, moving forward to embrace the shaken woman. "It's all right."

"But you don't know, do you?" she said in a quavering voice, shaking her head.

"I know," he said, his voice hushed and soothing. "I know." But how could he? He wasn't a mother.

I turned to walk away, my eyes blinded with tears, and bumped right into the woeful little man from the church. His eyes were red and he used a bandanna to wipe them.

"I'm so sorry," I muttered, trying to step out of his way without flattening him.

"Honk if you love Jesus," he whispered. Then, "Oh Lord,

pray for us sinners and our salvation. This is my penance. She is gone and I will have eternity without her."

He left before I could say a word, pressing himself against the wall and sliding away from me, around the corner, into another room, almost running from the grieving mother and her mourners. It felt like the last straw for me. I would've opened my mouth and shouted out for Raydean had she not at that moment materialized beside me.

"I see you met Wannamaker Lewis," she said, nodding toward the little man.

"Not exactly," I answered. "It was more like he babbled and I tried to stay out of his way. Why? I thought you didn't know who he was."

"Sierra, that was afore someone mentioned his name. Don't you know who Wannamaker Lewis is?" Seeing the blank look on my face, she continued. "The famous Honk-if-you-love-Jesus folk artist."

It came back to me then. Eccentric Lewis, the unwilling millionaire, or so everyone supposed, as his work was now featured in trendy galleries around the country.

"Today's trend, tomorrow's garage sale," I said.

"I don't think so, Sierra," Raydean answered. "I invested a bit in his work myself. Of course," she added hastily, "that was afore he became famous." Raydean is very paranoid that someone will find out she came into a little chunk of money when her husband died.

"Let's blow this pop stand," I said.

Raydean scanned the room and nodded. "What's good for the goose is good for the gander. Never stay in one place too long," she said, heading for the door. "You'll gather moss. A psychologist told me that one time."

Thirteen

I didn't go to work that night after Ruby's funeral. I called Vincent and told him to let Marla have the house to herself for a night; the Tiffany could do without me. I was expecting him to fight me on it, but he didn't. I guess he knew it wouldn't have done any good.

I shut all the blinds, pulled the curtains across the bay window in the living room, and started lighting candles. That's what I do when I'm depressed: I light candles, put on sad music, and dance. I wandered over to the CD player and started hunting up just the right music. Fluffy walked into the room and climbed up onto the futon, ever the observer.

"I don't get it, Fluff," I said, heading for the kitchen. "Ruby's dead and nobody seems to know what happened. And, you know," I said, pulling a jug of my father's homemade wine off the counter, "not one person knows why or who." I poured a hefty portion of Chianti into a Flintstones jelly glass and opened the kitchen door to let the cooling night air circulate through the trailer. When I walked back into the living room, I found Fluffy was actually listening, her moist brown eyes reflecting pools of sadness. "It's up to us, girl," I said, taking my first swig of wine. "We should be able to figure it out."

Fluffy sighed. She knew I was right. She also knew it was going to mean a lot of activity and trouble. Fluffy has a delicate temperament. Stress makes her cranky. I sat there next to her, stroking her tiny body, drinking Chianti from Pop's cellar, and listening to music. In the back of my head, I was turning over the facts of Ruby's death. I hadn't just run into the trash bin in my attempt to reach Ruby. I was pretty sure I'd been hit or pushed. There ought to be some memory, some sound or scent that would help me identify the killer.

"I got an idea, Fluff," I said. "I'll go back out to the race-track tomorrow. Surely something will come to me. At least I can talk to people, see if anyone saw Ruby with anyone, or saw John Nailor." Fluffy growled low in her throat. Probably thinking it was dangerous to sniff around a crime scene. I ignored her and drank the rest of my wine. It felt warm going down, spreading through my body and easing all the tension of the day.

I got up and poured another glass, realizing that I ought to stop at one and that I ought to eat something, but not doing either. The music was calling me. I walked softly into the middle of the living room. Sarah McLachlan was singing "I Will Remember You." I reached up and unfastened the clip that held my hair in a neat bun, shaking my head gently to let my hair fall down around my shoulders. I closed my eyes and began to move.

I unfastened my robe, tossing it onto the futon and danc-ing in my panties and bra. The tears came again, running unchecked down my cheeks as I danced. At some point I thought of John, but it wasn't the vision of his kiss that held me. Instead I remembered his arm around the woman at the racetrack, the way he held my gaze, deliberately, before he bent down and kissed her.

I leaned over, my hair spilling over my head and almost sweeping the floor in a blond waterfall. The room was golden with candlelight, the only sounds being Sarah McLachlan's voice and that of my feet as they moved across the floor.

I played the song again and again, dancing through my visions and feelings, forcing my body to work out the pain. I was sweating, my breath coming in short gasps. Ruby's face floated before me, the piano softly carrying me from one image to the next. I whirled slowly around, my hair spinning a golden wheel, my arms extending the circle. I opened my eyes as the song again came to a close. John Nailor stood in the doorway of the kitchen, his arms folded across his chest, watching.

We didn't speak. Instead he covered the short distance between us with a few steps, gently folding me into his arms and standing silently as the sobs that had been held back for so long finally came.

At last I felt the surge of emotion ease and then stop. I lifted my head and took the handkerchief he offered. I was standing in my underwear, sweaty, my nose running and my eyes swollen from crying.

"I must look like hell," I said, breaking free of his arms and crossing the room to get my robe from the futon.

"Not really," he said calmly. His white oxford-cloth shirt had black mascara stains on the shoulder now.

"How long were you there?" I asked.

"Long enough." He picked up my glass of wine from the bar that divided the kitchen from the living room and drank.

"So, don't you knock?" I pulled the sash on my robe tighter and began gathering my damp hair into a bun.

"Sierra, everybody needs to let it go sometime. It's nothing to be ashamed of." He crossed the room to the futon and sat down, pulling me with him. For a second, I felt dizzy. I wanted him to touch me again, and yet I didn't want him to ever touch me again. I didn't want to feel the way I did when he kissed me, as if our bodies were melting together and I might lose myself.

I straightened up and looked into his eyes for a brief second. "All right," I said. "This has to stop. I don't know what this thing is between the two of us, but I'm not going to do this." He smiled and reached out to touch the side of my face. His fingers burned a trail down my cheek, softly caressing my neck.

"You're not, huh?" he whispered, his face moving dangerously toward mine.

"No," I said, my voice squeaking an octave higher. "No!" I pushed back again. "You've got some questions to answer, Nailor. For one, what were you doing at the track?"

John shook his head. "I'm not going there with you, Sierra," he said. "I can't."

"If it had to do with your job," I continued, "Wheeling would've known about it." John said nothing. "Are you in trouble?"

He laughed, but I could tell he didn't find the question funny. "You could say that," he said.

"Then let me help you."

"I'll handle it on my own, Sierra. It's nothing I can't take care of. I just want to make sure you stay out of the way."

"Who killed Ruby?" I asked suddenly.

"Sierra, I told you, I don't know anything about that. Just let Detective Wheeling do his job, all right?"

"Well, I can't do that," I said. "He's not doing his job. That's the whole problem."

"You don't know that," he said. "The police aren't going to come running over here to let you know what they're doing."

"I can see that," I said sarcastically. "You could tell me if they were doing something, but you boys are all in the same club, no matter what. Even when —"

"Even when what?" he interrupted. "Even when I've got personal feelings involved, Sierra? Is that what you were going to say?" He reached out and grabbed both of my hands, pulling me closer. He bent his head and kissed me, letting go of one hand to reach up and cup my chin.

My heart was pounding and my body was screaming, "Go

for it, forget all this other crap. You want him. Go for it!" His hand moved down my neck and across my robe, gently circling my breast. I felt myself moan softly.

"No! Damn it, Nailor! You're not going to do this to me!" I pushed him away. "Answer my question!"

I'd made him mad, but I didn't care. He opened his mouth to speak, but the phone rang, startling both of us.

"Who could that be?" I said, reaching across him for the phone. "It's one o'clock in the morning, for Pete's sake! Hello?"

"Sugar," Raydean said in a husky whisper, "you got company."

"Raydean," I sighed impatiently, "I know I've got company."

"No, honey," she said. "Additional company, outside."

"What?" John was close enough to listen to the receiver, and he moved cautiously toward the window.

"Outside, about to the corner, three lots down. There's a car there, been there for a while, with somebody in it. I'm thinking it looks like po-lices."

"Oh, man," I said, fuming. "All right, honey, thanks. I'll take care of it."

"Well, I just thought you oughta know, being as how you got inside company."

"Raydean, how'd you know that?" I asked.

"Night patrol," she said cagily. "I try to keep my eye on the universe."

"Well, good job, Raydean," I said, but she'd hung up.

John was peering out a corner of my window, straining to see the car down the street.

"Look, I'm pretty sure it's ours," he said, "but I don't want them to see me."

"Why? What's going on? Don't you think they saw you come in?" I asked.

"I don't think so," he answered. "I parked somewhere else and walked in, and I didn't see that car when I got here. Do you have another door out of here, one that doesn't face the street?"

"No, I don't," I said. "I think your only option's going to be the bathroom window. It's in the middle of the trailer and it's dark back there. You could walk out and around to get back to your car."

John nodded. "Shit!" he said, stepping away from the window. "This is all I need." He was up and moving down the hallway. By the time I reached him he was already clearing a dried flower arrangement off the top of the toilet tank and preparing to open the small window.

He slid it open, moving slowly to keep the sound to a minimum, then turned, saw me, and stepped down to stand beside me.

"We have unfinished business," he said.

"I have unanswered questions. Starting with why don't you want them to see you?"

He laughed quietly. "You don't give up, do you?" He kissed me again. "That's for next time," he said. A moment later I was staring at an empty window, the curtains ruffling softly with the breeze.

I went across the hallway to my bedroom and peaked through the curtains out into the street. The brown sedan was still parked by the side of the road. What are they doing watching me? I wondered. And what kind of trouble was John in that he couldn't risk being seen leaving my house?

Fourteen

$\mathcal{S}$unlight did not improve the appearance of the Dead Lakes Motor Speedway. Instead it played upon its every imperfection, and there were many. It is a dust bowl surrounded by gravel, burnt grass, and litter. A run-down, rust-infested playground for motorheads addicted to whatever speed they can attain with their patched-together vehicles.

I drove my newly repaired Camaro across the track entrance, shuddering as my tires bounced on the metal plates installed in the clay drive. I expected the track to be quieter than it had been when Ruby and I made our last appearance, but if anything it was noisier. I drove carefully across the track and into the pit, where cars were lined up in front of their trailers and once again men hung over the hoods, gobbled up by the cars' gaping mouths.

A sign hung over the pit entrance announced: TIME TRIALS TODAY. "Now, that's an aspiration," I said to myself. "Time trials my ass—they can't even keep those wrecks together long enough to make an entire race and they want to tempt fate by timing them?"

I looked through my windshield, which was rapidly becoming covered with road dust, searching for the main office. As near as I could tell, there wasn't one, so I parked and decided to make the rest of the trip on foot. It was probably better this way, I reasoned. I'd probably find more people to talk to.

I had one goal in mind: I was going to find someone to give me the straight scoop on Roy Dell Parks, and not one of his groupies or pit crew. I needed someone who would tell me about the true Roy Dell, the man I voted most likely to have killed Ruby Diamond.

Because this mission would involve mostly reluctant men, men who wouldn't want to discuss their feelings and thoughts, especially about someone in their own outfit, I had chosen several Sierra secret weapons: my Superbra, designed to get even the most reluctant male to address at least one part of my anatomy; a micro miniskirt; a tiger-striped spandex body-suit, with appropriately plunging neckline; and finally, long, long blond hair, arranged so that it would fall softly over my shoulders. I was going for the vulnerable and troubled young-girl look.

I walked up to the first person I spotted, a guy with long, stringy blond hair, bent over a tire rim, efficiently putting on a new tire. He wore a flannel shirt, even though it was easily ninety degrees, baggy khakis, and high-topped black basketball sneakers.

I walked up behind him, straightened my shoulders to en-hance my natural attributes, and placed one hand on my hip, ready to put the act into motion.

"Excuse me?" I called. "Could you help me?" I sounded so helpless I could've puked, but it was for a worthy cause. So imagine my surprise when the boy whirled around and I saw that he had tits. Not only tits, but he was a she, and she was about seven months pregnant.

"Yeah," she said, straightening and wiping the sweat off her forehead with a hand that left thick black smudges. "What d'ya need?"

My shoulders slumped, my hand dropped from my hip,

and I'm sure my mouth hung down to my chest. A pregnant tire changer? Wasn't there some law against that?

"Should you be doing this?" I asked.

She rubbed her belly casually and laughed. "Why? 'Cause of this?" I stared at her bulging stomach. "Honey, this ain't the first and it won't be the last. I worked right up till Virgil practically fell out on the ground, and it didn't hurt him none." I looked at the tire and then back to her. They seemed like mighty big tires, and even though there was nothing small about her, the tires had to be heavy. "I don't carry 'em, if that's what you're thinking. I just fix 'em. Now, was that what you were wanting? 'Cause if that's it, I'll be getting back to work." She turned around and would've gone back to the tire if I hadn't spoken.

"No, no, that's not it. I didn't even know you were . . . when I called to you." She looked back around, sighed again, and pushed a few stray strands of hair off her forehead.

"Well, then?" she said.

"Well, I was looking for the office, or wherever Mickey Rhodes works."

"Over there." She pointed toward the snack shack.

"In the snack shack?"

"No, not exactly in it. There's two parts to it. Mickey's offices are in the top, over the shack."

"Would you mind if I asked you a couple of questions about the other night? My name's Sierra Lavotini," I said, stepping forward and not giving her a moment to say no. "My friend Ruby was killed here the other night."

The woman looked around, as if hoping someone might step forward and save her from the conversation.

"Well, I don't know," she said.

"What's your name?" That's the same thing I always ask the customers when I want to get them into a conversation and eventually into a table dance. Once you get their first name, you've got a commitment to a conversation.

"Ann. And I wasn't here that night, so I can't help you."

"Well, Ann, I don't even know why I'm here, to tell you the truth." I shrugged my shoulders and bit the inside of my cheek. Tears welled up in my eyes. "You see, Ruby's mom, well, she don't think the cops are doing right by Ruby. You know what I mean?"

I suddenly had Ann's full attention and sympathy. Her hand crept to her stomach and she rubbed absently, putting herself in Ruby's mom's place.

"Mrs. Diamond, well, Ruby was her only baby, and I don't know what it's like to lose a child, but I can imagine." I paused, letting Ann have some time to imagine the loss of her little Virgil. She shuddered and I went on. "She asked me to come over here and just see if I couldn't piece together anything that would help her find out more about her baby's last moments on this earth. She wants to know if anyone, anyone here, could know who would do such a thing to her only child."

"Aw, man," Ann said, sighing, "that's awful." Tears had formed in her eyes and all thoughts of tires had vanished. "Well, from what I hear around here, Roy Dell was the last to see your friend, but he wouldn't do such a thing."

"What makes you say that?"

"Oh, everybody loves Roy Dell," she gushed. "Sure, he likes the ladies, but who could blame him?" Ann frowned and shook her head. "All those female fans, decked out, just trying to get his attention. It can go to a person's head. Besides, his wife treats him like a dog."

The image of Lulu Parks dragging Roy Dell out of the Tiffany popped into my head and I laughed. "Yeah, I saw her drag him out of a club one night. She sure gets angry about him and the ladies."

Ann's frown deepened. "She did what?"

"She marched right into the Tiffany Gentleman's Club, where I worked with Ruby, and dragged him right out."

Ann nodded slowly. "That was for show, pure and simple," she said. "Lulu doesn't love him, never has, never will. She loves his name and his sponsor money, but she don't love him. Why else would she—" Ann stopped talking abruptly.

"Would she what?" Don't clam up on me now, I prayed. Ann was clearly ambivalent, shifting from one foot to the other and chewing on her bottom lip.

"Well, I don't think that's important," she said, her cheeks turning scarlet.

"Ann, you never know what's important. It's just this kind of thing that the police don't hear that might help Ruby's mama."

"Well, I don't see how," she said, reluctant, "but all right. I know for a fact that Lulu doesn't love Roy Dell Parks. She cain't because Brenda the snack shack girl caught her old man, Frank, with Lulu not one week ago."

"No!" I looked shocked. "Are you sure?"

"Sure? Hell, yes, I'm sure. Brenda and me are tight. I was one of the first ones she told."

"Brenda caught them together?"

Ann's eyes widened and she looked behind her, as if ensuring that no one would overhear her. "You wouldn't believe the mess! See, Brenda was the closer that night at the snack shack, so she was here late. She wasn't in any hurry to get home, either, 'cause Frank had lost his race. He's bad to drink when he loses. And when he drinks he always takes it out on poor old Brenda."

I remembered the two women at the snack shack talking about their husbands. One of them must have been Brenda. Frank had to be the same Frank who seemed to be so loyal to his buddy Roy Dell. Go figure, playing up to Roy Dell and boinking his wife for good measure.

"Well, Brenda was on her way out to the Dumpster, carrying out the trash, when she hears this kinda laughing, moaning sound. She figures it's a couple of kids fooling around by the picnic tables, so she coughs and tries to make some noise so they can hear her coming and break it off."

I nodded understandingly. Sure, that's what anybody'd do. I was picturing the area with the picnic tables, an ideal rendezvous spot for a couple of teenagers looking to neck before they went home.

"Well, you can just imagine. The sound wasn't coming from a picnic table. It was coming from the corner behind the Dumpster." A chill ran up my neck. Just like Ruby, I thought. "When Brenda rounds the corner to heave the sack of trash into the bin, she flat trips over her husband and Lulu. Frank's pants were down around his hairy legs, his butt shining in the moon, and Lulu was minus her top. Let me tell you, I wouldn't never want to see that sight! It's been all I can think of, every time I've seen Frank since!" Ann shuddered again.

"What did she do?" I asked.

Ann looked sad and shook her head. "You got to know Brenda and Frank. I don't know why she stays with him. Got a bad case of the 'But I love hims,' I suppose. This wasn't the first time something like this had happened. Frank just turned his head and looked over his shoulder at her. Then he told her to get on home or he'd beat her ass."

"You have got to be kidding!" I would've skinned the asshole alive.

"No. Brenda said she just started crying and left. She sat up all night, waiting for him, and when he finally got in, he was knee-walking drunk and mean as a snake. By the next morning, he acted like it never happened and they went on just like always. Brenda swears she loves him, and that if it weren't for the alcohol, he'd be a faithful man. I say that's a load of crap." Ann was clearly disgusted.

"I thought Frank was Roy Dell's friend?" Ann looked at me as if I were a stupid child.

"Around here, ain't nobody your friend. Racing's a tough business. You can be drinking with somebody one night and pushing them up the wall at a hundred miles an hour the next. It's just business. Frank'd skin his mother to be where Roy Dell is. Maybe screwing his wife is just a way of moving in on his territory."

But what was in it for Lulu? I wondered. I turned to ask Ann about that, but she was quickly grabbing a tire iron and starting to work. Another man was approaching us, wheeling a tire.

"You ain't got that yet?" he yelled to Ann.

"Keep your pants on," she snarled. "I'll have it in a minute." Our conversation had ended and I knew she wouldn't risk saying any more. Not now at least. The man was staring at me and starting to smile. Time to move along, I thought, heading for the snack shack.

Lulu and Frank. Go figure. What would Roy Dell have done if he'd known that? What if he did know and started messing with Ruby to pay his wife back? No, I couldn't see that. He was too nice to Frank and intimidated by Lulu. He was clueless, I knew that for certain.

As I rounded the straightaway, about a football field away from the snack shack, I had a hallucination. It had to be a hallucination, because there was no other way to explain what I was seeing. A familiar chestnut-skinned figure drove slowly past in a beat-up old Ford pickup. Her hair was hidden by a ballcap, but the profile was unmistakable. Carla Terrance—John Nailor's ex, former DEA agent, and my sworn enemy—was here in the Panhandle.

No way. I shook my head and stared harder at the slow-moving vehicle. Our eyes met for a brief second, hers narrowing to tiny slits while mine widened. No doubt about it. Carla was back in town, up from Miami, and if I was any judge, she wasn't here for pleasure. So what was the DEA doing here? I wondered. And could it have anything to do with John?

Carla gunned the truck and shot off out of the pit, probably worried that I'd blow her cover. Well, at least I had something to go on with Nailor.

The snack bar was closed, a metal partition pulled tight from the ceiling to the countertop. I looked at the metal fire escape steps leading up to the roof deck and Mickey Rhodes's office. Maybe Mickey had something to say. I started climbing, my high heels clicking noisily against the metal steps. The noise from the pit seemed louder the higher I climbed, and the smell of exhaust filled the air.

The deck was a tribute to excess and was clearly the track owner's sanctuary. It was much larger than it had seemed from the ground, with wrought-iron tables and chairs, padded stadium seats lining the rail that overlooked the track's finish line. There was even an all-weather bar sheltered by a tin roof. What Mickey didn't spend on the track, he poured into his entertainment center. The same was true of his office. I pulled open the thick wooden door and entered an empty reception area that was so thickly carpeted and insulated that the outside track sounds vanished as the door swung shut.

There were different sounds coming from one of the two rooms that branched off the short hallway behind the reception area. I could hear a woman's high-pitched laugh and a man's voice bantering and clearly enjoying himself. Before I could stop myself, I had moved to the edge of the doorway. I'd know that voice in my sleep. I'd heard it in the darkness of my trailer. John Nailor was perched on the edge of a desk. Behind it was the brunette he'd kissed.

I opened my mouth to speak, staring from her to him and back to him again. He had stiffened, but his face hadn't changed. It was the same as always, inexpressive, but was that a flicker of fear that I saw in his eyes?

"May I help you?" the brunette asked, tossing her head and slowly removing her hand from its resting place on John's thigh. She wore bright red lipstick and had huge brown eyes, but her skin was tight and little lines marred the edge of her mouth and eyes.

"You know, if you're looking for Mr. Rhodes to pay you, it won't happen before the thirtieth. No exceptions. I'll sign checks then and not a day sooner." She was a prissy little thing, I thought. And that is fear I see in his eyes.

"Well, I'd hoped to —"

"Look," she said, not waiting to hear what I really wanted, which was a good thing, since I was having trouble remembering my name or breathing. She rolled her eyes at John, as if to say "See what I have to deal with all day?" "You've got to be patient. Mr. Rhodes will see to it that everyone gets their money, but not until the thirtieth. I know the money's late in coming, but it will be here and griping won't get it here any faster."

I might've said any one of a thousand things, but I didn't. I let the little snip believe I was another wife there to collect her husband's money. I looked at John one last time and managed to gasp out "Fine," before I turned and walked away. Give him the benefit of the doubt, my head said. Kill the bastard, said my heart.

Fifteen

I had just passed the Dead Lakes, heading for Chipley, when I noticed the car in my rearview mirror. I was going fast, but it was moving even faster. It was a black sports car with tinted windows, the kind you expect to roar past you with the thumping beat of a bass line throbbing out over the sound of the engine. A hothead. A young kid with a big stereo, always in a hurry, zooming up behind you and then pulling out across the double yellow line and passing you in a blaze of speed, never mind that there might be a car coming from the opposite direction.

I didn't need the aggravation, so I accelerated, pushing the Camaro out to almost eighty, expecting the kid to follow at a distance. It didn't seem to phase him. He kept up, creeping closer, until his bumper was a few feet from mine.

"Asshole," I muttered into the rearview mirror. "If that's the way you want it, the road's all yours." Gradually I slowed down, but he didn't pass. He stayed on my tail, almost touching me. I slowed down more, until I was doing under forty, but he stayed on my tail. I rolled down my window, motioning for him to pass me, but he didn't. When I slowed to thirty, he hit me.

It was a jarring tap to my rear bumper, just enough to force me to fight the wheel. Before I could pull over to let him pass, he hit me again. This time he hit harder, punching my left rear bumper, shaking the car so hard that the wheel jumped from my hands. I was out of control, the car flying off the side of the road, narrowly missing a stand of pine trees.

"Son of a bitch," I yelled. The car roared past, screaming toward Chipley. I sat there, my head resting on the steering wheel, fighting tears. It was not my day. Hell, if you wanted to be technical, it wasn't my week. Run off the road by a psycho teenager, brushed off by a man I was realizing I knew less and less about, my friend murdered. What was left? What kind of screwy life was this?

"Am I just doing something wrong here?" I was falling back on my Catholic upbringing. When all else fails, and you can't explain current events, it can only mean one thing: You pissed off God. "All right, I thought we reached an agreement. I come to church on the big days, I confess my sins to you on a semiregular basis, and you agree to cut me some slack. This don't feel like slack here. Not to be disrespectful or nothing, but I could use a break. One little break, that's all I'm asking." I listened. There was only the sound of crickets or locusts whining in the heat.

I threw the car into reverse and carefully backed out onto the macadam road. I'd had enough for one day, and I still had to go to work. I was not looking forward to that. The rest of the day was a wash, as far as I was concerned. I was going to lock myself inside my trailer, pull all the blinds, and go to sleep until I had to crawl out of bed and go to work. I thought about my bed the whole way home. It was about time that I took control of my universe, I preached to myself. No more little Miss Passive. Not Sierra Lavotini. A new day was dawning and I was the sun.

How God must have enjoyed listening to that. How She must've been laughing Herself silly. Fate was waiting on my parking pad when I got home—in the form of a late-model dark blue Lincoln with Pennsylvania tags. Slightly salt-rusted, not from the ocean, I was sure, but from the harsh Philadelphia winters and the overly zealous street crews that throw salt everywhere in their attempt to fight off winter's snow and ice.

"No," I moaned. "Not them. Not now." There was no avoiding it. It was my parents' car. As I pulled into the driveway, I could see two heads, one just hitting the headrest, the other, taller, commanding the driver's seat. The doors flew open as I pulled up the parking brake, my mother jumping out of the car in her rush to get to me.

"Sierra!" she yelled, her voice a high-pitched shriek. "It's me!"

No, it's freaking Elvis, I thought uncharitably.

She grabbed me in a bear hug, her gray curly head reaching up to my shoulder. As I wrapped my arms around her, I was suddenly aware that I was glad to see her. My mother always smells faintly of freshly baked bread and olive oil. I bent my head, resting it gently on top of hers. For a moment I was home, back in Philly, and the problems of the world had all gone away.

The sound of the car door slamming made me look up again, expecting to see my father, and instead looking into the clear brown eyes of my baby brother, Al, the policeman.

"What are you guys doing here?" I asked.

"Sierra," my mother said, her voice muffled by my shoulder, "you never called us back. You call up and say those strange things about needing a moose. What was I to think?" Behind her back, my brother rolled his eyes.

"Ma, don't tell me you drove down here to see if I was all right?"

My mother pushed herself off of my shoulder, grabbed my arms, and stared up at me. "Are you telling me not to worry about my baby?" Behind us my brother stifled a laugh with a cough. "Don't tell me what I did was wrong, because I get enough of that from your father and your brothers." Al coughed again and Ma whipped around to glare at him. "That'll be enough out of you, Mr. Have-No-Respect-for-His-Own-Mother!"

Al turned scarlet. "Ma, I drove you here, didn't I? I took off work for you."

"Humpf," Ma snorted. "A big-shot police officer. The fire department wasn't good enough for him. The girls I introduced him to weren't good enough for him. No, he's gotta go across town to date a college girl. And to what avail, Mr. Lovelorn?"

Ma didn't wait for an answer. She turned back to give me a piece of her mind. "Your father thought I was crazy coming down here like this. Your brother Francis tried to back him up. It isn't enough Francis Xavier's following your pa's steps to be chief, no, now he's gotta stick his nose into your father's and my relationship."

This was pure vintage Ma. The longer it's been since she saw you, the longer the opening lecture. We all knew not to take it too seriously. She would let you know for sure when she was really angry. You wouldn't be standing in the room with Ma when she was seriously mad. Dishes flew, pots, glasses. She'd only been angry a time or two in my life, and this wasn't one of them. This was just her way of saying hello. The last time Ma had been angry, really angry, was when a certain waitress down at the Sons of Italy Social Club decided to move in on Ma's territory with Pa. Now, that was a pretty picture, I hear, although I was not there to witness the confrontation of one Leonora Mostavindaduchi.

". . . and so I should have cause to worry," Ma was saying. "You lost weight. You're not eating. And look at those circles under your eyes. Alfonso," she said, whirling on my brother again. "Why do you stand there like an idiot? Start unloading the groceries. Can't you see she's starving?"

Al smirked and turned to the trunk of the Lincoln. As the automatic lock clicked and the trunk lid began to sigh open on its hydraulic hinges, he reached in and started grabbing what can only be described as the entire interior of Little Frankie's Italian Market.

Fluffy, who had not yet run out of her doggie door to welcome me home, now stuck her head out for a look-see. She got one glimpse of my mother heading like a runaway train toward the door and knew this was no place for a chihuahua.

"You still got that little rat-dog, eh, Sierra?" Ma huffed. "A girl like you, she don't need something you might trip over and squash. You need a good guard dog, that's what." From behind the door I heard Fluffy growl.

I rushed ahead of Ma and unlocked the door, dreading her initial reaction to my trailer. At least when you have little furniture, the place stays neat.

"Oh, my," Ma said, sighing and stepping into the kitchen. She took a moment and stood, with me and grocery-laden Al behind her. She looked at the kitchen, clean and white, with its elevated table and barstools by the bay window. She edged slowly over toward the living room, examining the knickknacks on the shelves above the pass-through counter that divided the two rooms.

"Oh, my," she said again as she stopped in the entrance to the barren living room. Slowly her gaze swept around the room, taking in the mirrored wall, the lone futon, and the stacks of books that ringed the walls.

"This is where you practice, eh, Sierra?" Her voice was softening. She nodded her head like she was drinking in my life and understanding.

"Yeah, Ma," I said, "this is my living room. See, I've got my stereo here, and my books, too, so I can read when I want to."

Ma laughed. "Still with them books, eh? You were always one with the books." She gazed down the hallway toward the bedrooms but apparently decided against a full inspection. "I'll look down there later," she said. "Right now, we gotta get some food in you. Looking like a stick, Sierra," she said, turning and walking into the kitchen. "That ain't good in your profession. Right, Al?" she called out the back door. Then I heard an abrupt "Oh," and Ma whirled toward me. "Looks like you got company, honey." Al came through the door, toting more groceries, and behind him, also heavily laden, was Detective Wheeling.

Wheeling set the groceries down on the counter and smiled at Ma. She was instantly charmed and smiled back. Al looked guarded. He smelled a fellow police officer and knew from experience that a police officer in his sister's life usually spelled trouble. He was making a mental "Aha, I knew she was in trouble again" to himself.

"Detective Wheeling," I said, "this is my mother, Mrs. Lavotini, and my brother Al."

Ma wasted no time filling Wheeling in on her priorities. "Good," she said to him, "another mouth to feed. What's with you people down here? All I've seen so far is skinny people." Ma was poking her head into bags, pulling out jars and cans and big bags of celery and tomatoes. "I can't talk to you right now because I've gotta start cooking, but you young people go sit, talk, and pretty soon we'll eat."

Wheeling opened his mouth to say something, but didn't. Instead he smiled at me, knowing I was caught between a rock and a hard place. Talk to him, or make a scene and face my mother.

"Ma, I don't have a lot of time," I said. "I've gotta leave for work soon." Not exactly true, I had an hour, but Wheeling didn't need to know that.

"Nonsense!" Ma shouted. "That's the problem with you

people. You never take time for what's important. Always rushing, you are." Wheeling was grinning now.

"Let's talk," he said. His tone didn't allow for any other options. He stepped past me into the living room. Al went outside and returned with two suitcases, slowly walking past us and heading down the hall. He was straining to overhear, I knew. It was a Lavotini trait. I glanced back toward the kitchen. Ma was chopping onions, but she wasn't humming like she always does when she cooks. She was trying to listen in, too.

I led Wheeling over to the bay window. I didn't like the look in his eyes. We were headed for trouble and I knew it.

"All right," I said, taking the offensive, "cut to the bottom line. I don't want you here asking questions and getting my family into this. I answered questions at the station. I'll be happy to come down there again."

Wheeling just stared for a moment and when he did talk it was in a low, deadly serious tone. "You're in big trouble, Ms. Lavotini," he said. A chill ran up my spine. I was aware of Al, listening in the hallway, and knew that Detective Wheeling knew my brother was listening, too.

"Hey, you think telling me I'm in trouble is gonna frighten me?" I said. "You didn't grow up in Catholic school. Every day some nun was telling me I was in big trouble." I tried to laugh, but it fell flat. "They always wanted you to confess to some sin you hadn't committed. Just like you, eh?"

Wheeling wasn't smiling. "You want a bottom line? Here's your bottom line: I know John Nailor was in this house last night and I know he was at the racetrack this morning when you were there. I want an explanation."

"For what? He can't come see me? I can't bump into him in public?" My heart was racing and I could feel my neck start to flush. "Why don't you go ask him why he was here?"

"Oh, I intend to," he answered. His voice was tight, controlled, and underneath, very angry. "But right now, I'm asking you."

"You know what I think?" I said. "I think you've already talked to your partner, and now you're double-checking. Otherwise, it makes no sense, you coming to me before you go to him. Or can't you find him?" I saw the flicker in his eyes and knew I'd scored. "You can't find him. Well," I said, throwing up my hands in mock surrender, "what can I say? He's a friend. He stopped by to visit."

"And left by the back window?"

"Hey, that's all you get. You can ask your partner if you want more." Why didn't Al step in and run interference here? I wondered. "And while we're at it, why don't you go ask Nailor's ex–old lady what's what?"

Wheeling looked genuinely puzzled, then angry.

"Miss Lavotini, you put Detective Nailor at the scene of a murder. Now he's sneaking in and out of your house in the middle of the night. Then he's back at the scene today. I've got to wonder if I don't have a dirty cop in my department. I've also got to wonder if I've got all the facts about a homicide I'm working. Now, here's how it goes: You tell me what's going on between you two, and you get honest, or you may find yourself charged as an accessory after the fact in a murder. And if I find out that your story and Detective Nailor's don't fit, you may be looking at a much more serious charge."

"Talk to my attorney."

"I'm deadly serious, Miss Lavotini," he answered. "You pull an attorney into this, and any help you might need from me goes out the window."

My ears were buzzing. I felt hot and very scared, but he didn't need to know that.

"Detective Wheeling, call my attorney. I don't chat without him present." Now Wheeling looked furious. "I think you should leave." I turned and walked toward the kitchen door.

"Ma, Detective Wheeling can't stay for dinner."

Wheeling walked up to my mother, and I found myself holding my breath. "A pleasure meeting you, ma'am," he said. Al was walking quietly through the living room and into the kitchen, standing with Fluffy by his side. They were silent, but both managed to look protective.

As he started down the steps, Wheeling looked back up at me, squinting into the late-afternoon sun. "Don't try and make this into a game. You and Detective Nailor could be in some very large trouble."

"See you in the principal's office," I answered.

He didn't say anything else and I didn't wait. I closed the door and headed back to the living room. Ma was cooking, but Al was standing by the bay window, waiting for an explanation.

My brothers are just like my dad. They think because they're male, it's their duty to protect me and Ma. This has led to some head-on confrontations, especially between me and the oldest, Francis. All of them do it, even Al, the one brother younger than me. He's the worst lately, maybe because John Nailor went to Philadelphia a few months back when I got in trouble and asked my policeman brother a lot of questions about me. Al and John got along, but Al didn't take too kindly to me being involved enough in a homicide that the police came asking questions.

"So, you're wondering what that's about, eh?" I asked.

"I don't think I got to wonder, Sierra," Al said in a low voice so Ma couldn't hear us. "You and John are in some kind of trouble and it involves a homicide." He was giving me the same hard look Wheeling had given me. "Sierra, is John a bad cop?"

"No!"

"Then why didn't you talk to that detective?"

"I didn't want . . . I didn't think . . . I hadn't . . ." I sputtered around for the right explanation.

"In other words, Sierra," Al said, suddenly the police and not family, "you don't know what he is. Sierra, don't cover up for someone you don't even know if you can trust. You're hurting yourself here, kid. Don't go letting your feelings get in the way of telling the truth, 'cause the truth is going to come out, Sierra. You don't need to be caught in the middle of a police investigation."

"Sierra, could you come here?" Ma's insistent call from the kitchen saved me from answering Al. I didn't know what was going on. Nobody was choosing to share that with me. I was just hanging out there in the wind. Maybe John was just using me. Maybe he was into something wrong. On the other hand, maybe he was working on something that he couldn't share with his fellow officers. But who was left taking the risk and trying to cover for someone I couldn't be sure I could trust? Me, Miss Doesn't-Know-When-to-Quit Lavotini.

Sixteen

It was going to be an actual relief to leave the trailer and go to work. Apparently, after Detective Wheeling stormed off, the thunderclouds began to gather over Ma. She smelled trouble and nobody was gonna rest until she'd gotten to the bottom of it.

"What's going on, Sierra?" she said, just as soon as I entered the kitchen.

"Nothing, Ma. He's got a hot temper, that's all. He's imagining things."

Ma turned away from the stove and crossed to the sink, a heavy stockpot full of water and noodles pushed out in front of her. She dumped the pasta into the colander and slammed the heavy pot into the sink. She didn't like my answer.

She turned on the water full blast, squirted in some soap, and decided to have her say.

"Sierra, I am not about to have my own child look me in the eyes and lie!" She whirled around, staring at me, just the way she used to when my brothers and I were young. "You look here, Sierra," she said, gesturing toward her face. "You look in my eyes and say that again. Can you look at me and say you don't know what's going on with you and the police? Is your conscience clear?"

A little twinge started up in my gut, moving fast toward

my throat. I gulped. Funny as it may sound, I don't lie to Ma. I swore off it when I was eight. She is just too much of a force to be reckoned with.

Al wandered into the kitchen, led by his nose, which smelled Ma's sauce simmering away on the stove, full of garlic and butter. For a second he looked like he was going to open his mouth and save me, but then Ma reached out one oven-mitted hand and whacked him.

"Don't start!" she cautioned. "Let your sister dig her own hole. Let her lie to her mother, if that's what it's come down to."

So I told her. What else could I do?

Ma never stopped moving. She's that way. She can't sit still, especially when she's worried about something, and Ma was plenty worried. When I got to the part about Ruby dying, Ma sucked her breath in across her teeth, the spoon she held pausing motionless over the sauce. She looked at me then, deep into my eyes, her own face filled with pain.

When I got to the part about John, and him kissing the brunette, and then him coming to the trailer and kissing me, she turned two shades of dark red. She carried the steaming platter of noodles and white sauce over to the table, whipped the garlic bread out of the oven, and motioned me and Al to the table.

"You love him, Sierra?" she asked. She was serving Al's plate, seeming to pay more attention to it than to me, but I wasn't fooled. Al was drilling a hole in the table with his eyes, trying to act like this was any other dinner conversation.

"What is love, Ma?" I said.

She reached across with one swift move and whacked me upside the head with her wooden noodle spoon.

"Ow! What'd you do that for?" There are certain rituals that human beings perform for absolutely no reason. I had to ask the question; it was part of the ritual. For my trouble, I got a second whack.

"I don't know, Ma," I said. "I don't know him well enough to love him."

Ma put down the spoon and looked at me, her eyes locked on mine, suddenly shiny with tears or something else.

"Aw, Sierra," she said softly. "You got it bad."

The room was completely still for a long moment, the air filled with steamy, spaghetti smells. Finally, Al had the good sense to choke on his pasta. Ma reached over and smacked him good-naturedly. "What's the matter with you?" she cried. "Your sister's in love and all you can think to do is stuff your face? Have a little respect!"

"And you," she said, her attention turned back to me. "Eat! *Mangia!* You ever see a happy man with a skinny woman?"

We all laughed, the tension broken for the time being. But I knew I wouldn't have long to wait for the next round of questions. It was far better to eat and run off to the Tiffany, where there was only one question: How much money can I make them guys cough up tonight?

By the time I roared down Thomas Drive and into the Tiffany parking lot, I had switched in my head from Sierra, her mother's daughter, to Sierra, Mistress of the Night. No matter what was going on in the real world, me and the Fluff still had bills to pay and pasta to buy. You gotta have a good head if you're gonna rule the night.

I always notice the change in myself when I start getting ready to leave the house. I stand taller, pulling myself up by the tops of my shoulders, brining my breasts up into focus. I move slower, deliberately. I powder and wax and shine every square inch of my body, because at the Tiffany, my body is a temple and I'm looking for worshipers, preferably rich ones with loose, floppy wallets oozing money.

Don't take me wrong here. I like most of the guys I meet. I don't mind talking to them and hearing all their problems and dreams, but the bottom line is this: It's my freakin' job. No more. No less.

So, by the time I hit the backstage dressing room, I was moving to the music, zoning out on my own inner space. I was a green. Therefore, I found it only appropriate to dress like Cleopatra. I wound a little rubber snake around my arm, threw on a black wig, and wrapped my body in a toga. Simple but effective.

Ralph, the stagehand, cranked the smoke machine as I walked out. I've been trying to convince him and some of the guys to carry me out on their shoulders, but Ralph says he can't, his back would go out. I know that's not true, but I don't bust him about it. Truth is, Ralph's young and probably doesn't think he could control himself. He's afraid he'd embarrass himself onstage. So I say, what the hell, live and let live. But it would be a powerful entrance.

Instead I stood there, surrounded by smoke, and reached one hand up to make the snake on my arm wiggle, like maybe it was real. Then I started moving and swaying to the music, my hands slowly caressing my thighs. With one fast jerk, just as the music built and froze for two counts, I ripped away the toga.

There I was, standing out on the edge of the runway, wearing nothing but a gold thong bikini and a snake. That's when I noticed the boys from the racetrack. I had to notice them. Meatloaf was so excited his body was jerking and I thought he was having some kind of a seizure. Frank was leering and standing a little too close to the edge of the stage. The rest of Roy Dell's crew was right behind Frank. But where was Roy Dell?

I looked up and caught Bruno the bouncer's eye. This was a crew that didn't respond well to structure. However, Bruno was one of those structures that didn't respond well to customers touching the merchandise.

True to form, Frank was the first to make a move. He took a step forward, bringing himself right up against the twinkle lights of the runway, and reached out a thick, muscular arm.

Bruno, materializing beside Frank, slowly reached his Goliath-sized arm over Frank's shoulder and wrapped his fingers around Frank's wrist. No words were exchanged, but the look of pain that crossed Frank's face pleased me.

"Step back," Bruno said, his voice a flat monotone of seeming indifference.

Frank didn't move, but little beads of perspiration began to pop out on his forehead. You could almost see the little kid in him want to say, "Make me." Bruno felt Frank's reluctance and squeezed a little tighter on his wrist. The skin beneath Bruno's fingers turned a grayish white. I was starting to feel sorry for Frank.

Slowly, very slowly, Frank began to withdraw his hand from the edge of the runway. Just to taunt him, I lost my bikini top. Meatloaf started to drool, oblivious to Frank's predicament. Mickey Rhodes broke off whatever high-level conversation he'd been having with Vincent and took two quick strides over to the area where his employees were in imminent danger.

I bent at the waist and reached my arms out in front of me, slid into a slow split, then rolled onto my stomach and arched my back. Even Mickey stopped for a second to appreciate true artistry in motion. That's when I believe Meatloaf lost his entire paycheck to my thong, Frank got tossed by Bruno, and Mickey Rhodes saved half the track workforce from also getting kicked to the curb. He wedged himself between them and me, staring them down until they backed off and proceeded one at a time to offer me twenties in the most gentlemanly fashion. Like lambs led to slaughter, I sighed to myself, and who better to lead them than Cleopatra herself?

Marla was primping in the mirror when I returned to the dressing room.

"That big boy'll tip good if you play to him," she said matter-of-factly.

I wasn't in the mood to hear Marla's opinion of who to work. I've got radar for that kind of stuff. I can smell a heavy tipper coming eight hundred miles away. So I ignored her.

"I saw him give dear, departed Ruby a hundred-dollar bill not two weeks ago." Marla was sly. She was watching me out of the corner of her eye while appearing to straighten her cleavage, stuffing most of her artificial enhancements into the uppermost portion of her bra cup.

I couldn't help it. I had to know. "Which big boy are you referring to?" I asked, picking at a slice of cold pepperoni pizza that someone'd left behind in her rush to hit the stage.

Marla sighed in exasperation. "I believe you know him as Meatloaf," she said, "but his Christian name is Albert."

"Get out! Albert!"

Marla frowned. She fancies herself a social worker and laughing at someone's *Christian* name was like slandering them.

"Wish he'd give me a hundred dollars," Marla muttered. "I listened to him going on and on about Ruby just the other night. You'd think Meatloaf actually thought they were an item!"

Marla had me and we both knew it. I was drawn into a conversation with her against my better judgment. Sooner or later, Marla'd want something. She didn't usually disseminate public service information without an ulterior motive.

"What'd he say about her?" I asked.

Marla gave me her that's-for-me-to-know-and-you-to-find-out look, tossed her long black hair, and pretended to ponder.

"You know, I've been thinking it wouldn't hurt you none to let Vincent put my name up ahead of yours just one time," she said.

"Kiss my ass, Marla," I said, cool as a cucumber. "Your name can come ahead of mine when I move on, retire, or die. Until then I headline. You don't." I edged a little closer into Marla's personal space, something that made her acutely anxious on account of she knew it would take me no time whatsoever to wrap my hand around her hair and yank it until she cried or told me whatever it is I wanted to know. "What did Meatloaf say about Ruby?"

Marla dropped all pretense of preening in the mirror and whirled around to face me, at the same time backing up toward the stage door.

"He said he shouldn't have let her slip away, or something like that. I don't remember exactly. He was mumbling something about protecting. All's I know is he didn't give me a big tip, and I listened to him moaning and wailing for a good ten minutes."

I wasn't listening. I was gone, out the door looking for Meatloaf. Pushing past men who grabbed at my silk kimono, I rushed to get to the table where I'd seen the Dead Lakes pit crew. It was empty. Glasses of half-melted ice and empty beer bottles littered the tabletop. I spun around, looking back at the runway, but there was no sign of Roy Dell's crew.

"Damn!"

"I know, honey," the waitress said, strolling up. "They stiffed me, too."

I must've seemed confused because she kept explaining. "When the little guy got thrown out, the whole rest of the lot followed behind him like yard dogs following the supper dish. Their boss over there made 'em all go home," she said, nodding to where Mickey Rhodes sat with Vincent.

"It shouldn't be much longer," he was saying to Vincent as I approached their table. "And you can take that to the bank."

"All's I want to take to the bank," Vincent replied, his jaw muscle twitching, "is the money."

I should've stopped myself, but impulse control is not my long suit. I had crossed the room and was standing by their table before I'd thought about what I was going to say. So I wound up standing there like little Joey Romano the time his mama chewed him out in the street for stealing an apple off a cart down at the Italian market in South Philly. He'd just stood there, his mama wailing on him, with this goofball, quasi-nonchalant look on his face, like maybe every kid gets his ass whipped in the street by his mama at age eleven. I had the same expression on my face now, I just knew it.

Vincent only looked up when he saw Mickey had stopped listening to him and had turned his attention to me.

"What, Sierra? What? I'm busy here." Vincent puffed out his chest like maybe he was really important. He was doing it for Mickey's benefit, but Mickey couldn't see past the tips of my 38DDs.

"Where are the boys?" I asked, looking only at Mickey, like maybe he was gonna get lucky if he told me.

Mickey squeaked and found his voice. "I sent those animals back to Wewa. I saw how they were acting and I apologize for them."

I leaned over, resting my hands palm down on the tiny table, and stuck my chest as close to his face as possible without asphyxiating him.

"That's too bad," I purred. "I was hoping to talk to them."

"You were?" Mickey seemed shocked. "A lady such as yourself ought not trouble herself with morons!"

I let my face droop down into a look of deepest sorrow. "Aw, I guess you can see right through me, Mr. Rhodes."

"Mickey, call me Mickey," he gasped.

"Mickey, if the truth be known, one of the girls was just telling me how close Meatloaf was to my dearly departed friend Ruby. I just thought maybe if I talked to him, it would relieve some of the pain we're both in." A little tear rolled down my cheek, prompting Mickey to reach for a handkerchief and offer it to me. He looked uncomfortable with my distress, and I couldn't blame him. I was doing my best to seem inconsolable.

"Sierra," Vincent sighed, "this ain't hardly the time—"

"Eh, bite me, Gambuzzo!" I snapped, completely blowing the moment I had worked so hard to create. Vincent jumped up out of his chair, Mickey along with him. Vincent was looking to hurt me and Mickey to defend my honor should it actually come to blows.

I stared at Vincent and he stared right back just as hard. We were both breathing heavily. In fact we were all breathing heavily, but Mickey was panting for another reason altogether. In that tense minute, I remembered that it wouldn't do to lose my cool right now.

"Screw it!" I snapped finally, and seemed to give in. "It's the grief. I'm overwhelmed." Vincent appeared to be considering publicly humiliating me when I was at my weakest, so I added, "But what with Ruby dying and me having company from Cape May"—I looked straight into Vincent's eyes, indicating that he should know Moose had sent in his henchmen—"I just can't be held responsible for my emotions."

Mickey sighed and reached out to pat my arm. Vincent looked downright frightened, because at that moment his wanna-be mobsterism was encountering the possibility that the real thing was in town.

"Whatever." Vincent gave up.

"However," Mickey replied, "however I can be of service."

I bent my head over Mickey's handkerchief and turned

away. "I'll be all right," I said. "These things just take time."

The music started up, Marla skipped out onstage, and I was forgotten. Wherever Meatloaf was and whatever he knew, it wasn't going to be discovered by me tonight. Tonight was a dead loss, except for the wad of money I'd collected off the dirt track dummies.

Seventeen

I was tired. My feet ached. All I wanted was a good night's sleep. It was all I could think about—the way my sheets would feel against my skin, the hum of the central air, the darkness of my room. It was stupidity at work in its most elemental form.

In Philly you learn: Don't go out and not watch the street. Don't walk across a dark parking lot to your car thinking about anything but who might be out there and what you'll do if they confront you. You stop thinking about that, and eventually, some wise guy'll try and make you a victim, and it'll happen sooner rather than later.

I was standing by the Camaro, my key in the lock, when I heard him coming up on me fast, running. The damn key wouldn't come out of the lock. I was disoriented because my mind had been wandering. I couldn't even get to my Mace. He was on me before I could move, slamming me against the side of the car, throwing something over my head, and pulling me to the ground.

"Son of a bitch!" I yelled, my voice muffled by the thick fabric over my head.

"Shut the fuck up!" he growled, his voice thick. "Feel this?" Something round and hard pressed into the small of my back. He had a gun.

I nodded. My throat tightened as my heart threatened to burst through my chest. It was hot and close under the blanket. I couldn't breathe. I was going to suffocate.

"I brought you something," the voice said. "Something to make you think."

I waited for him to hurt me, knowing that I couldn't get away.

He was winding something around me: a rope. He pressed it tighter as he pulled it in and knotted it.

"You ask too many questions," he said. "Let the dead rest. It ain't got nothing to do with you."

I bit my lip hard to keep from crying out. He shoved me against one of my tires, pushing himself away from me. Where was Bruno? Why wasn't he out in the lot? He was almost always outside at closing time, making sure we got to our cars safely.

My assailant kicked me then. Right in the ribs, knocking the air out of my chest, leaving me dry-heaving as I lay on the warm asphalt. Son of a bitch. Then I heard him leave, heavy footsteps running across the lot, toward the thin ring of oleander bushes that divided the Tiffany's parking lot from the endless string of tattoo parlors and strip-mall stores.

I lay there, waiting for the air to return to my lungs, struggling to move my arms out of the rope that bound them, and finding I was making progress. The rope rolled upward as I freed myself and pulled the thick fabric away from my head. With one final tug, I jerked free and cool. Beach air filled my starving lungs.

I sat there, gasping, staring at the drab olive-green wool blanket that the creep had used to cover my head. At my feet lay a Barbie doll, naked, one breast severed crudely and red fingernail polish dripping down her body to resemble blood. In one hand, Barbie held the head of a small brown dog, just like Fluffy.

A warning or a promise? I sat there, leaning against my car, still too weak to move, holding the Barbie doll.

"You rotten bastard," I gasped out into the darkness. "I'm going to find you. You got Ruby, but you ain't gonna get me." I eased myself slowly to my feet, gathered up the blanket, the rope, and the doll, and tossed them all into my backseat. My entire body was shaking.

"Yeah, you go on and hide in the darkness. You sneak up on people smaller than you and take them when they're not looking, when they're feeling safe. You just go on and do that!" I could hear my voice sounding shrill, bordering on hysteria. "But watch your back, you miserable lowlife, 'cause I'm coming."

Fat lot of good it did me, saying that out loud to the darkness. Chances are he was far away by now, hiding from us all. It didn't really matter. Those words were what picked me up off the ground and reminded me of who I was. I was a Lavotini and Lavotinis don't run from bullies. They may regroup, they may call in their brothers to help, but a Lavotini doesn't stand by and let her friend's murderer go free.

Ruby's killer had just made a serious mistake. He had sought to frighten me off with intimidation and had instead given me that false sense of courage that comes from intense rage. It was time to call in the big guns and quit eatin' shit.

I jumped into the driver's seat and chirped the tires as the Camaro screamed out onto Thomas Drive. I should've gone back inside. I should've told Vincent or called a cop or anything other than what I was doing now. But I couldn't stop myself. I was shaking and driving too fast. Besides, what good would it do to tell the cops? I'd only end up reading about it in the paper. Hell, that's probably what had gotten me roughed up: the newspaper article that named me as an eyewitness. And now that I thought about it, maybe Roy Dell and the boys hadn't screwed up my car. Maybe someone had done it on purpose.

I was talking, loud, with the window open and the wind fighting to shove the words back down my throat. I talked and screamed my way across the Hathaway Bridge, past the used-car lots and cheap hotels that line Fifteenth Street, past the police department where who-knows-what was going on.

"And I don't see you people doing anything except putting my life in more danger," I yelled out as I drove past.

I cut through side streets, winding my way to the Lively Oaks Trailer Park. It was completely dead, a rarity for a trailer park, even at three A.M. Here and there a streetlight lit up the trailers, reflecting off the taillights of the cars that sat still on their parking pads. I saw eyes everywhere, staring out of the darkness, watching me. Now I was acting hyper-vigilant.

Two huge glowing eyes stared at me as I pulled up onto my parking pad and cut the lights. Fluffy. Her entire body radiated disapproval. Where have you been? she seemed to say. *They* are still here.

"I know, girl," I said, climbing the steps slowly, clutching my side with one hand and reaching out to her with the other. "But we need family right now. We're gonna need all the help we can get."

Fluffy sighed and pushed through the doggie door, not waiting for me to unlock the door and step inside. Fluffy had her pride after all. She didn't think we needed anybody's help.

"Wonder where you got that attitude?" I muttered into the dimly lit kitchen. Ahead of me, Fluffy sighed again loudly, walking on toward the bedroom, her sharp little claws clicking across the parquet floor.

Eighteen

*I*t was not even fully light outside when I convened the first meeting of the War Council. Fluffy, disdainful of the whole idea, had chosen to sleep in, racked out on her satin pillow at the head of my bed. But Ma and Al were overjoyed to be included. All right, so maybe the word *overjoyed* is a bit strong, but they were both in the kitchen, sitting at the table, thick white mugs of Italian roast in their hands.

I don't know how Raydean got in on the Council. I long ago quit trying to figure out how she knows when something's about to kick off. She just appears. Call it a psychotic's sixth sense, or call it paranoia, if you will. Whatever the extrasensory perception, Raydean had appeared just after I turned on the kitchen lights and flicked the switch on the coffeemaker.

Ma was bleary-eyed, her hair still in little yellow plastic curlers and her pink-flowered flannel bathrobe pulled tight around her midsection. She insisted on baking cinnamon rolls from scratch, but used the cheater's ingredient: quick-rising yeast. To her, it was almost a cardinal sin. In order to serve the very best, one must slave and suffer. Quick-rise didn't offer enough pain to produce truly good rolls. From the look on Al's face, it didn't matter. A roll is a roll to Al. But then, he's a cop. They never watch what they put in their mouths.

Raydean came prepared. For what, I don't know, but she was prepared for any and all circumstances. She wore a clear plastic rain hat and carried an old-lady purse in her left hand and a shotgun in her right. Her floral house dress was rumpled, its pockets bulging with tissues, and because this was an important meeting, she wore white ankle socks over her standard knee-high hose. I figured she was coming up on time for her Prolixin shot down at the mental health center. In fact, we might be walking a thin line between time for the shot and past time for the shot. The gun was a sure sign that Raydean was losing touch with reality and expecting an alien invasion by the Flemish.

The four of us sat at the table, a plate of Ma's steaming rolls between us, discussing strategy.

"I don't like this," Al mumbled, his mouth thick with cinnamon roll.

I rolled my eyes. He kept insisting that we call the cops to let them handle this.

"Al, this ain't Philly. This ain't one of your APE cases. There is no acute political emergency about a stripper gettin' whacked at a dirt track. Panama City doesn't have the manpower to pursue it—"

"What?" Al boomed. "What? To pursue it like you can, Sierra?"

"Yeah," I said, but he knew I was bluffing.

"Alfonso!" Ma screeched. "Are you saying you can't help her? You would turn your back on blood to give your allegiance to a police force that isn't even your own? Is that how you were raised?" Ma shook her head, but it wasn't a Protestant shake. It was Catholic. It implied: "Aha! So that's how come you walked away from your own father and brothers, denied your heritage, and left the fire department to become a cop. What are they, these cops? A cult?" Al didn't even look up. He didn't have to. A Catholic head shake is a tremor you feel deep in your guilt-ridden soul.

"Don't go there, Ma," he cautioned. "Don't even start with me. It don't have nothing to do with that. It's about who can do the most."

Ma shook her head again. "A punk beat up your sister last night," she began. "That same punk killed her friend. The way I see it, this is now a personal matter. Do I have to call your father? Do I really need to tell him about this? His own son, walking away from the family?" Again. The word hung in the air, unsaid. You would leave us *again*?

Al sighed, the Vatican treatment too much for him to handle. "All right, Ma. All right." He reached for another roll, but Ma slapped his hand.

"Here," she said, reaching for the thickest roll with the most icing. "Is better."

Raydean leaned across the table and looked Ma in the eye. "You're one to go down the river with!" she said. "I got me a plan."

Ma smiled at Raydean. Maybe Ma hadn't noticed that Raydean was batshit. Maybe to her wearing a rain hat on a sunny day and toting a shotgun was just being well dressed.

"Let's us cruise up to that racetrack and do a little investigating."

"Aw, no, Raydean," I said smoothly. "I was thinking you and Ma might hold down Command Headquarters here so if we needed you, we could call for backup."

Al had the good sense to nod his agreement, but Raydean saw right through it. "Horsepucky!" she said. "Me and your ma ain't holding down no desk jobs! I got an idea or two of my own."

Ma seemed to have lost her mind, 'cause she was nodding her head as if Raydean was making sense.

Raydean pushed her rain hat a little lower on her forehead

and cut her eyes over at Ma. "What say we stake out Lulu? If that old girl's running around on my nephew, he oughta know about it!"

Ma's lips tightened and I knew she was remembering a certain Mostavindaduchi woman down at the Sons of Italy Social Club in South Philly.

"I don't hold with infidelity," she said. "I'll pack the provisions."

With that, Ma stood up, tightened her bathrobe belt, and glared at me and Al as if daring us to try to stop her. I wasn't saying a word for two reasons. One, I didn't figure Lulu to be any threat, especially to Raydean, who was family. And two, I knew Ma would smack me if I tried talking back, and I hadn't had enough coffee yet to stay safely out of her way.

"I'll get the car, lamb chop," Raydean said to Ma, and left.

Ma wandered off to the back of the trailer to make herself presentable.

"Why didn't you stop her?" Al demanded, roll crumbs dropping like rain down his shirt front.

I whacked him quick, just like Ma would. "Why didn't you, burgerhead?" Al rubbed his head and said nothing.

"I'm thinking you should go up to the track and nose around Roy Dell's crew," I said. "Maybe you can get a line on Meatloaf." Al frowned like he was having second thoughts. "Unless, of course, you'd rather have the *po-lice* do it." Al glared at me. "All you gotta do is act like a fan. It ain't rocket science!"

"And what are you gonna be doing?"

"God! You'd think you was Pop or Francis! I'm not doin' anything that could be in any way construed as dangerous!"

Al wasn't reassured. He knew me. "What exactly are you going to be doing?"

I sighed and looked like he'd caught me in the act. "I'm taking Fluffy to be groomed, if you must know!"

Of course, that wasn't quite the whole story, but Al didn't need to know everything.

Nineteen

To me and Fluffy, there ain't nothing better for the soul than a good ride in the country, T-tops off, the breeze circulating through the car, and the radio pumping out something that rocks and is maybe a bit naughty, like Bonnie Raitt. It's times like that when me and the Fluff are closest. Female bonding, I call it. I think Fluffy felt the same way, 'cause when I looked over at her, she was smiling. Either that, or the wind was ruffling her lips. I wanted to believe she was happy. In fact, I needed to believe she was euphoric on account of what I was about to do to her, my very own best friend.

We'd ridden over to Wewahitchka, after I'd spent the morning combing through the yellow pages looking for dog groomers named Iris. There was only one. The way I figured things, since Ruby'd been killed in her hometown, I couldn't overlook her past, and the only bit of her life that remained a mystery was her first three years, her biological parents, and her roots.

I was considering any other, last-minute options, and Fluffy was considering the sky and the little fleecy clouds that danced across it. I looked over and felt a little sad, but in the end, what I was about to do would be for the good of us both. We were looking to find a killer, after all, and in a case like that, some sacrifice is necessary. Ruby's biological mother could know something that would help me figure out who would have a motive to kill her. If not, Fluffy and I still came out ahead, because Fluffy would be clean.

I pulled up in front of the Doggie Palace of Pampered Love and cut the engine.

"Fluff," I said, "I would've told you about this earlier, but you woulda ducked on me."

Fluffy was definitely not smiling now. She smelled doggie fear in the wind, and her wide-brimmed ears were pinned back flat against her tiny head.

"It was the only way I could think of for us to meet Ruby's original mother," I said. Fluffy began to growl, deep and low in her throat.

"I know, I know," I said. "You hate dog groomin'. Well, sugar, there's parts of my job I don't like either, but a girl's gotta do what a girl's gotta do sometimes, even if it means letting someone clip your ear hairs."

Fluffy barked, one shrill, glass-shattering yip of terror. Above all else, Fluffy hates the dog groomer. For her, it's kind of like seeing the gynecologist while also visiting the dentist.

I snuck a peek at my watch. We were right on time for our noon appointment. I reached over and snatched Fluffy up in my right hand while opening the door with my left. It was best to barrel on ahead and not let Fluffy stew any longer.

The Doggie Palace of Pampered Love was a tiny bungalow covered with pink peeling paint and ivy that scampered up over the porch rails and up the side of the cottage. The Palace sat on a shady side street, surrounded by pin oaks. It would've been almost romantic, if not for the sound of a thousand yapping dogs and the smell of disinfectant.

As we reached the foot of the stairs, the door burst open and an elderly woman emerged carrying one pure white miniature poodle under each arm. Fluffy took one look at the matching pink hair bows and attempted to break free.

"Fluff, I won't let them put no sissy pink hair bows on you!" But we both knew I was lying. I'd do anything to find out more about Ruby Diamond.

We stepped into the little house and Fluffy began to shake. In front of us stood the image of Dorothy Lamour a hundred pounds heavier in a brightly colored muumuu, with a huge synthetic magnolia blossom in her hair.

"This must be Fluffy!" she trilled.

"And you must be Iris Stokes," I said, a big smile pasted across my face.

She hadn't been hard to find. There was only one Iris Stokes listed in the phone book, and when I saw the Doggie Palace of Pampered Love listed right beneath her name, I knew I'd have a cover for asking every question I could think of.

Iris Stokes reached for Fluffy. I held my breath, waiting for Iris to scream out in pain as Fluffy sank her sharp little canines into her hand, but it didn't happen. Fluffy was paralyzed with fear.

"Come on, darlin'," Iris crooned, leading the way into her grooming room. "You's a little scared, but Auntie Iris is gonna take such good care of you." The muumuu rippled, shaking the brightly colored lotus blossoms. With a practiced movement, Iris set Fluffy down on a metal table and proceeded to fasten her collar to a little lead that ensured Fluffy's cooperation by holding her prisoner.

"My, my, my," murmured Iris, peering into Fluffy's ears. "It's been a long time since you had any attention of a personal grooming nature."

Fluffy let out a loud, agonized moan of pure terror.

"Fluffy," I said, stepping forward, "the lady hasn't even touched you!"

Fluffy rolled her eyes up at me.

"Full treatment?" said Iris.

I nodded, and Fluffy started to yowl.

"Mind if I watch?" I asked. "Sometimes it calms her down." I shot Fluffy a look, the kind of look that I hoped promised a wonderful treat if she cooperated.

Iris didn't seem to hear. Instead she gathered up clippers and combs, bottles of goop and sprays, all designed to turn Fluff into a real lady.

"Ham!" she bellowed suddenly. A thin man materialized from the back room. He was elderly and walked gently, as if he were afraid of snapping in half.

"This little darling needs a bath," Iris said, smiling. "And make sure she has a little time in the whirlpool, too." Fluffy moaned again. Iris reached up, unsnapped her collar, and handed her over to Ham. He hummed something tuneless and walked off with my baby safely cradled under one of his bony arms. There'd be hell to pay for this little trip.

"How'd you hear about us, hon?" Iris asked, eyeing me like I was perhaps an exotic bird. Couldn't blame her really. I was wearing a tiger-striped tank top, black stretch stirrup pants, and five-inch black stilettos. The way I figure it, every outside appearance is an opportunity to promote good public relations.

I let the sadness inside me well up and play across my face.

"Ruby Diamond's mama told me about you," I said.

The change in her was instantaneous. Gone was Dorothy Lamour, and in her place a grieving mother. She tried to hide it, but there was no way to hold back the tears that welled up in her eyes. She fumbled and dropped a pair of scissors.

"She told you about me?" Iris asked softly, waiting to see which way I'd take the question.

I took a step closer to her, close enough to reach out and touch the soft folds of fabric.

"Ruby and I were like sisters," I said. "I want to know who killed her, don't you?"

The room was as still as the air outside. Both of us holding our breath. In the distance, I could hear Ham shuffling around, talking gently to Fluffy and running water. Iris's breath rushed out of her lungs in one huge sigh.

"I wouldn't have given her up for the world, but I had no choice," she said, and began to cry. "It was years ago. I had no family to help out. My husband went crazy and left us. I already had a little boy. How was I gonna feed two young'uns? I didn't know what to do."

Iris's anguish was real. Her hands clawed at the fabric of her dress, and her eyes stared off into the past.

"The boy was older. He could half fend for himself, but Ruby Lee was just a baby. I couldn't leave her to go find work." Iris was shaking now, her entire massive body quivering with remembered pain. "So I did the hardest thing I ever done in my life. I dressed her all up in her pretty pink sunbonnet and this little pink checked dress with pearly buttons, and I took her up to social services. I left her there with them."

Ham chose this moment to wander back in with Fluffy, cuddled up in a pink towel, only her head sticking through. Iris and I looked up and both burst into tears. Ham, not certain why the sight of a chihuahua swaddled in a blanket should cause such distress, did the only thing he could, the only thing any man would do. He pretended it wasn't happening.

He stepped forward to the metal table, gently deposited the trembling dog, and clipped her to the harness. Now and then, as he completed his task, he'd look up at Iris, concern playing across his features, but he never met her eye directly. Finally, at a total loss, he left. Iris seemed unaware that he'd even entered the room, but she stepped mechanically over to the table.

"It's all right, sugar," she crooned to Fluffy. "No one's gonna hurt you."

She wasn't talking to Fluffy.

"They found her a good home," Iris said. "Wewa's a small town. You'd a thought they'd place her farther away, and at first they did. Sent her off to stay with a family in the county somewhere, wait out the time for me to change my mind, or find money that wasn't never coming." Iris's eyes glowed with frustration and grief.

She picked up the clippers and began to shave Fluffy. Fluffy didn't have much hair to begin with, so I figured it wouldn't hurt her to have an imaginary shave. Fluffy seemed to feel differently, but she stood absolutely still.

"What happened to Ruby's father?" I asked. "Why didn't he send child support?"

Iris looked up from her task, her eyes dull with hopelessness. "He was in a mental institution. By the time I could get on my feet, she was gone." Iris picked up a spray bottle and spritzed some cologne on Fluffy, who sneezed loudly. "I knew where she was, of course. Jane Diamond all of a sudden had a little girl, been wanting a child all her life and couldn't have one. Couldn't have a dark-haired, big-eyed little girl till she got mine." Iris shrugged. "I got what I deserved. We all did."

"What do you mean?"

"I lost my baby. It was my fault. And Jane Diamond got her. Loved her like she was her own, and in time, she was. I had to watch my baby grow from a distance, saw her graduate high school, saw her leave for her senior prom." Iris looked up at me for the first time. "Don't get me wrong. I'm not saying it should've turned out any different. What could I have given her?" She looked around the tiny grooming room and shook her head. "I got remarried, but it didn't work out. He even adopted my son. But that ain't no guarantee. He run off

about six years later. By then, I'd been to grooming school."
Iris sighed and began to work on Fluffy's ears.

"Fool me once," she muttered, "shame on you. Fool me
twice, shame on me. When number two left, I was ready. Me
and Michael made out all right, squeaking by. Then Ham
came along."

With a start I realized Ham was husband number three.
Old rail-thin Ham. Iris seemed to read my mind.

"Yeah, him. He's older, just like my first husband, but he
ain't crazy." She chuckled to herself. "Now, he's a might slow
on the uptake, but he loves me and he ain't going nowhere.
Ever'one I ever loved is gone." She stopped and sighed. "Even
Michael. He got himself into some trouble, and now he don't
speak to me." As if on cue, Ham began his tuneless humming
in the back room.

"What happened to Ruby's father?" I asked. "Did he ever
leave the institution?"

Iris looked disgusted. "Oh yeah, he left all right. Them
legislators over in Tallahassee got the big idea it was wrong to
keep nuts in the nuthouse. Developed a thing called deinsti-
tutionalization. You know what that means, don't you?" She
didn't wait for me to answer. "It means, 'We ain't spending no
more tax dollars on you people. Go back where you came from
and bother them people.' "

My heart quickened. Ruby's insane father returned to Wewahitchka. How had he felt about her being adopted?

"So he came back here? To Wewa?"

Iris nodded slowly, opening a plastic container full of
brightly colored hair bows.

"Yep. He came back. Acting like it was the Fourth of July
and Christmas all rolled into one. Just as crazy as a Betsy Bug."

"How long . . ." I couldn't even figure out what question
to ask first.

"He'd been away fifteen years when he come back, his

151

hair all wild and his eyes lit up with a fire. Wanting to see his young'uns." Iris snorted. "Couldn't even remember we was divorced! Fat lot of good that did!"

"Where is he now?"

"All over town," she said. "All up in *Time* magazine. All over the news. All over everywhere."

"I don't get what you mean," I said.

"Honey, you ever hear tell of the Honk-If-You-Love-Jesus artist?"

"Wannamaker Lewis? Ruby's father is Wannamaker Lewis?"

Iris nodded and picked a vibrant yellow bow, peeled a little patch off the back of it, and stuck it firmly in the center of Fluffy's cue-ball head.

"The walking one and only," Iris said. "Multimillion-dollar daddy." She laughed softly to herself. "All the money in the world and he couldn't save her. 'Course, he didn't make any of it until after he was released, but still, she's dead and he's not. Somehow it don't seem fair."

Iris turned her attention back to Fluffy. "Don't you look special!" she said. "Let's shine that coat up a bit." She reached for a small tube of grease that squirted out clear and smelled like a whorehouse. "This'll do you!" she said, but Fluffy moaned.

"Did Ruby know about you and her father?" I asked.

Iris glanced up, her eyes sharpening to little pinpoints. "No! No way was I gonna put her through hell twice! I don't know how her low-life of a father found out, but I do know the only decent thing that man ever did was leave his daughter alone. Him, me, Ruby's new mama, Michael, and Ham were the only ones ever knew where Ruby went. That's just how it had to be."

Iris turned her attention back to Fluffy, who'd had enough of Iris and the Doggie Palace of Pampered Love to last her a lifetime. She was raising up her front paws and attempting to pull the hair bow off of her head.

"Darlin'!" Iris exclaimed. "That ain't ladylike! Come on, now!" With a practiced hand, Iris slipped Fluffy's rhinestone collar around her neck while at the same time undoing the snap that kept Fluff a prisoner. "There!" she said. "All purty for Mama!"

Iris gently placed Fluff in my arms and stood right in front of me, her teary, red eyes staring directly into mine.

"I can't charge you for this," she said, "on account of how you're gonna find out who hurt my baby. You're gonna come back here and tell me," she said, "and then I'm gonna kill him. I couldn't keep her. I couldn't save her. But by God, I can avenge her!"

Iris's eyes smoldered. Her heavy body trembled with rage, and for a moment her face was so red, I considered calling 911. Then Ham shuffled back into the room, humming, and the moment was broken.

For a second, the Doggie Palace of Pampered Love had seemed full of rage and violence, but just as quickly, it returned to pinkness and light, as if a cloud has passed briefly over the sun. Danger seemed as far away as Ruby's childhood. But like childhood, the illusion of safety vanishes all too quickly. Me and Fluff were heading for big trouble. On one level I knew that, but did that make it right to drag my family and friends in along with me?

Twenty

*F*luffy wasn't speaking to me.
We were driving down the little side streets of Wewa, the wind
blowing through the T-tops just as it had been an hour ago,
but for us, the mood was broken. The yellow hair bow had
blown out the window and become a distant memory, but
Fluff's encounter with Iris Strokes was obviously still fresh in
her mind. At least we were focused on the same mental image,
but Fluffy was dealing with the trauma to her psyche, while I
was thinking of another, more deadly trauma.

Ruby Lee Diamond had lived and died in a public fish-
bowl. The way I figured it, Iris Stokes was dead wrong if she
thought no one but insiders knew who Jane Diamond's
adopted daughter was. How hard could it have been to figure
it all out in a tiny spit of a town? Maybe Ruby was the only
one who didn't know what half the town knew. But now I
knew, and there was one more link to follow. Ruby Lee's crazy
father.

Finding Wannamaker Lewis wasn't going to be a problem.
Wannamaker didn't want to be missed. The Honk-If-You-Love-
Jesus icon had positioned himself with the canny shrewdness
of a professional retailer, right in the heart of town, at the main
crossroads, next to Wewa's only grocery, gas, bait, and tackle
shop, the Dixie Dandy.

His studio was a rundown shack that had once sold Tupelo honey. At least that's what the sign that hung precariously from a pin oak still promised to deliver. The dirt brown hut sported a rusted tin roof, and it might have gone unnoticed if Wannamaker hadn't taken steps to ensure that didn't happen.

The entire lot was crammed with whirligigs: wooden cutout Uncle Sams painted every color of the rainbow, huge bears covered with Scripture, and his trademark HONK IF YOU LOVE JESUS placards. One whirligig in particular stood out, jutting into the road. It was Jesus, with mobile arms that swung in circles with the wind. At least it must've been Jesus. It was a good physical likeness, but there the resemblance to the traditional figure ended. Jesus wore a tie-dyed robe, had fire in his eyes, and an American flag was painted squarely across his chest. Floating above him was a halo and two angels, one with a flashing neon sign that said, OPEN. HONK IF YOU LOVE JESUS!

Sister Mary Catherine would've had plenty to say about this. I crossed myself as a precaution and pulled into the parking lot. Fluffy, sensing perhaps another encounter of a personal nature, jumped down off the seat and crawled to the back of the car so I couldn't grab her.

"To each his own, girl," I said. "If you don't want an extra dose of precaution, if you are not concerned about eternal damnation, then stay in the car." My answer was a low growl. Fluffy was a heathen and proud of it.

BEWARE! a sign proclaimed, as I stepped out of the car. SATAN IS EVERYWHERE!

"Damn straight," I muttered.

JOHN 3:16, another placard read.

"Lavotini 24:7," I said back. I wandered up onto the porch of Wannamaker's studio, looking for signs of life other than the eternal kind. A ceiling fan whirred slowly inside the studio, moved by the breeze that gusted through the paneless windows.

"Anybody home?" I called, stepping gingerly across the wooden porch planks.

"Yoo-hoo, Mr. Lewis?" I waited another moment, until I was sure that no one was around, and started back to the car. "Too bad for you," I said out loud. "I just love Jesus!" Still no response. That didn't make sense. If Lewis's folk art was worth so much, what was it doing just sitting out in his parking lot unattended? Where were the security guards that hovered around the fancy galleries they always showed on TV?

I reached the Camaro and had my hand on the door when Fluffy started the dog equivalent of screaming.

"He ain't here," a deep voice boomed, scaring me into jumping a good two feet straight up in the air.

I whirled around to face one of the biggest, darkest, and tallest men ever to fill a pair of tattered overalls.

"Good grief! Holy Mother of God! Were you trying to scare the living shit out of me, or is it just something you do naturally?"

The man stared at me for a moment, as if it were taking a while for the circuits to connect and formulate an answer.

"It's his nap time," the man said slowly. "Don't take nothin' and you won't go to hell." He stood there, not moving, too close for comfort. There was something not quite right with this cookie. Then he smiled, a beautiful toothy smile that warmed his face. "Jesus loves the little children," he said. "Come back after nap time."

"I will," I said, sliding behind my door and slipping into my seat. Fluffy was still screaming at the top of her lungs, and I wanted to.

"Bye!"

I cranked that Camaro up and spun out of the driveway. Fluffy, emboldened by our departure, leaped up onto the back-seat and balanced her front paws on the open window ledge.

Her bark changed to a deeper promise of murder and mayhem.

"Yo, Fluff," I yelled, "you keep that shit up and I'll bring you back with me the next time."

There was an abrupt silence from the backseat.

I pulled into the Dixie Dandy parking lot, to the side farthest away from Wannamaker Lewis's studio, and stopped by a phone booth so I could look up Roy Dell. If Raydean and Ma were serious about staking out Roy Dell's house, then it was probably time for me to check on them. Knowing Raydean, they were inside drinking tea. Knowing Ma, she was cooking Lulu a real meal and lecturing her on the values of fidelity and the penalties for committing mortal sins.

I couldn't have been further from the truth.

Roy Dell lived off of State Route 20, away from the racetrack, in a little cluster of brick and wooden-sided house that had been someone's attempt at a subdivision in the late 1960s. Roy Dell's place in the one-street neighborhood was not hard to find. It sat at the end of the cul-de-sac, scrubby pines and knobs of grass springing up like errant groundhogs, a big split-level with its siding painted Roy Dell's vibrant racing yellow, just like his race car.

The piece-of-shit yellow Vega sat in a position of honor in the front yard, its back two wheels up on cinder blocks. Various hulks of cars and car parts lay littered across the front yard, sandwiched in among the used racing tires that had been painted a house- and car-matching yellow and filled with stringy portulacas. It was a vision of poor taste and a monument to sloppy living.

You could view the entire street from the top of a little rise that led down into the Lucky Days Subdivision, a fact that I found faintly disturbing on account of how Ma and Raydean would have no good surveillance point that wouldn't leave them exposed to their subjects. Ahead of me, just outside the entrance to Roy Dell's little neighborhood, sat Raydean's ancient Plymouth Fury. The car was deserted.

"Something's wrong, Fluffy," I said. "It don't feel right around here. They wouldn't just leave the car and walk onto Roy Dell's property. No, if they felt good about things, they'd have driven right up to the front door. Especially Ma with her corns."

Fluffy, still unsure of me, stood on the backseat, sniffing the air. From the look on her face, and the way she bared her teeth, I was thinking she saw things like I did.

"Time for a little reconnaissance," I whispered. I backed the Camaro down the street, away from Raydean's cop-mobile, and parked under a thin stand of pines. I leaned down and grabbed a pair of aerobics shoes from under the front passenger seat and pulled off my stilettos. Then I reached under my seat and started rooting around for a weapon, just in case.

I know, if ever there were a case for carrying concealed, it would be me. Dancers are life's little idea of target practice, and so most of us carry, but not me. The way I see it, an attacker would only use the gun to kill me. The truth be told, I was scared of guns. But for some reason, I wasn't scared of knives.

My fingers sought and found the Spyderco that lay just under my seat. They curled around the smooth casing, caressing the steel back of the blade. You grow up in Philly, and you learn how to defend yourself with your own hands. A knife is just an extension of my fingernails. My brother Francis gave me the Spyderco. He didn't say much and I know it set him back a pretty penny, but it was his way of letting me know that while he accepted my decision to dance, he would still worry about his baby sister's safety.

It was now my turn to worry about Ma and Raydean.

"You stay here, Fluff," I said. Of course, Fluffy was gonna

do what she wanted to do, but it gave me a sense of being in control just to say it.

I got out of the car and started creeping down the street, sticking close to the side of the road and trying not to be seen. When I came up even with the Plymouth Fury, I realized I had every reason to be worried. The front and backseat were littered with pieces of pine branches. An empty Piggly Wiggly grocery sack lay on the front seat along with an empty package of black shoe polish. Ma's purse was open, the contents scattered in with the pine needles. Worst of all, Raydean's shotgun lay out in plain view on the backseat. Those two wouldn't walk off leaving their valuables unattended. Where in the hell was Ma?

As if in answer to my question, an ear-splitting scream filled the air, a scream of terror that could not be mistaken for anything else. It was followed quickly by another unmistakable sound: gunfire.

I took off running as hard and fast as I could, and headed for the glaring yellow house, headed straight for the source of the sounds. I looked up as I hit the driveway just in time to see two soldiers and a naked man. An ugly, naked man.

I jumped behind Roy Dell's Vega and peered up over the hood. The naked man streaked by me and there was a horrible moment as I realized I knew him. Frank was running full out, heading past the front of the house and making for the back side of it. Following behind him were the soldiers, Ma and Raydean dressed in camouflage that had to date back to World War II, judging from their pine-covered helmets. Their faces were blackened with shoe polish, but their eyes glared out as they ran by, too intent on their quarry to notice me. Ma was carrying something black and square in her left hand. My ma and Raydean, chasing old caught-in-the-act-again Frank. I would've laughed had it not been for a sudden complication.

The front door slammed open, flying back against the wall,

as Lulu burst out upon the scene, a shotgun in her hands and a murderous look in her eyes.

Ba-boom! The gun discharged and half the flowers in one of the tires scattered to the four corners of the earth. *Boom! Ba-Boom!* She fired off two more times, and then, as she located Ma and Raydean, she laid her head alongside the barrel and took careful aim.

Lulu did not look like an amateur. She was gonna kill somebody.

At a moment like this, time slows to a crawl. I saw Lulu site Ma's backside, but I was already in motion. I had the advantage of Lulu's attention being focused on Ma and Raydean. She didn't see me coming, and she didn't hear me as I climbed on top of Roy Dell's Vega and launched myself into the air, flying toward the porch and the barrel of the shotgun. Too late, I connected. *Ba-boom!* The gun fired wild, deafening me with its roar. Lulu, now on the ground, was puzzled and incensed. She turned her attention to beating the living crap out of me, which wasn't going to be hard to do, given Lulu's size and strength.

I heard a dull roaring sound and I figured I was about to die from Lulu sitting on me. The sound got louder, though, and for a second, my attacker was distracted. I shoved her and she rolled sideways, moving just enough for me to reach my hand into my pocket and wrap my fingers around my knife.

"Baby!" a voice yelled. We both looked over. Frank had materialized in his black Firebird, which must've been parked out of sight behind the house.

"Baby! Throw me some pants! I gotta get outta here!"

Lulu looked up, torn between doing what Frank wanted and killing me. That's when she slugged me hard across the jaw and struggled to stand up.

"Don't you move none," she said. "I'll be right back to kill your ass!"

Yeah, like I was really gonna stay lying there on my back, waiting to get my ass kicked.

"Sierra! Stop him! I can't get a good shot!" Ma's voice cut through the haze of red pain. Sweet Jesus, tell me Ma didn't have a gun!

I jumped up in time to see Ma with a black camcorder held up to her left eye, trying to get Frank on tape.

"Ma, what're you doin'? This ain't a wedding down to the Social Club."

Raydean was right beside her, grinning. "Sierra," she cried, "we caught him bringing the mother ship in for a landing!"

Frank, suddenly aware that the army was again after him, gunned his engine and popped the clutch, jumping the car forward across the front yard. Only one thing stood between him and freedom: An unmarked police sedan sat squarely in the middle of the driveway and Detective Wheeling stood behind the passenger door, his gun drawn and a seriously pissed-off look on his face.

Lulu picked that moment to come flying back out onto the porch, her shotgun aimed at the spot where I'd just been, and a pair of jeans slung over her beefy shoulders.

"All right, you!" she yelled, not waiting to see if I was still there. *Ba-boom!* The spot on the porch floor where I'd been lying burst into splinters. I vaulted over the back side of the porch just in time and hit the ground in a crouch. Raydean and Mama, being not quite the fools they appeared to be, ducked down behind Frank's car.

"Freeze!" Detective Wheeling screamed.

"Baby! Don't do it!" Frank cautioned. "He'll shoot you! Drop the gun!"

Lulu looked out into the driveway and saw the barrel of the Glock 9mm, appeared to think for a bare second, and then dropped the gun, a smile quickly replacing the homicidal look on her face.

"Hey, Officer, what's doin'?"

Wheeling wasn't having any of it. He remained hunkered down behind the roof of the car, a radio mike in his hand, barking into it. Then he put it down and started issuing orders. In the distance, sirens began to wail as Wewahitchka's only police car came to the rescue.

"Put your hands in the air! Now!" Lulu raised her hands like a placid schoolchild. "You!" Wheeling yelled to Frank. "Cut the engine and get out of the car!"

Frank shut down the car immediately, but didn't move to leave it.

"Get out of the car, now!" Wheeling yelled, the adrenaline rush evident in his red face.

"Aw, man," Frank said, and sighed. "Do I have to?"

"Get out of that damned car right now!"

Slowly the door swung open, and as I saw it from my position lying on the ground alongside Lulu's porch, one bare foot hit the ground, then another. There was still-as-death silence for about thirty seconds, and then the sound of Detective Wheeling laughing.

"You think that's something," Raydean called out, "you oughta see what we got on videotape!"

Wheeling shook his head slowly and raised up a little from behind his car.

"Where's Roy Dell?" he called out to Lulu.

"He ain't here," she answered.

"No, duh!" said Raydean, cackling. "That boy don't know what he's missing!"

"But he will," said Ma, patting the camcorder.

I crossed myself as an extra precaution. I knew Ma was thinking back to the Sons of Italy–Mostavindaduchi fiasco. Poor Pa, I bet he never speaks to another woman again in his life, let alone smiles at one.

Wewa's finest arrived at that moment, and a young deputy

sprang from the car, his gun drawn and a wild-eyed look of pure terror in his eyes. Here he was, at his first gunfight. He looked at Wheeling, then saw naked Frank.

"Damn!" he swore. "What you got here?"

Wheeling looked over at him. "What, boy, you never seen a naked man? Go up on that porch and retrieve that shotgun, would you?"

The young man cut past Wheeling and cautiously approached Lulu, slipping up onto the porch and grabbing the shotgun tenderly.

"Now," said Wheeling, stepping out from behind the car and walking a few feet up the drive. "Would somebody care to explain what's going on here?"

Raydean took a step forward and looked like she was about to tell all, but then she stopped suddenly. "Hey," she said, "ain't you that boy from over to the drugstore?"

"The very same one," I answered, stepping out from the side of the house.

"Uh-huh!" Raydean snapped. "I thought as much. Alien!"

I smiled at Wheeling. "There's really not much to this at all," I said smoothly.

"Now, there's a damn lie!" Lulu spit, but just as quickly remembered that she'd been caught in flagrante delicto, and shut her mouth.

"Does anybody here want to press charges against anybody else here?" Wheeling asked, slowly running his eyes over all of us one at a time.

No one spoke. I hesitated, then decided to tell him the details about Lulu and Frank later, when Ma wasn't around to get any more involved than she already was.

"Well, fine then," he said. "I'm just interested in catching up with Roy Dell, Ms. Parks. Where might I find him?"

"Why do you want him?"

Wheeling stared at her hard for a moment. "I have a warrant for his arrest," he said finally.

Lulu stepped to the edge of the porch. "On what charge?"

"The murder of Ruby Diamond," he answered, his eyes never wavering from hers.

Lulu seemed to teeter for a moment, then grabbed on to the porch rail for support and leaned forward. "That's the most ridiculous thing I ever heard in my life! Roy Dell never laid a hand on that slut!"

"I got evidence to the contrary, ma'am. I'd appreciate you letting us know if you hear from him, on account of I'm sure you wouldn't want to be an accessory after the fact."

Lulu opened her mouth to say something, then just as quickly closed it.

"Now," said Wheeling, turning to face the rest of us, "I'm thinking y'all ought to disperse."

Raydean and Ma started to walk off toward Raydean's copmobile, obviously anxious to put as much space between themselves and Frank as possible.

"Hey!" Frank said. "They got something of mine! I want that film!"

Lulu tossed Frank his pants and he started struggling to pull them on while Raydean and Ma quickened their pace to a dead run.

"You'll have to take care of that later," Wheeling said to him. "I need to talk to you."

"Can't it wait?" Frank was looking over Wheeling's shoulder and seeing his recent past getting away from him, forever preserved in Ma's camcorder.

" 'Fraid it can't," Wheeling answered calmly. "I need you to sign that statement you gave us yesterday." I was starting to walk away after Raydean and Ma, but I was also trying to overhear. "And I need to talk to you, too, Ms. Lavotini."

I spun around and looked back at Wheeling, who hadn't even turned away from Frank as he spoke.

"I figure you got your hands full, right now, Detective. Catch up with me later." After all, he couldn't actually detain me, not unless he was going to arrest me.

"Don't leave your trailer," he said, his command voice returning.

"How about this, Detective. I won't leave the country."

I could tell he was mad. The dull red flush was moving across the back of his neck. There'd be hell to pay later, but for now, I had a videotape to watch.

Twenty-one

*R*aydean must've flown back to Panama City. Her car was securely parked on her parking pad, the canvas cover concealing it from alien invaders, when I pulled onto my own parking pad across the one-lane street. No sign of life came from either trailer, but I knew Al had just come back because Ma's car was still making ticking noises like it does when you shut it off.

Fluffy was all too glad to be home. She bailed out of the car, flew up the steps, and was through the doggie door before I could cut the engine. So much for companionship. I guessed she'd had enough for one day. But somehow I knew my day was only beginning. It might've had something to do with the look on Al's face when I walked into the kitchen. He was sitting at the table, scowling, a laptop computer open in front of him.

"Hey," I said cautiously.

"Did you see Ma?" he barked. "Did you see her just now? Cause I'm thinkin', you know, somehow Sierra's behind this. Ma is looking like a freaking escapee from World War II!"

"Yeah?" I leaned against the counter and tried to look calm, like it was no big deal at all for our saintly mother to turn to blackface and camouflage.

"She was running, Sierra. Running like someone was after

her. And she stonewalled me. Wouldn't tell me bupkiss. Just said she had to take a shower. She's been in there ever since." Al was plainly exasperated.

"Well, what's it been, Al? Five minutes? It takes time to get that shit off your face, and she's all sweaty—"

"Sierra, can it. What happened?"

I figured there was no easy way around it, so I told him. Of course, certain, shall we say, nonessential details were left by the wayside. I didn't think Al would approve of Lulu shooting at Ma, or Ma videotaping Frank at the golden moment with Lulu. I merely intimated that Ma and Raydean had encountered Frank and his honey in a compromising position.

"I don't believe you, Sierra."

"Be that as it may, Al, that's my story and I'm sticking to it." I laughed, like there wasn't a care in my world, but I stepped over to the window and peered out through the gauze curtains. It wouldn't take Frank any time at all to find out where I lived and come barreling down the road. Raydean was Roy Dell's aunt, after all. Frank would at least come looking for her.

"What you looking at?" Al barked.

"Nothin'! Jeeze, will you take a pill!" I looked over at my brother and realized he'd hooked his laptop to my phone jack. "Hey, is that long distance?"

"No!" he grumped.

"Al," I said, sliding into the seat next to him, "what's really bothering you?"

He looked up for a brief second, then away. "You know that the guy you sent me to find out about, Albert a.k.a. Meatloaf, has a record?"

"No, how could I know that?"

"I just thought maybe with your connection at the police department, you might know."

"How'd you find out?"

Al spun the computer around so I could see the screen. E-mail from a buddy in the department back in Philly.

"So what's he done?" I asked, because Al quickly spun the computer back to face him and started tapping.

"Assault and battery, on a female," he answered.

"How much time did he do?"

Al looked up at me. "None. For some reason, the charges got dropped just before it went to trial. Technically, it's not supposed to still be in the system, but my buddy's got a connection with NCIC." Al was looking puffed up, like he knew things none of us regular citizens would ever know.

Ma picked that moment to reappear, traces of shoe polish stuck in her ears.

"What's all the yelling?" she asked, as if she hadn't heard every word through my paper-thin walls. "Youse two got low blood sugar. That's your problem. You need to eat!" Ma was on a tear, whipping out pots and pans, and running water for noodles.

"Don't you got work, Sierra?" she asked. "It's going on five o'clock. You gotta get out of here soon. Go on and take your shower. I'll call you when supper's ready."

There I was, in my own house, taking orders from my mom the espionage queen! What was wrong with this picture?

"Ma, we gotta talk," I said.

She gave me an anxious look from her spot behind Al, making a chopping motion at her neck, like I should slit my throat. Don't talk. Okay. I understood.

"Yeah, you're right, Ma," I said. "I need a shower."

By the time I returned, transformed into Sierra, Wonder Queen of Desire, Al and Ma had settled into an uncomfortable silence.

We struggled through dinner, with each one wanting to say stuff but not wanting the other to know. Al followed me out to the car as I was leaving for work, frowning.

"Don't go near that Meatloaf guy," he said. "He's dangerous."

"I can handle Meatloaf."

"Sierra, no you can't. That woman he assaulted?"

"Yeah?"

"She was a dancer."

A cool breeze blew across the parking pad, making me
shiver. "All right, Al, I'll watch my back extra special. But Al,
you gotta do one thing for me, all right?" It was my turn.

"What?" Al was plenty suspicious.

"Ma and Raydean kinda pissed off Lulu and her boyfriend,
Frank. Just on the off chance that he takes a mind to pay back,
would you watch Raydean's place?"

"I knew it. I just knew it. There's always more, isn't there,
Sierra? You just never tell me the whole story."

But I was gone by then, gunning the car into reverse and
laying a patch down the road just like we used to do up in
Kensington when Bridge Street was quiet. I looked at Al in
the rearview mirror. He wasn't laughing.

Twenty-two

The night called for something special. The Tiffany was jumping. Vincent Gambuzzo, smelling a big take on the door, was walking around like a stuffed panda bear, puffing out his chest and trying not to stumble on account of the RayBans he wore even in the darkest parts of the club. Roy Dell and the racetrack crew were conspicuously absent. But I'd given Bruno, the steroid-impaired bouncer, a heads-up on Meatloaf and Frankenstein. He'd be ready to bounce their sorry tails off the sidewalk should they show.

There was a surprise waiting for me when I got to the club, a surprise I'd been working for months to score. My source, Dickie the Deal, had come through on procuring tonight's costume. I didn't know how he'd done it, and I didn't want to appear even curious, but I was grateful to the tune of one hundred large. I counted out five twenties and handed them to Dickie on the back fire escape. He shoved the brown-paper package into my hands and fled, anxious not to be recognized.

"It'll fit," he called over his shoulder, "even with them va-vooms of yours, it'll fit!"

I laughed and ran inside. It fit all right. Right down to the silver cuffs, it fit.

When I stepped to the edge of the stage and signaled

Ralph to cut on the smoke machine, he looked up and for a moment was frozen in admiration.

"Where in the hell . . ." he started.

"You don't even want to know," I answered. Then I adjusted my hat, gave my belt a little twitch, and wandered out onstage as the opening strains of Fiona Apple's "Criminal" started pumping up the audience. Officer Sierra was reporting for duty, fully decked from the hat to the black polyester shirt to the gear belt. The only things nonregulation: the micro-miniskirt, the five-inch stilettos, and of course my black lace G-string.

The crowd went wild. Especially when I pulled my fake pistol and blew them all a kiss over the end of the barrel. Oh, yes, I was in complete control.

"You're all under house arrest," I cooed, whipping out my handcuffs. "Any troublemakers in the house?"

Bruno barely beat the crowd down to the edge of the runway, positioning himself between me and them.

"I like you!" I said, to an innocent-looking young businessman. "Show me your wrists, lover boy!"

He didn't think, he just offered his wrists, his hands clutching dollar bills, and let me cuff him to the pole at the end of runway. "What're you gonna do to me?" he squeaked.

As little as possible, I thought, but to his face I just smiled. "Relax, sweetie," I said, running my hands down the length of his body. "I'm gonna frisk you, and then Officer Sierra is gonna turn you loose. Ain't nobody gonna hurt you." The crowd at the foot of the stage laughed, and my victim turned bright red.

"Hurt me, baby!" a man's voice cried. "Oh, hurt me bad!"

I uncuffed my prisoner, stepped back, and pulled the baton out of my gear belt. The music rose. I caressed the baton, stuck it slowly back into my belt, and ripped my skirt off with one quick move. There was a collective sigh from the audience.

I pulled my hat off, and my hair tumbled down around my shoulders. Slowly, very slowly, I started to undo the buttons of my uniform, all the while leaning my back against the pole and sliding up and down. I licked my lips and looked hungry. Even Bruno was watching.

"You've been bad, bad boys," I said, and lost my bra.

The men were going wild, and I was collecting a G-string full of bills. If things kept up like this, my costume would earn its price many times over. I squatted down and swiveled my thighs out toward the runway so my admirers could stuff in whatever money they had left, and then, as I straightened, I saw him.

My body feels John Nailor's presence and there ain't squat I can do about it. When our eyes locked across the room, I felt my temperature rise by a good two degrees. He was watching me the same way he always did, like a hungry animal. But this time, he was an angry, hungry animal. I guess he takes police work seriously. Maybe he didn't take to my salute to his boys in black. Whatever. I tipped my hat and winked. The boy needed to learn how to take a joke, develop a sense of humor.

I stood up and walked slowly down the runway, ever closer to my fans and John Nailor. As I walked, I began unbuckling my gear belt, taking my time, and lingering just a little too long on the buckle. The belt broke free and I tossed it to Bruno, who grinned like he'd captured a prize. Then I slipped my thumbs under the thin straps of my G-string, looked out at the boys, and made like I was going to yank it off.

They were screaming and throwing money. I smiled this little impish grin like "Hey, ain't this fun? Now I'm gonna do something special for you and only you." Each man was just sure I was looking at him. At that exact moment, Ralph put on the smoke machine full blast, and I disappeared back up the runway in a puff of smoke.

"Damn, Sierra!" Ralph said as he helped me shrug into

my purple silk kimono. "Damn!" I peeked back around the curtain. The smoke had cleared and, true to form, John Nailor had disappeared.

"Damn!" I said.

Marla chose this moment to make her appearance, strutting up like an alley cat with hemorrhoids.

"I see you warmed them up for me, honey," she said, preening in her silver B-52 bomber outfit.

I scowled over at her. She was about to have Ralph hook her up to an elaborate set of guy wires so she could fly out over the crowd and pretend she was a plane. I failed to see the appeal. She called it her salute to our flying men in uniform on account of how half our trade some nights is men from Tyndall Air Force Base. But I don't see why she bothers, since them boys don't tip worth your time and effort.

"Marla, learn to walk in them shoes and you might have half a shot at an act," I said.

She sniffed and walked on by, trying to balance on seven-inch platform stilettos while counterbalancing her silver wings. Some act!

I took another look back out into the house as Marla flew out over the runway. No sign of Nailor. Well, that wasn't a surprise. He'd turn up again, and from the way his jaw was twitching, I figured it would be sooner rather than later. Wonder why he'd come to the club? Was he trying to reach me? Did he need to tell me something? I flashed on the image of him in my trailer, in the darkness of my kitchen, his arms on either side of me, pinning me to the wall, his lips connecting with mine.

"Whew! Don't go there, girl," I whispered. "You don't wanna be the victim of a spontaneous combustion!"

But I couldn't get him off my mind. I found myself looking for him for the rest of the night every time I walked out onto the runway. By the time I was ready to leave work, I was practically sweating. Why in the world did that man have such an effect on me?

Vincent Gambuzzo stopped me as I was leaving. I could tell he'd been just waiting to get me alone. He could've come and found me any time during the night, but instead he positioned himself by the back door, knowing I'd be close to the last one to leave. I always am, on account of how I take time to put my costumes away neatly and prepare for the next night. I see that as the mark of a professional. Take care of your stuff and it'll take care of you. My new costume was a case in point.

"Sierra," Vincent said, suddenly looming up on me in the darkened hallway, "what was that cop doing back in my club?" Vincent hated having the heat in the house. He figured it cut into his business. He particularly hated John Nailor, because Nailor saw right through Vincent, down to his small-time attitude and wanna-be posturing.

"Vincent," I said, "looked to me like the man was a paying customer. He had a drink in his hand, didn't he?"

"A Coke, Sierra," he groused. "It was a lousy Coke!"

"So? What do you care? You charge the same for a soda as a beer!"

Vincent wasn't satisfied, I could see it, but he let it go and leaned in closer. The man had a serious case of garlic breath.

"What're you doing about our situation?" he said softly.

"What situation?" I was playing dumb and stalling while I manufactured something.

"You know. Ruby."

"Ah, *Ruby*," I said, acting like it had slipped my mind, just to make Vincent a little nuts. "Didn't I tell you I had company?" I said. "Who do you think it is?"

Vincent raised an eyebrow and nodded appreciatively.

"They getting anywhere?"

"Let me put it to you like this," I said, leaning back from his face and making a show of not wanting to be overheard.

"The big one's on-line with his network, communicating. And the short guy's going around cranking up the heat. Everything that was in the frying pan is in the fire now!" Vincent didn't need to know I was talking about Al and Ma.

He smiled. "That's why you call in an out-of-towner for things like this," he said. "We needed the large talent. Convey my gratitude to your uncle Moose."

"All's I can say at this point, Vincent, is that things are really cooking around my house."

"That's all I wanted to hear," he said.

I walked past him, out into the night, shaking my head. Vincent was never gonna get it. The lights could be on forever, but nobody was home at his house.

I stepped down off the back steps and started toward my car. Just as I thought, a shape sat in the passenger seat, waiting. I smiled. Nailor could no more stay away from me than I could from him.

I forced myself to saunter slowly toward my vehicles, as if I weren't in the least bit interested. Nailor was slouched down, wearing a cowboy hat, probably thinking it was an adequate disguise in case Detective Wheeling was watching. I shook my head. The guy was pitiful.

I flung open the driver's side door, tossed my bag in the backseat, and sank down behind the wheel.

"You know, that's a stupid disguise," I said, but my voice trailed off as soon as I realized the man in my front seat wasn't John Nailor.

"I know, ma'am," Roy Dell Parks said, "but it was the best I could do given that the law is on my tail and I'm wanted for murder."

Twenty-three

Roy Dell looked worse than usual. Stubble climbed up over top of his beard, running up his cheeks and giving his face a dirty, unkempt look. His clothes were filthy. His hair was about the same, standing straight on end, wiry and a grayish yellow. His breath smelled of liquor and his eyes were bloodshot. But that wasn't what worried me about Roy Dell. It was the gun in his shaking left hand that had me concerned.

"What's the gun for, Roy Dell?"

"Insurance, sugar," Roy Dell answered. He didn't look any too happy. In fact, he looked about half in the bag and totally crazy. "Start your engine," he said. "I think better when I'm moving." He hefted the gun up a few inches for emphasis, his finger sliding around the trigger.

"Roy Dell, put that gun down!" I was trembling. How could Raydean's nephew be a killer?

"I give the orders now," he said, his voice rising above my Camaro's engine, "and if I want to stick the barrel of this gun down yer purty little throat, I'll do it!"

"You the man," I answered, and peeled off out of the parking lot onto Thomas Drive. There was a clinking noise as we jumped the curb. Roy Dell was carrying more than a gun. A fifth of Jim Beam rolled across the floor on the passenger side.

Roy Dell was drunk, and that made him a loose cannon. I didn't know what he'd do.

"Head for the bridge," he commanded. "I wanna go to the Oyster Bar."

"No, you don't," I said, before I could stop myself. "You're a wanted man. That'd be piss-poor planning on your part."

Roy Dell seemed to be thinking. "Just drive," he said, sighing. "I got the world on my mind! And don't try anything smart. I get to feeling mean when I drink. A girl like you don't need to make me angry."

I cut across the back edge of Panama City Beach, the cool night air blowing through the open windows. It was a lovely night for a drive, but I could've done better for company. Roy Dell's thoughts must've run along the same lines, because he wedged the gun under one thigh and reached for the bottle. There was only a few inches left, so I figured Roy Dell was well on his way to passing out drunk.

"You think you got problems," he said finally.

"Did I say I had problems?" I answered, swinging onto the Hathaway Bridge. I was eyeing a car in the distance behind us. A car that had somehow followed me no matter what turn I took to get to the bridge. A car that kept a careful distance, just like its driver had been taught in surveillance school. My stomach flipped over and my temperature started to rise. He was back there, all right.

"Sierra, you're driving in your car, held at gunpoint by a drunk wanted for murder. I'd say you were thinking you had problems." Roy Dell swiped at his eyes. He'd either caught a June bug slap in the face or he was beginning to cry. My money was on the latter.

"But I got it worse'n you," he said. "They think I killed that precious angel. Ripped her head half off with my own naked hands."

"Hey!" I cried. "That's enough!"

"Then my old lady gets caught screwing my best crew man! Damn, I wish that hadn't a happened." Roy Dell pulled on the bottle. "He was the best backup driver I ever had, and now I'm gonna have to kill him. And top it all off, she's got him lying about me. Saying I was places I wasn't. Sayin' I coulda killed that precious girl."

"Roy Dell, you are a slob and a drunk, but I do not buy that you are a homicidal maniac." For one thing, I thought, you are too stupid to be a homicidal maniac.

"Watch me," he growled. "I'll kill his ass! She weren't much to look at, but she's all I got. Hell, I know she don't love me like a good woman oughta." Roy Dell was crying. I snuck a look sideways, and there they were, huge fat tears cutting streaks down his grimy cheeks.

"Roy Dell, if you cared so much about your wife, how come you were chasing up after Ruby?"

"You wouldn't understand," he said slowly, his words slurred around the edges. "It's a man thing. Ain't you read none of that Mars and Venus shit?"

I snuck a peak in my rearview mirror. He was a half a block back, following carefully as I wound my way toward Bayou Drive, down along Saint Andrews Bay, in and among the most beautiful houses in Panama City. My body was suffused with moist heat, and my heart rate was approaching the danger zone.

"Roy Dell, why are you in my car?" I had business to transact with a certain cop and this low-life was delaying my future.

"My aunt Raydean said you'd help me. She said, 'Take it on the lam and find Sierra. She'll know what to do.'"

"And you took her advice?"

"Well, where in the hell else do I have to turn?" he yelled. "You think I like being in this position?"

"All right, all right! Calm down. She's right, I'll help you, but you need to help me, too. You can't go waving a gun at me and think I'm going to be falling all over myself to help you."

Roy Dell seemed to think on that for a minute. "All right," he said finally, "we'll do it your way."

I needed time to think and it was going to be hard to do that with a cop on my tail and crazy, drunk Roy Dell Parks in my car. "Why do the cops think you killed Ruby?" I asked suddenly.

"Beats me!" Roy Dell finished the bottle and heaved it out the window. Behind me, John Nailor swerved to avoid the shattering glass.

"Hey! That's littering!" I yelled into the wind. "I'd appreciate it if you'd dispose of your trash in the proper receptacles."

Roy Dell must've taken offense because he reached between his legs and pulled out the gun again. "I will not blow off my testicles!" he said.

"You're hopeless," I said. "Here's what we're gonna do. You're gonna stay hidden for the time being until I can figure out what's going on and get you hooked up with my attorney. I'm gonna slow down when we get close to the park, and I want you to jump out and start running. Call me tomorrow at noon and I'll tell you what to do next."

Roy Dell laughed. "That is the dumb-assedest plan I ever heard of!"

I looked over at him. "Look in your rearview mirror," I said. "You see them cute little headlights? That's my boyfriend, the cop." Roy Dell's face paled and he right away craned his neck to look.

"Jesus!"

"Jesus ain't gonna help him what doesn't help himself," I answered. "Now, you see why I gotta get rid of you in a fast but hopefully inconspicuous way? I'm trying to help you, Roy

Dell." I held my breath, hoping he'd go for it and not decide I was somehow an enemy.

"If you put me out, he'll be after me in a car and I'll be on foot!"

I took another curve and began to double back toward Eat at Joe's restaurant.

"Roy Dell, let me handle him. Please? Can you lose yourself if I drop you? 'Cause I'm gonna drop you right . . . now!" I swung into the tiny park, spun around and slowed to a crawl. Roy Dell, used to flinging his body out of race cars that were in the process of self-destructing, opened the door and half jumped, half fell out onto the hard ground, slamming the door shut behind him.

The Camaro had done a one-eighty and now sat directly in the path of John Nailor's unmarked sedan, our headlights lighting up the thirty feet that separated us.

Nailor jumped out of his car, his hand reaching behind his back. He moved quickly to my passenger side door and yanked it open, still staring out into the darkness of the park.

"You think you're just slicker than owl shit, don't you?" he yelled. His jaw was twitching and his face was red with anger.

"What're you talking about?"

Nailor leaned down and plucked Roy Dell's gun off the seat. "You care to explain this?" he said. "You got a license to carry?"

"Hey, that isn't concealed. And besides, it isn't mine!"

"Damn straight, it ain't yours!" He was livid. I don't think I'd ever seen him that angry and I knew why. He didn't have control of the situation and I did. Pure and simple. It was a man thing, I guessed.

He slid into the passenger seat, almost levitating with rage. "You know you were just aiding and abetting a probable felon? You know you're now an accessory after the fact?"

"Before, after, what's the difference? The man hid in my car and held me at gunpoint, what choice did I have? Besides, the poor fella needed help. Who could he turn to?"

"You?" Nailor laughed bitterly. "That's desperate, all right."

"Well, go get him if you're so freakin' fired up! He couldn't have gone too far. He's on foot and unarmed and drunk. We're around the corner from the jail. Go get him, big man!"

Nailor glowered at me. I fully expected him to hop out and run, but instead he just sat there.

"What makes you so sure Roy Dell killed Ruby?" I asked.

"Because Frank said he couldn't find Roy Dell just before race time. Said he was missing for ten whole minutes. Frank says Roy Dell wasn't himself before that race, that he was acting strange."

I shook my head in disgust. "And you believed him? If you're looking for suspects, well, Frank's looking just as good to me. You know he was screwing Lulu? Maybe him and Lulu decided to off Ruby and make it look like Roy Dell did it."

Nailor was watching me like I had suddenly suggested he fly to Mars. "How would you know that?" he asked. "You know, you shouldn't be nosing around in a police investigation. It's dangerous, Sierra. This is a murder investigation."

"Maybe you need to hang out with them tiny, petite, brunette types. The kind that aren't in danger of ever taking care of another human being or putting themselves at risk. Maybe what you're looking for is a trophy."

I was pushing him way further than I knew I should, but I couldn't help myself. I'd had enough.

"You don't know a thing about her," he said.

I took that as an admission and zoomed in for the kill.

"What'da I gotta know about a Junior League bimbo?" I said. "Girls like that are a dime a dozen."

"Right," he said.

"Right? You tellin' me I'm right?" I couldn't believe my ears. John Nailor was copping a plea.

"Have you wondered why I'm spending so much time with her?" he asked.

" 'Cause you're tired of tall blond women with brains and looks?"

He threw his head back and laughed, a deep, strong, genuine laugh that warmed me all the way through.

"Yeah," he said, "something like that. I'm tired of beauty and brains and heat." He said that last word while his eyes were practically looking straight through me. Suddenly it was way too warm for comfort in my little car.

"So? What're you doing chasing her?"

Nailor sighed. "It's business, Sierra. I'm into something I can't talk about. She's part of it and that's all I can say, and you can't repeat that, you hear?" He looked serious and for the first time I noticed something else. Pain?

"What's so wrong you gotta lie to your partner?" I asked softly. That was it. That was the source of the pain. Nailor's eyes darkened and he looked down at his lap. He couldn't face me with whatever it was.

"I'm over a barrel here, Sierra," he said. "I had to do what I was told . . ." He broke off and looked out the window.

"Who's giving the orders?"

He didn't answer for a few moments. Then, "It's the wrong way to go about doing the right thing, Sierra. But I don't get a say in how this goes down. I'm the puppet and if she says 'dance,' then I gotta dance."

"Who's 'she'?" I asked.

There was almost a chill in the night air. The sky was filled with stars. And this wasn't the man I knew. John Nailor never danced to anyone else's tune.

He shook his head and wouldn't answer me.

"It's Carla, isn't it? This is a DEA investigation."

His eyes flickered, an admission. "What are you talking about? Now you're making stuff up," he said, but his voice had changed, suddenly anxious.

"Carla, your ex. I saw her at the racetrack. You can't tell me she's not back in town. I bet she's got you by the short hairs, big guy. You're working for her, aren't you?"

I knew he wanted to talk, but instead he stayed silent. He wouldn't look at me.

"This ain't you," I said. "You're in trouble, aren't you?"

"I wish it was that easy," he said.

I reached over and touched the side of his face, letting my hand slide around the back of his neck as he slowly looked up at me, and then moved closer. I turned my face to his and felt his lips melt into mine. He reached over and pulled me to him, hungry and insistent. It was as if we'd been starving. There was an urgency to our movements. His lips moved across my face, down the side of my neck. His hands slipped under my shirt while mine fumbled with the buttons of his starched, oxford-cloth shirt. I wanted him. I had never wanted anyone or anything the way I wanted him at this moment.

"Wait," he said suddenly, looking around as if coming up for air.

I moaned. "Not now! What?"

"Sierra, we're in the middle of a public park with our headlights on!"

I didn't care. I would've taken him right there, if only he hadn't forced me back to reality. He turned to me, running his thumb along my bottom lip, just like he had the other night. I moaned again involuntarily.

"Come on," he whispered. "I'll follow you back to your place." His eyes were dark wells of energy. Oh God, I couldn't wait.

"Your place," I said. "We have to go to your place!"

"We can't," he said. "Come on, let's go to your place. I'll be careful. No one'll see us."

"John, I can't. I have company."

The temperature dropped a good ten degrees instantly. "What do you mean, company?"

I laughed. "My brother Al and Ma are staying with me for a little while."

"Damn!"

I pulled my shirt back into place and straightened up. The mood was quickly evaporating.

"What's wrong with your place?"

"It's too dangerous," he said suddenly. "In fact, I don't know what I was thinking. This is too dangerous." He'd buttoned his shirt and now he picked up Roy Dell's gun. "Do you know how to use this?"

"No, I don't believe in guns."

He sighed and shook his head, then shoved Roy Dell's gun into his waistband.

"But I do know how to use this!" I said, whipping out my Spyderco and snapping it open so the shiny steel blade hovered an inch from his navel.

"Put that thing away before you hurt somebody, most likely yourself!"

"Hey! I'm a frustrated woman, all right?" I flicked the knife shut and started to shove it back in my pocket.

He leaned over just then, slipped his hand behind my head and kissed me. Long and slow and deep. I sighed and melted against him, drinking in the smell and taste of his body against mine, half thinking maybe I could slip him past Ma and Al. But it was over before I could say or do anything. He was gone, walking away to his car, not looking back once.

I sat there and watched him back out of the park and onto

the road. I was gripping the steering wheel with both hands, my heart pounding. Every spot where he'd touched me still burned. I wanted that man, and one day soon I was gonna have him.

Twenty-four

All hell was breaking loose at my house. It was four A.M. when I pulled up onto the parking pad, and every light in the trailer was on. Every light in Raydean's house was on, too, but that was nothing new when you consider that she spent a lot of her time patrolling for alien invaders. From the looks of her lawn and front door, she'd finally proven her point: alien life did indeed exist. The place was seriously trashed.

It wasn't until I'd stepped out of the car and was approaching the back stoop that I noticed the damage to the right rear corner of the trailer. An entire Godzilla-sized bite had been taken out of the siding, leaving a gaping hole that yawned into my laundry room. Either the aliens lived off vinyl siding or someone had made a king-sized crater into my house.

Al met me at the door, an ugly black gun poking out of his beefy hand and a look I'd never seen before on his face.

"We had company," he said.

"They do that?" I said, pointing to the hole in the side of the house.

"Nah, Raydean did that one. They did that," he said, pointing to the tire-mark trench spun out into Raydean's yard, the broken birdbath, and her blown-apart front door barely hanging on its hinges.

"Frank?" I asked.

"No, Sierra, the flippin' Flemish!"

I pushed past him into the kitchen. "There ain't no call for sarcasm," I said.

"Isn't there? Isn't there?" Al was losing his cool. "Why don't you take a look on your sofa and tell me if I have a right to be pissed off!"

I turned and walked around the room divider into the dimly lit living room. Ma was lying on the sofa, a clean white patch of gauze on her forehead, stained red with a quarter-sized spot of blood. Her skin was every bit as white as the bandage and she appeared to be unconscious.

"Ma!" I screamed, and flew to her side, dropping down beside her. I saw Fluffy then, cuddled up by Ma's shoulder, guarding her.

Ma's eyes flew open and she seemed to have trouble focusing.

"Sierra? Is that you?"

"Oh, my God, Ma!" I started to cry. "Oh, Ma, I'm sorry! It's all my fault."

I could hear Al behind me, muttering something like "Damn right, it's your fault!" But I didn't need him to tell me I'd pulled my own mother into danger.

"Sierra?" Ma called weakly.

"Yeah, Ma," I said, grabbing her hand, "I'm right here!"

"What did you say?" she whispered.

"I said I'm right here." I moved closer by her side. Al stepped up to the edge of the futon and covered Ma with a blanket that had fallen onto the floor.

"No," said Ma, "I mean what did you say before that?"

"I said I'm sorry, Ma."

"Really?" she whispered.

"Really. I really, really am. I'd do anything for this not to have happened, Ma. I'm so sorry!"

"Good!" she cried out suddenly, her voice startling my brother and me. "Then tell your brother to keep that damn blanket off me and get me a glass of Pa's Chianti! Jeez! The way he's been acting, you'd a thought I was dead and buried, not hit by a tiny piece of debris!"

With this, Ma sat up, glared at my brother, and gave me a little shove. "He insisted, Mr. Know-It-All, that I lie still, just the way they trained him in first-aid school for cops. Well, I told him and told him, bring me a glass of wine to thicken up my blood and I'll be fine. But no! Years I got of taking care of the sick and injured. Suddenly, Mr. Philadelphia Cop knows better than all of his ancestors before him!"

"Ma!" Al looked shocked and hurt. "I was looking after you!"

Ma gave him a look like she wasn't quite sure, and then smiled. "I know. You was doing all you knew to do, but I'm telling you, and Sierra will back me on this, that your father's Chianti will fix anything that ails you."

"She's right, Al," I said, rising to my feet. "That's what we could all use here, a little vino."

"Deal me in, lamb chop," said a rusty voice from one of the bedrooms. I looked up at Al.

"Hey," he said, throwing up his hands, "what else was I gonna do? She had no door. I wanted her to be safe. She's gotta stay here."

"I'm not faulting you, Al. You done good."

"You shoulda seen him, Sierra," Ma cried, suddenly proud. "When that hooligan drove up in his car and shot at the door, Alfonse came running out, his gun held in the air, just like them cops on TV."

Al was bringing over the jug of Chianti and four wine-glasses. "I coulda gotten a clear shot off, too, if youse guys hadn't come running out into the street like Rambo! And you hurt like that, Ma. You shoulda been layin' still."

At this moment, Raydean wandered out into the living room, her hair set in pink plastic curlers, covered by her rain bonnet, and her feet covered in huge bunny slippers, pink slippers with little smiley bunny faces. Her nightgown was a pink quilted throwback to a Sixties rummage sale, and her face was just as pale as Ma's.

"Is it snack time?" she said, her face breaking into a wide grin. "I always like snack time the best. Next to art therapy, of course." She looked over at Al, as if seeing him for the first time. "Hey, you're that new guy, aren't you?"

Al was too stunned to correct her.

"Don't you worry none about what's in that bottle," she said, pointing to the wine. "Them nurses are all the time dosing us with antipsychotics. It'll slow you up a little, but sooner or later you'll be your old self again. Trust me! I done more time in these HMO Nazi death camps than you'll ever know! Just do everything I do, and you'll be back out on the street in no time!"

Al set the glasses down gently and pulled the cork out of the Chianti bottle. Ma was watching Raydean, a confused look on her face.

"Come here, honey," I said, softly. I got up off the floor next to Ma and led Raydean over to the sofa. "Drink some of this."

Al gave me a sharp look. "I gotta draw the line there, Sierra. She shouldn't be imbibing. Not in her condition."

Raydean cackled. "That's kind of you, sonny, but my child-bearing days are over. I ain't in a delicate condition, just fat!"

I pressed the glass into Raydean's hands and realized she was icy cold and trembling.

"Bottoms up!" she cried, and started to swig Pa's Chianti.

"Raydean, sip it, hon. That's potent stuff you got there."

Raydean looked at the three of us, then over our shoulders, as if making sure no one could overhear. "You know," she giggled, "if this is such powerful stuff, maybe we might oughta slip some to that prissy social worker what runs group!" She leaned in close to Ma and patted her knee. "Girl needs to get out more! Always sitting upright, with them little professional pumps and her long skirt, her hair pulled up so tight it makes her eyes bulge out. No wonder the poor thing can't find her a man!"

Ma couldn't help herself, or else Pa's wine was taking effect. She tittered like a schoolgirl.

"You know I'm right, don'tcha, lamb chop? I say we grab the young one over there and make a run for it. But wait till after lunch—with what they're charging, I figure we ought to get our money's worth!"

Raydean's glass was empty and her eyes seemed to droop. As I watched, she swayed slightly.

"Come on, honey," I said, standing up and reaching down for her hand. "Let's go lie down for a little bit."

Raydean stood up slowly and looked over at Al. "Don't frown so, sonny! Nap time's part of the program. They call it relaxation therapy, but we all know better!"

I led her off down the hallway to the room Al had been using. The twin bed was turned down and covered with fresh sheets. Al's doing, no doubt.

"Here we go," I whispered, gently pushing Raydean back against the mattress. "I'll get you all nice and comfy."

Raydean smiled a sleepy smile, her eyes already closing.

"Sierra?" she said.

"What, hon?"

Raydean snuggled deep into the covers, then reached out one hand to me. "Don't leave just yet." Her voice quavered and cracked with unshed tears.

"Sure, honey, sure. I won't leave you." I sat down beside her and gently stroked the back of her hand.

Raydean's face relaxed. "You're gonna sing to me, aren't you, Mama?" she said.

I sat there, staring at the wrinkled, childlike face. She'd never been this bad before, and it frightened me.

" 'Jesus loves me, this I know . . .' " The words came unbidden to my lips, spilling out, the old song that Ma would sing when we were little babies. " 'For the Bible tells me so.' " I turned off the bedside lamp and sat in the darkness, singing, tears slowly spilling down my cheeks. What in the world had I gotten us all into?

Twenty-five

*B*acon was frying, and buried underneath its aroma was the smell of strong Italian Roast, waiting for me to wander into the kitchen and claim my cup. When we were little kids, that smell would wake me up every morning, along with the AM radio, KYW "All News, All the Time." I'd wander down the steps and there would be Pa in his sleeveless undershirt, sitting at the kitchen table, drinking coffee out of his thick white mug.

Ma always hummed while she cooked. She never woke up in a bad mood and she always started our day off on the right foot. "You gotta eat protein," she'd say, slapping a full plate of eggs and bacon down before us. "You need brain power. Them Sisters ain't gonna like it if you show up without your thinking caps!"

I wandered out into my kitchen, the clock screaming that it was no longer breakfast time, but instead, lunchtime. There she was, at the stove, fixing a frying pan full of bacon and eggs.

"Hey, sleepyhead," she cried. "Sit down. You need some brain power!"

I just stood there staring at her. Ma was no spring chicken. She was what? Fifty-six? And here she was, up with less than seven hours of sleep, cooking my breakfast.

"Sit, sit!" Ma carried a steamy mug to the table and

plopped it down. "Coffee! You look like you can use it."

"Ma, what are you doing? You oughta be in bed." I looked at the spot on her forehead where she'd been injured and saw an ugly purple bruise radiating out from behind the Band-Aid that covered her cut.

"Nonsense!" she said. "I got a little cut where a piece of the door hit me last night. It's no big deal."

I cinched the belt on my chenille bathrobe and stepped over to the table. The coffee was calling me.

"You need your rest," I said, sounding, I knew, like an ungrateful kid.

Ma snorted. "Listen. I raised five kids, and your Pa was a fireman. You think I know from rest? Sierra, last night was no different from any other night at home. Have you forgotten that?"

I must've just looked at her 'cause she kept on going. "No, maybe you wouldn't know. Sierra, your Pa's a fireman, so're your older brothers. When he gets in—and most often with him working second now, it's at all hours of the night—he needs me."

Ma stirred the eggs and half turned so she could face me and the stove at the same time. "He don't deliver eggs, Sierra. He saves lives. He's got a dangerous job. When he comes in, I'm there." Ma pulled strips of bacon from the pan. "And now with your brothers working, too, I'm there for them. No need in them going home hungry and waking up their wives. They got little children. There's no call to go waking up everybody. I'm there." Ma looked proud. "Rest ain't no big deal," she said.

I looked out the kitchen window, across the street to Raydean's trailer. It looked even worse in the daylight.

"Where's Al?"

"I sent him off to bed," Ma said, presenting me with a full breakfast, complete with her homemade cinnamon rolls. She was in her element. "You know that boy sat up all night?"

Ma was bustling around the kitchen, wired on caffeine and nerves. I'd seen this before. She always bustled when she was nervous.

"Aren't you eating?" I asked.

"No, no, I'm not hungry. I'll get something later." That confirmed it. Ma never ate when she was worrying.

"I'm gonna take care of some things today," I said. "It ain't gonna be like this much longer. Frank'll leave us alone." I had a sudden thought. "Ma, did Al call the police last night?"

"Of course!" Ma looked surprised that I would even ask. "That nice man, Detective Wheeling, came out, and he and your brother talked for a long time."

Well, maybe that was a good thing. Maybe it would keep Frank away from us for a while, at least long enough for me to figure out what was going on and how it all tied in with Ruby's death. Somehow, I just knew it all worked together. If I could find out more about the racetrack or Ruby's past, I could probably find her killer. I looked up at the kitchen clock again. Twenty after twelve and I was due at work by seven. It was time to get moving.

"Ma," I said, "when Raydean wakes up, I need you and Al to take her to the mental health center. She's due for a shot, and once she gets that, she'll be back to her old self."

Ma clearly didn't believe me. "They won't lock her up, will they, Sierra?"

"No, Raydean just gets like this sometimes." That wasn't exactly true. I'd never seen her quite this bad. I was scribbling the directions to the mental health center on a piece of paper when the phone rang.

"Sierra," Roy Dell said, "it's me! What's the plan?"

I had no plan, but Roy Dell didn't need to know that.

"Where are you?" I said.

"I'm across the street," he said, "in Raydean's garage. I'm using my mobile phone."

I looked back out the window to the garage. The double doors were slightly ajar, and as I watched a thick hand emerged and waved briefly.

"I see you!" he said. "You see me?"

"Roy Dell, quit fooling around. You wanna advertise your presence? Don't you think there's a reward out for finding you? I mean, you are wanted for murder." There was a gasp from the stove area, as Ma whirled around to give me her full eavesdropping attention.

"I'm gonna go take a shower and then I'll be over to get you," I said. "When I pull up in the drive you come out and hop in the back seat. And make it quick, too!"

"You ain't gonna dump me out of a speeding car again, are you?"

"Roy Dell!" I hung up. I had no idea what I was gonna do with him, but dumping him out onto the highway didn't seem like a bad idea at this particular moment.

"Sierra!" Ma said, all poised to lecture me on perpetrating a felony.

"Ma, it's neither here nor there, 'cause whatever you're about to say, I already know. Just pretend we've had the conversation and I am duly warned."

I got up and started moving.

Ma was sputtering as I left, too worked up to say what she was thinking. A good thing for both of us.

To his credit, Roy Dell could move when he had to. He streaked from Raydean's garage into the back of my car almost before I could switch from drive to reverse.

"Duck down and stay down!"

Roy Dell did exactly as I asked. I shot out of the driveway

and laid tracks down the tiny street, heading for the highway and Wewahitchka.

"Is he the best in the business, Sierra?" he asked.

"Is who the best in the business?"

"The lawyer you're taking me to see." Roy Dell's voice was muffled, but I could still pick up the anxiety. I'd forgotten all about telling Roy Dell I'd take him to see Ernie.

"The very best," I said. Once again, the image of Ernie Schwartz naked and playing the ukulele on my kitchen counter came unbidden to my mind and I laughed.

"Then why are you laughing?"

"Aw, I ain't laughing on account of that. And besides, we aren't going to Ernie's place now."

"And why not?" Roy Dell demanded.

"On account of I need to ask you some questions and make a stop or two first. You've got some information I want and I'm your only hope of help, so I figure you'll be glad to answer a few questions, right?"

There was a pause, then a muffled "Right," followed by a heavy sigh.

"You can sit up now," I said after a few minutes. We'd left the city limits and had moved rapidly into the country. No one was around to see us, and even if there had been, it wouldn't have meant anything to them.

Roy Dell raised his shaggy head level with my front seat and peered out at the pine trees and telephone poles that zipped by.

"Where're we headed?" he asked.

"Two places. First to Wannamaker Lewis's house, and second, to the speedway."

Roy Dell half leaned into the front seat. "The track! We cain't go to the track! They'll be all over that place looking for me!"

"Maybe," I said, "but it's a risk I'm prepared to take. I've gotta know more about what's going on there. Don't worry," I added, "I'll throw a blanket over you. There's a nice green one in the backseat."

Roy Dell turned around and reached for the blanket I'd saved after I'd been jumped in the parking lot. "Hey, this looks a lot like one of my blankets," he said. "Yeah, this is just like the one I keep in the back of my car."

My heart began to pound and my mouth went dry. "Of course, that isn't your blanket, is it?" I asked. I waited for the denial.

"Hey," he said slowly, "this *is* my blanket! Lookit right here!" He was back in my face, the blanket clutched in his fist. "See that burn mark? That little one?"

He showed me a hole that looked like a cigarette burn. "That's from the first time me and Lulu . . . Well, you know." He broke off and sank back into the seat, lost in his memory. "She liked to smoke afterward. You know . . ."

The image of a naked Lulu and Roy Dell rolling around on the blanket, one sweaty clump of too-white flesh, made me shudder.

"How'd you get my blanket, Sierra?"

"Where'd you lose it, Roy Dell?" Cat and mouse.

He was silent for a few minutes, thinking. "Well, it's always in the trunk of my Vega, out to the track. It's good luck. I checked on it before ever' race. I don't think it was lost."

This was pointless. Roy Dell didn't have the brain cells to lie about a blanket, let alone a murder.

"Roy Dell, we're coming up on Wewa. Where does Wannamaker Lewis live?"

"Huh?" Roy Dell sat up again and moved in between my two bucket seats. "I reckon he lives the same place he's always lived."

"That ain't exactly helpful, Roy Dell!"

"Oh, right." He scratched his beard and peered out the

windshield. "Up yonder," he called out. "See that little road running off to the side there? Take that. You'll see it down there on the right." Roy Dell suddenly vanished behind the seat.

"Where are you going? There isn't a soul around!" The road wound through what must've once been the center of town and was now a collection of almost disintegrated Victorians.

"You never know," Roy Dell said. "Folks around these parts worship me! I am, after all, the King of Dirt."

"Sheeze!" I sighed and slowed the Camaro to a crawl. I'd found Wannamaker Lewis's house all by myself. It was dead ahead, painted up worse than his in-town shack. Every inch of the house was covered with brightly painted figures and crooked black letters. The mailbox was painted red with the word BEWARE crudely lettered on its side. Scrubby pines and tall, aging magnolias shadowed the backyard, hiding the house from its neighbors. Big azaleas and boxwoods crowded the tiny front yard, nearly hiding a short wrought-iron fence.

I pulled up in the driveway and cut the engine.

"Would you look at this," I breathed.

"Ain't it some shit!" Roy Dell said from the safety of my backseat. "Neighbors just flat out hate it, but they cain't do a thing about it. Ol' Wannamaker's the richest man in town and ever' one of them knows it. Cain't nobody risk getting on his bad side."

"Why not?" I was looking out the windshield. The house looked vacant and deserted.

"On account of he's nuts, and they're all working him to get his money. He ain't got no family." Not that you know about, I thought. "They're all just hoping he don't leave it all to his cat or nothing. So they kiss up to him and act all nice, all the while hoping he'll die." Roy Dell laughed to himself. "You ask me, that coot'll live to be a hundred. His kind always do! And another thing, he's on to 'em all. That old boy may be crazy, but he's sharper than the preacher's tongue on Sunday!"

I was losing interest in Roy Dell. "I'll be back in a minute," I said, and left him to his musings.

I stood by the side of the car for a second, just trying to figure the best way into Wannamaker Lewis's house. Huge magnolia trees flanked the gate in the front yard and the azaleas crawled around and under their spreading tree limbs. It was going to be like walking through a wall of green fire, trusting you'd come out alive on the other side.

"Hell, the paperboy must do it every day," I muttered, assuming, of course, that Lewis took the paper.

I inhaled deeply and pushed off toward the house, darting through the open gate and plowing through the bushes and branches that grabbed at my clothes and hair. It was a battle, and I looked like I'd been in a catfight by the time I arrived on the porch, but at least I'd made it.

The front porch was littered with parts and pieces of Wannamaker Lewis's artwork. Little cans of paint sat around, some empty, some closed back up and lining the porch rail. But it was the front door that frightened me. Glaring out, painted to take up the entire doorway, was an avenging angel. Us Catholics didn't have nothing on Wannamaker's vision of God's wrath.

She was a beauty, all right, snakes for hair, a sword in one hand and a column of fire balanced in the other. Her eyebrows could've stood serious plucking, and her nose was long and hooked, but her lips were bloodred and smiled a terrible smile. You could almost hear her saying "Vengeance is mine!" The tip of her sword was painted over the doorbell. RING HERE IF YOUR CONSCIENCE IS CLEAR, said the crudely lettered sign.

I reached one tentative finger out and touched the button, half expecting it to be booby-trapped. It rang just like any other doorbell, screaming through the interior of the huge darkened house.

I peered into one of the windows, but they were too dirty to see through.

"With all the money you made on art, you'd think you'd take care of the place," I said aloud. "So I guess you're not home, huh? It must not be nap time." I turned around to leave. "I'll just mosey down to your studio and see if I can catch you there." It helped to speak aloud. Made the house a little less creepy.

"Too late!" a voice said suddenly. "Too late!"

I whirled around and stared back at the front door. The angel's eyes blinked, red and rheumy with age. He was watching me.

"Mr. Lewis," I said, "my name is Sierra. We met at Ruby's mother's house after the funeral. I'd like to talk to you."

"For Wannamaker so loved the world that he lost his only daughter," the old man said, his voice coming softly through the door.

"I'm sorry, Mr. Lewis. She was my friend."

I stood there, staring at the angel's eyes. They blinked once again, then disappeared only to be replaced by their painted version. Pretty awesome peephole. There was the sound of metal on metal as the lock was turned and the door slowly swung open to reveal the little wizened farmer from the funeral, tears rolling down his cheeks.

"You can come in," he said. "I don't bite." He stood back and beckoned me inside. "See," he said, as I stepped over the threshold, "the eternal fires do not burn here!" He turned and led me into a parlor.

The room was filled with antiques—settees with rump sprung seat cushions, tables, and lamps—all dripping with dust and cobwebs. I gingerly sat on the very edge of the chair he indicated, barely waiting for him to settle before I began talking. This was not a place where I wanted to tarry.

"Mr. Lewis, I want to find out who killed your daughter."

"Satan," he answered calmly.

Two could play this tango, I thought. "Satan's agent," I corrected. I silently thanked the Sisters for my theological background. "I want to meet this agent of Satan," I said. "I want to see him returned to hell."

Wannamaker's eyes caught fire, and he leaned toward me. "I have many enemies," he said. "Rich prophets make enemies."

I was starting to think I should've brought Raydean along as an interpreter. "So you're saying someone knew Ruby was your daughter and killed her to get to you?"

"In my house are many mansions," he said softly.

"Mr. Lewis, did you ever talk to Ruby? Tell her you were her father?"

Tears flowed down the little man's cheeks. "No," he whispered, "but I would have one day. I wanted to take care of her, but I didn't want to hurt her." He was openly crying now. "Iris gave her away!" he moaned. "I didn't know. I never knew her, only him."

He jumped up, the tiny chair he'd perched on fell over onto its side. "I should've gone first!" he yelled. "My Son of Satan wanted to take me first! But no, He had to take her! Had to be sure I was all His! My kingdom shall be yours, I said, but He wants it all, everything. I must pay! I must be broken! I must die!"

Wannamaker's eyes were wild and, as he jumped and screamed, he moved closer. He reached out suddenly and grabbed me by the shoulders, shaking me in a grip that was powerfully strong. His hands were like iron.

"Let go!"

He didn't. Instead, he was in my face, spewing spittle and screaming. "Vengeance is not for Him!"

"Wannamaker, let me go!" I yelled, but he couldn't hear me.

"Come on," he said, suddenly releasing me, abruptly calm. "I'll show you where it is."

"Where what is?" I stood, towering over the little maniac. My instincts said leave. The man was obviously a fruitcake, and the dusty, smoky smell of his house was starting to make me sneeze.

"The will," he said simply. "In my house are many mansions, all for her and He knows it, too. All for the angel." He turned and darted out of the room leaving me to follow as best I could.

I heard him clattering up the stairs and I followed the sound, out into the broad front hallway, up the sweeping staircase, my hand reaching out now and then for the dusty banister.

"Mr. Lewis?" I called.

"Up here," he answered, his voice muffled and far away. "Come on . . . it's . . . in a safe," I thought he said, but I couldn't be certain.

I was becoming aware of something. The dusty, smoky smell was stronger. I stopped for a second to get my bearings and to listen. As I did, I looked toward the end of the second-floor hallway. Smoke had started to billow out of a doorway. The house was on fire!

"Fire!" I screamed. "Mr. Lewis, where are you? The house is on fire!" I heard a scrabbling sound, like the footsteps of someone running. I started opening doors, looking into dust-covered rooms, screaming for Wannamaker Lewis, but he didn't answer me.

I reached the doorway to the attic and pulled it open. Behind me, thick, gray smoke rolled down the hallway. I made my way up the steep stairs, calling for Wannamaker and getting no answer.

The attic was empty except for pieces of furniture and dusty boxes. I went on anyway, looking behind them, hoping to find Lewis hiding. What I found instead were drugs. Hidden behind a stack of boxes, piled high in a four-by-four square, was brick after brick of what appeared to be cocaine, compressed and tightly wrapped with plastic.

There was no time to look further. In the distance I heard the crackling of fire. I had to get out of the house. I had to find Lewis and get us both out. I ran down the stairs to the second floor. The sound of a gunshot stopped me cold. Was someone shooting? Or was it the sound of something exploding with the heat?

Someone screamed, maybe Wannamaker? The smoke was thick now, and I was choking. "Get down, Sierra. Remember, crawl along the floor!" My dad's voice spoke in my head. I dropped to my hands and knees, trying to recall where the staircase was, feeling my way along the hallway. Somewhere downstairs, I heard another explosion that sounded like a gunshot. How long before the whole place exploded?

I was shaking and choking and crawling backward down the steps. I reached the bottom. I was only a few feet from the front door, I remembered that, but could I reach it? I could hear the flames now. I stood up as I reached the bottom step, ready to run. The hallway was filled with smoke and I felt lightheaded. Where was I? Where was that door? I sank down slowly, feeling for the bottom step. Maybe if I just rested for a moment, I could remember. Maybe if I closed my eyes just for a second . . .

Twenty-six

It was nice where I was, because he held me. Sweet cool air filled my lungs and warm arms held me.

"Sierra," he whispered, "wake the hell up!"

What was wrong with him? Didn't he know Harrison Ford shouldn't speak like that to his beloved?

"Harrison!" I heard my voice whine. "That's not nice!"

"Open your eyes, Sierra!" Nailor's voice commanded. "This isn't Hollywood!"

I opened my eyes and found myself with John Nailor under the sheltering shade of a low-hanging magnolia tree. Outside, beyond our hiding spot, the sounds of men's voices and machines could be heard.

"What's going on?" I said, coughing and pushing myself up.

Nailor grabbed my arm and pulled me back against the tree trunk. "Don't get too close," he warned. "I don't want us to be seen. We're in Lewis's backyard. The firemen are putting out what's left of the fire. The place is crawling with police and firemen. I don't want anyone to see me."

I peered out again. From where I sat, it was hard to see. Pine trees and huge, ancient azaleas covered the backyard as they did the front.

"How'd I get here?" I asked, turning to look at Nailor for the first time. He was covered with black sooty streaks, but beneath that his skin was gray. The lines around his eyes were deep and etched with fatigue.

"Wait!" I called out. "Wannamaker's in there! We have to go back and get him." I started to pull away, but he held on to me.

"Sierra, Wannamaker Lewis is dead. Someone shot him. His body was three feet from the steps where I found you. Didn't you see him?"

I slumped back against Nailor. Dead? Shot? It was as if my mind simply could not accept his words.

"I was coming to watch the house," Nailor continued, "what I could see of it. When I got here, I saw your car parked a ways down the street and figured you must've been inside Lewis's house. When I realized it was on fire, I came looking for you." He said it simply, as if he'd said, "I saw you were out of eggs, so I stopped at the store." *I came looking for you.*

"Hey," I said, gazing back out at the flashes of color and motion surrounding Wannamaker Lewis's house, "you said my car was down the street? That's not where I left it. And what about Roy Dell?"

Nailor straightened a little and winced. "What about Roy Dell?"

"Are you hurt?"

"What about Roy Dell?" He ignored my question like I'd ignored his.

I was still staring outside and motioned Nailor to keep still. Three men, two firemen and a man in plainclothes, were walking deeper into the backyard, staring at the ground and then back toward us. As I watched, the plainclothesman stooped down and touched something on the ground.

"Looks like they're headed this way," I whispered. "They're following something." Nailor said nothing. I turned around to see if he'd heard me. He was gone. In the place where he'd leaned against the tree trunk, there was a wide splotch of blood.

I couldn't let them find the bloodstain, or they'd know I hadn't been alone. If John didn't want to be seen, then there was a reason. Maybe the gunshots I'd heard had been directed at him and not Lewis. I had to protect John. But I couldn't let him stay out there alone, without me.

I reached out and touched the blood, letting some run onto my finger. Then I rubbed my bloody finger around one nostril. "It's a good thing I went to Catholic school," I said softly, on the off chance that somewhere nearby Nailor was listening. " 'Cause stories like the one I'm about to tell ain't easy to come by." Then I pushed the branches aside and wandered up to the men.

"Where am I?" I cried softly. "What happened? Where's Mr. Lewis?"

I figured it to play out exactly as it did. These three guys, intent on figuring where the blood drips were leading to, thinking they were hot on the trail of an arsonist, come up on me, Sierra Freakin' Lavotini, the Queen of the Blond Amazons. A maiden in distress with a bloody nose. Good thing it wasn't the Panama City P.D. on the job. With them, my reputation precedes me, and I would've been out of luck.

To further complicate their lives, I swooned, requiring their immediate attention. They didn't need to know that I worked men over like this for a living. No, for the next thirty minutes, they were heroes. Plying me with oxygen and water, listening to my story of stopping at the house to buy a Jesus whirligig, then the fire breaking out and Mr. Lewis vanishing. It was masterful, but I had to silently promise to do an Act of Contrition as soon as possible. The Sisters would've been pleased. After all, it was for a good cause.

I gave them my name, but not the real one. And my address, also bogus. And implied maybe I'd like to hear all about being big strong firemen sometime. Then I wandered off down the street, making for my Camaro, hoping I wasn't too late to double back and find Nailor. There was too much blood under that tree for it to have been a surface wound. I was pretty sure he was hurt, and hurt bad.

Nailor was right about the car having been moved. It sat a half a block away, the keys still in the ignition. Maybe Roy Dell had moved it when the fire started, but where was he?

I cranked the car and pulled slowly out into the street. Behind me, the firetrucks blocked the road. As I looked in my rearview mirror, an ambulance pulled up and EMTs went running for the house. They'd found Wannamaker Lewis.

I crawled down the street, edging around the block, trying to figure out where Wannamaker's lot edged up onto his back neighbor's. Nailor couldn't have gotten far without help. I parked when I judged I was near enough to approach Wannamaker's house from the rear. A ramshackle Victorian cottage stood on a lot that mirrored Lewis's yard. At least I wouldn't need to contend with neighbors or dogs. Only snakes and rodents lived on this estate.

I got out of the car and stomped off through the tall grass and bushes, hoping I was warning all wildlife to get out of my way.

"John?" I called, pitching my voice low. No answer, then in the distance, a moan.

I ran in the direction of the sound, listening and alternately calling his name. I found him lying on his back, twenty feet from the tree where we'd sat hiding.

"Hey, it's me, Sierra. Open up them big brown eyes." I knelt by his side. He didn't answer me. "John?" I reached out to touch him, trying to support him into sitting upright, but instead finding his back soaked with blood.

"Oh God, oh God!" I moaned, rocking back on my heels.

I was fighting back the urge to cry and trying to figure out what to do. "All right! All right! We're gonna get you some help," I said, but I don't think he heard me. He didn't move. He didn't cry out when I slipped my arms under his shoulders and began dragging him slowly across the yard.

I don't know how I dragged him to the car. He was a dead weight, but I was suddenly powerful. It felt effortless. It seemed to take forever, but I wasn't tired. I was determined. When we reached the car, I knew I was done for. There was no way I could pull him into the backseat all by myself.

"Honey," I said, resting him upright against the car, "I need you to listen to me. I need you to come back and help me. Help me help you, John."

He moaned and his eyes fluttered. "That's it," I said, "just one little move and I've got you in the car. Okay? On three. One, two, three!" I pulled, he pushed, a little. I pulled harder and he was in the car, lying on my backseat.

"All right! Good! Just rest, sweetie. We'll be at Bay County in no time."

"No!" he said, his eyes flying open. "No! No hospital! I'm all right!"

"Are you out of your fucking mind?" I yelled. "You're fucking bleeding all over my car!"

"It's a surface wound," he gasped. "Went clean through. It's just my arm. Sierra, don't take me to the hospital. Take me home!"

He was out again. Cold. I was sweatin' and he was out cold. What was I supposed to do? He said no hospital. Maybe those gunshots really had been meant for him. He was in trouble, I knew that much. And then I knew: Ma. She would know. I'd take him home all right. Home to Ma.

Twenty-seven

*I*n my former life, as a little girl, I'd wanted to be a nurse. Now, seeing us both soaked in blood, I knew what a joke that had been. My heart was racing. The car was hot, and the air sticky sweet with the scent of blood. I wanted to throw up.

I didn't think he was outright bleeding to death. I think blood spurts out in spasms when you've cut an artery or some vital blood vessel, but I don't know, because I'd given up on my medical career when I learned about bedpans. All I could do now was drive. That was something I could do very fast and very well. It was twenty-some miles back to the Lively Oaks Trailer Park. I think I made it in just over fifteen minutes.

John hadn't said a word the whole trip back. He hadn't moved. He hadn't regained consciousness. I, on the other hand, said plenty.

"You know," I said, "you shoulda been straight with me up front that you was hurt. We coulda wasted less time that way. But, no, you're too macho or whatever." When that didn't work, I moved on to threats and intimidation. "If you wake up," I said, "if you let me take you to the hospital, I'll dance naked on your bed every night for a year." When that brought no response, I started a new conversation. "Okay, God," I said, "it's me again. Only this time, listen, it ain't for me. It's for him. Honey, don't let this one die on me. Not so much on account of me, but on account of he's a good guy. He ain't never hurt nobody. And look, Ruby's gone. Isn't that enough dying? I don't know if you knew Ruby was gonna die, or nothin'. I'm not saying you did. Maybe you were busy and it slipped by. Maybe it shouldn't have happened. Whatever. I'm not blaming you. I'm just saying, 'Hey! Listen up! Don't let him die.' "

Sometimes you gotta get people's attention.

I didn't need to get attention when I drove up. Maybe that was on account of me laying on the horn. At any rate, Al came running down the steps as I pulled up, the ugly gun back in his hand.

"Sierra, what the hell's with the horn? Hey, you got blood all over you!"

"I need Ma," I said. "Look!" I jumped out of the car and flipped the driver's seat to reveal John Nailor passed out on the backseat.

Al stuck his gun in his waistband. "You shouldn't have done this!"

"I didn't do it, burgerhead!" I said, lapsing back into our childhood name-calling. "He's shot, we gotta get him inside." I went on before he could start in with the cop-interrogation routine. "He said he can't go to the hospital."

Al gave me a look and must've seen something in my face, because he didn't ask another question. By the time he'd reached into the backseat, Ma was on the stoop. When Al pulled out of the car and turned around, he had John cradled in his arms. Ma looked from me to Nailor and went into action.

"Put him in Sierra's room," she barked. "Sierra, run out to the Lincoln and get Pa's first-aid kit out of the trunk. Al, move it! Don't jar him!"

By the time I was back with the kit, which was more the size of a small suitcase on account of Pa being an EMT, Ma was working. She had John on his side, with Al holding him, as she cut away his shirt with a pair of scissors.

"Oh, Jesus, Mother Mary, and all the Saints," she breathed. "Sierra! Towels! I'll need warm water and a washcloth. Move it!"

I flew. I threw the towels on the bed and ran into my bathroom to run water. Al was supporting Nailor with part of his body and opening the first-aid kit with one hand.

"It looks like it went in the front," Al was saying, "with the exit wound here in the back above his elbow."

"Apply pressure there, honey," Ma said. "We've gotta stop the bleeding."

I brought a wet washcloth into Ma and stood there by her side, waiting for her to take it and feeling useless. Nailor moaned suddenly, and Ma and Al both stopped what they were doing, as if surprised to find that the gunshot wound was attached to a person.

"Hey," I said. I made my way up to the bed and knelt down. "Tough guy," I said softly, "it's me."

His eyes fluttered and then opened.

"That's Ma," I said when I saw his eyes connect with hers. "And Al's behind you, there. Welcome to Nurse Sierra's Home Health Care Center for the Physically Wounded and Terminally Stubborn, that, of course, being you."

He licked his lips and winced.

"Don't go making any speeches," I said. "We'll take donations when you're back on your feet." My God, he looked pale.

Ma looked at Al. "Is it stopping?"

Al carefully lifted back the edge of the towel and peered at the exit wound. "Uh-uh," he said. "Not yet."

"Well, keep it elevated while I try and put a tourniquet on." Then she looked at Nailor. "You're bleeding a lot," she said, her voice an even, calm monotone. "We'll get that stopped and you'll be fine." Her eyes seemed to soften, even as her hands worked to tighten the tourniquet around his upper arm. "It hurts, huh, sweetie?"

He nodded. "Not too bad." But his eyes made him a liar.

"Sierra, get the boy a little of your Pa's tonic," she said. "Thickens the blood." She nodded to Al to tighten his hold, then looked back at Nailor. "If you ate more Italian food and drank red wine regular, this sort of thing would go a lot easier!"

Nailor laughed softly. "Just need you to cook it for me," he sighed, and his eyes closed. Ma smiled, reached out, and grabbed the washcloth off the bedstand. Gently, she began wiping the soot and dried blood off his face and neck.

"You're a mess, son," she said softly.

I sat down next to Ma and waited until she was finished. "You want him to have this?" I said, pointing to the tumbler of Chianti I'd brought into the room.

"Al," Ma said, "we gotta prop him up a little."

It took the three of us to get him positioned, but finally Ma was satisfied. "That's good. Sierra, just give him a little sip at a time."

"You with us, here?" I said, a little louder than normal.

His eyes fluttered open.

"This is gonna help. You've had it before, but I didn't tell you it was good for you."

"What is it?" he whispered.

"Chianti. Thickens the blood." Al sighed and Ma reached out to swat him.

"Mr. Wiseguy," she huffed.

Nailor took a sip and choked, then another. "How much, Ma?" I asked.

She looked at Nailor and the tumbler I held in my hand, as if maybe she was actually calculating a dose. "At least half the glass," she pronounced. "We got a lot of blood needs thickening."

Nailor's eyes weren't opening, but he drank. Al was sitting next to him in the bed, keeping Nailor's arm elevated and pressure applied to the wound. I saw him lean closer to John and lift the towel. His eyes met Ma's.

"It might be slowing down," he said.

Ma nodded. "Thank your father for that, Mr. Know-It-All!" She looked at the clock and then back at me. "Sierra, don't you gotta be at work in an hour?"

"I'm not going to work with him hurt like this." Nailor appeared to be sleeping, his head slumped back against the pillows.

"Oh?" Al said. "And so you'd be telling your boss what? That your cop boyfriend got hurt and you can't come in? You wanna draw attention that something's not right?"

"No, Al, I'll tell him I'm sick."

"Oh," he scoffed, "that's real smooth. Were you sick yesterday? You think him and anybody else who's wondering won't know that's bogus?"

I hadn't thought about it that way.

"Sierra, you're in the middle of some deep shit, or haven't you noticed? Have you caught on yet that every time you do anything connected with finding out who killed your friend Ruby, that you or somebody else gets hurt?"

Or killed, I thought, remembering Wannamaker Lewis.

"This is dangerous, Sierra. We gotta play this one safe. Go to work. We don't want anyone coming around here asking questions, especially if we're gonna hide a cop with a gunshot wound."

"All right, all right! I'll go. You done with the sermon?"

"All's I'm asking is for you to use your brain. You kicked over a big can of worms, Sierra, and somebody out there don't like it."

Before I left, I walked back into my room and sat on the edge of the bed. He was sleeping, a lock of straight brown hair falling across his forehead. I leaned forward and gently kissed his cheek. His eyes popped open and he smiled slightly.

"You look beautiful," he whispered.

I was Sierra, Queen of the Night, my blond hair curled to fall across my shoulders, all powdered and scented, with gold glitter lotion perfuming my body.

With his good arm, he reached out and touched my cheek, his fingers trailing down my neck and across my shoulders.

"You know why I did it?" he said.

"Did what?" I had to lean closer to hear him.

"Kissed her."

"Yeah, why did you do that, you snake!" I was kidding, a little.

"I wanted to make you mad."

"Good job, sport! It worked."

He smiled. The bastard was actually smiling. "I know." Then the frown came. "If you hadn't been mad, somebody might've killed me. If you'd blown my cover . . ." His eyes closed. "Thanks," he whispered.

"Anytime, big man." I leaned over and kissed him on the lips. I'm a sucker for a pitiful man. "Go back to sleep. I'll be home as soon as I can." I couldn't tell if he heard me. He looked to be asleep again. "I'll crawl in bed next to you," I added. There was no reaction for a moment, so I started to leave. The sound of his voice surprised me.

"Naked, I hope."

"You just keep dreaming, sport. I'm more woman than you'll ever handle."

"Try me," he whispered.

I figured my detective was on the road to recovery.

Twenty-eight

*V*incent Gambuzzo wasn't happy. That was nothing new for Vincent, nor was the object of his displeasure — me — a surprise. I managed to piss off Vincent almost every time he saw me. It didn't bother me, but it bugged the hell out of him.

"Listen," he said, "Dead Lakes Motor Speedway is a big account. I'm looking to maintain a relationship and you ain't helping."

We were standing outside his office, just around the corner from the front door. People were walking past like it was Grand Central Station, and I could've cared less, but Vincent was doubly ticked on account of not liking his business known among the staff and public.

I stamped my black stilettoed heel, setting all the beads and bangles on my tigress outfit to jumping. "I don't give a good rat's ass what you think," I said. "There ain't money enough to make me go back out to that racetrack!"

Vincent's jaw was twitching, and behind the wrap-around sunglasses his entire face glowed a coronary red.

"Mickey Rhodes requested you," he said. "He wants to do a tribute to Ruby, sort of as a way to let the fans know that it's all right to come to the Speedway, that people are safe there. He thinks if you're there, it'll spread that message."

"Ain't my problem, Gambuzzo."

"You want it on the line, Lavotini?" he sputtered. "All right, here's the line: If your ass isn't up to that racetrack next Wednesday night, I'll . . ." He paused for a moment, long enough for me to open my big mouth.

"You'll what, Gambuzzo, fire me?"

"You're damn right!" he thundered.

"Oh, well, ain't that a fine business decision," I said with a sneer. "Fire your headliner on account of she won't go back to the place where another one of your dancers was murdered. How's that gonna look? Eh? Who you gonna find to work for you then, Vincent? A club owner who thinks no more of his dancers than to send them into harm's way!"

We were drawing a crowd. Tonya the Barbarian stood just behind me, her cavegirl club clutched in her hand like she might have call to use it. Marla had wandered up and clearly taken Vincent's side, but when Tonya snarled at her, she jumped back a good three feet.

"They know who killed Ruby," Vincent said. "And Roy Dell's a wanted man. He would no more show his face at the Speedway than in church. Dead Lakes is safe, Sierra. You're just showboating and I won't have it! Your ass'll be up there Wednesday night with a smile on your pretty little face, or you won't have a job to come back to. You work for me, Sierra, and this ain't Disneyland."

I could feel it welling up. I couldn't have stopped it if I'd wanted to. I had my pride. Sierra Lavotini didn't eat shit for nobody.

"You don't own me, Gambuzzo," I shouted. "And you can kiss my smooth ass, 'cause I quit!"

I couldn't believe it! I couldn't believe the words had come out of my mouth, but it didn't matter, 'cause I'd said 'em, and now I had to live by them. I spun around and stalked off to the dressing room amid cheers from my supporters and Vincent's voice calling over the top of them.

"Come back here, Lavotini! You can't quit! You're fired!"

I didn't look back. I just held my head high, walked into the dressing room, and started packing. Two years I'd given that man, and now I was done. I didn't need him. I could find a job tomorrow. Show-N-Tails had been after me for over a year to come work for them, and every other club in the country would be the same. I didn't need him!

I threw my costumes into my bag and started cleaning out my small portion of the makeup bar. I was cussing and talking to myself to beat the band. I wasn't even aware that anyone else had come into the room until I looked up and saw Ralph the stagehand standing behind me, his eyes the size of saucers, terrified.

"Well, what are you looking at?" I snapped, instantly sorry.

"Sierra," he said, his voice squeaky with trepidation, "please don't go."

I looked at him standing there, his red hair and freckles making him look like Opie Taylor from Mayberry, and my heart melted.

"I can't stay, Ralphie. I have to go. It's a matter of principle."

He gulped, looked me right in the eye, and said, "It's pride's what it is. You and Mr. Gambuzzo are always like this. Why're you going now?"

" 'Cause I said I would" sounded like a lame reason, and we both knew it. The other dancers were slowly filing into the room, standing behind Ralph and staring at me the same way he was. I was leaving them. Their mom was leaving.

"I'm sorry, guys," I said, slinging my bag over my shoulder. "I can't let him talk to me like that. I've gotta draw the line somewhere." I walked through them, out into the hallway, and out the back exit door. I left to the sound of complete silence, a first for the Tiffany Gentleman's Club.

"Keep walking," I said to myself. "Don't look back." My bag of makeup and costumes felt heavier with each step I took. The trip across the parking lot was endless. I threw my bag into the backseat, jumped into the driver's seat, and took off, spinning my tires the entire way out of the parking lot and onto Thomas Drive. Behind me, another car pulled out of the parking lot and in behind me. An unmarked sedan, black. Wheeling.

"Screw him!" I said into the wind. "Screw everybody! Screw the whole situation!"

I drove down the Miracle Strip, the stretch of Panama City Beach that hosts mega-hotels sandwiched in between mom-and-pop motels, go-cart tracks, and bars. Boys, standing alongside the road on the lookout for trouble, yelled out, but they barely even registered on my radar. I needed quiet and a place to think. I needed the beach.

I pushed on past the Strip, letting my foot rest heavy on the accelerator as I zoomed toward Laguna Beach. Wheeling was right behind me, following at a discreet distance.

"All right for you, then. See if you can do this . . ."

I swung down one of the side roads and picked up speed, zooming from corner to corner. I knew a few turns that Wheeling obviously hadn't anticipated. You don't grow up in Philly, with them tiny alleys and one-way streets, to be defeated by Panama City's little grid. I pushed ahead of him and abruptly swung into the Lotus, one of the beach's largest and most exclusive complexes.

My advantage was in having an owner's gate card, courtesy of a grateful patron who didn't mind letting a dancer have free parking right in front of the beach. Wheeling was just far enough behind me that he couldn't catch the rocker arm of the gate. He was momentarily stumped, but only momentarily.

Just long enough for me to wind my way into the parking garage, ditch the car and run out onto the beach.

It wasn't forever. I knew he'd find me. But I wasn't going to make it easy. I kicked off my shoes and started running, away from the lights that pointed out the strip and out toward darker Laguna Beach. In the dark, my Tigress outfit probably looked like a swim suit. But the tiny bells and beads clanked together to make me sound like a herd of housecats.

I ran and ran, not looking back to see if he followed me, not really caring, until I felt myself giving out, the rage seeping away for the moment. I sank down by the edge of the water, winded and panting. Then I glanced back. Nothing. If he was out there, I was as invisible to him as he was to me.

I looked out at the water. The crest of the waves glowed an eerie white in the light of the almost full moon. What was I gonna do now? I had a lap full of questions and not too many answers. Why did Roy Dell run off and where was he? Did he burn Wannamaker's house down? Did he shoot John? Did Roy Dell shoot Wannamaker? Why was there cocaine in Wannamaker's attic? Was that why John was nosing around Wannamaker's house and the racetrack? Was there some connection? I leaned back on my arms and tried to think.

I heard Wannamaker's voice in my head. "My Son of Satan wanted to take me first, but no, He had to take her." What if he hadn't been just babbling? What if Wannamaker was talking about *his* son, Ruby's brother, the missing Michael? Who was he, anyway? Where was he?

It had been stupid to tell Vincent I wouldn't go back to the racetrack. I had to go back out to that track. Everything stemmed from there.

I was so wrapped up in planning that I almost didn't see Wheeling trudging down the beach, a flashlight in his hand, following my tracks. He swung the light up as he got closer, hitting me full in the face with the bright light.

"Turn that off!" I yelled. "You know it's me!"

The light went out, and he sank down beside me, resting on his haunches. He did not look like a happy camper.

"You could've made this easier," he said.

"Oh, yeah, like I didn't already have enough of a pain in my ass by quitting my job, I should slow down and let you be that extra hemorrhoid. I think not!"

"So you quit, huh? Why?"

Why indeed. "It was a slow night."

Wheeling relaxed a little. Behind his thick mustache, he actually seemed to crack a smile.

"You're a pistol, Lavotini."

"You come all the way out here to tell me that?" I threw a shell out at the water.

"No, I came all the way out here to find out what you did with Roy Dell Parks."

"And I'm sorry for you, 'cause I haven't done a thing with Roy Dell Parks." I stood up and started brushing sand off my ass, taking it as an extra benefit that some of it was flying all over the detective.

"He was with you outside of Wannamaker Lewis's house," he said calmly. He stood up and folded his arms, an immovable force.

"All right, I'll bite. How did you know that?"

The smile was back, peeking out from under the mustache. "A source."

I almost went for it. I almost asked, "Nailor?" but that would've been walking into a trap or giving him information he didn't have. Instead I bit the inside of my lip.

"Why don't you guys let up off Roy Dell? He's a gnat on your windshield. You know he didn't kill Ruby. Why don't you focus on finding her real killer?"

Wheeling hadn't moved. He was less than a foot away from me, staring me down. "I don't know that," he said. "Frank

Collins puts him away from his crew and near the scene at just the right time. The rest of the crew all verified that Parks was late for the call to drive the car up to the starting line."

"That's enough for a murder warrant?"

"It is if a witness also heard your friend Ruby tell Parks to back off. Apparently, that made him angry."

"That's not what I told you!"

"Your story didn't altogether hang, now did it? You thought my partner was someplace he obviously wasn't."

What a smart ass he was! Still didn't believe me.

"Frank's lying," I said. "You and I both know he was fooling around with Roy Dell's wife. There's motive for lying right there."

"Then why'd Roy Dell run?"

I pushed past him and started walking back toward the car. He was right beside me, reaching out and grabbing my arm to stop me.

"Wait a minute!"

I spun to a stop, ready to take his head off, but he started first.

"Sierra, I'm not your enemy. I'm trying to apprehend the man who killed your friend."

"You do that by calling me a liar?"

"Who do you think I'm going to believe? My partner or you?"

I shrugged. "You gotta do what you gotta do." I started walking again, but slower, letting him keep up.

"I think you were mistaken," he said. "That's not the same as lying."

"Whatever." I looked over at him. "Wannamaker Lewis was Ruby Lee's biological father. Did you know that?"

"Yes, but Wannamaker Lewis died in that fire," he said. "You were there. Roy Dell Parks was there. Should I be making something out of that? You're damn right I should. I don't need to go looking for anything other than the obvious explanation." He hadn't waited for my confirmation.

"You think Roy Dell set the fire?"

"Don't you?" he asked.

I didn't answer him. I wanted to respond, to explain everything, but I just couldn't be sure, and with John's life on the line, I wasn't going to take a chance. If John had wanted to take his partner into his confidence, then he would've done so already.

We'd reached the parking garage, our footsteps the only sound in the orange-lit deck. He didn't say a word until I stopped by my car.

"If you see him," he said, his voice pitched low, "tell him I could help him if he'd let me. Tell him I'd know what to do. Tell him he ought to know that about me by now."

All of a sudden, I didn't think we were talking about a murder suspect.

"Roy Dell?" I asked.

"Anybody you think could use that message," he said, his face grim. "I don't leave people hanging out to dry, even when it looks like that's what they're doing to me. Situations can always be rectified. You tell Mr. Parks, or whomever, that I said that."

I reached out my hand and touched his arm. "I'll tell whomever what you said. Maybe you should think on the fact that things aren't always like they seem."

His eyes were hard. "I know that. I got more time invested in the relationship than you do. Trust is all you got to give in this world. Trust and your word. I gave my word, Sierra, and that means everything. You tell the son of a bitch I said that."

He walked away then, mad, hurt, and confused. He knew his partner was lying to him.

When Nailor recovered enough to answer questions, he was going to have to deal with me and Wheeling. What would make him lie to his own partner? Why would he be doing something undercover that his own department didn't know about? Something at the racetrack. Something that maybe had to do with Ruby's death.

I backed the car out of its parking space and started driving toward home. I didn't have a job. I was no closer to finding Ruby's murderer. And the man I'd figured was my best shot at a healthy relationship lay waiting for me in my own bed, too weak to move, and too stubborn to let me help him.

When I slipped into the trailer, it was just after midnight. Al was the only one up. He was sitting at the kitchen table, working a crossword and frowning.

"How's he doing?" I asked.

"I don't know. All right, I guess. He lost a lot of blood, Sierra. I'd sure feel better if he'd let us take him to the hospital."

"I don't think he feels a hospital's safe," I said. "I don't know what's going on, but I don't want to put him at risk. I trust him to know what's safe."

Al looked at me and shook his head. "Why you gotta always fall for the wrong guy, Sierra? Why you can't have a straight-up relationship?"

I reached for the Chianti bottle and Al's empty glass. "Beats me, Al. He's a good guy. I think we know that. He's just in trouble."

Al laughed softly. "And what guy gets involved with you ain't in trouble? It's like that 'chicken or the egg' thing. Which came first, trouble or you?"

"Good night, Al," I said wryly, taking my tumbler and heading for the back room. "I'll take the night shift."

"Don't do nothing to raise the boy's blood pressure," he called after me. "We finally got the bleeding to stop!"

I ignored him and tiptoed past the room where Ma lay

fully clothed on her bed, snoring. I softly pushed open my bedroom door and stepped into the room. Fluffy, who hadn't come out to greet me, sat up by Nailor's shoulder, on guard.

Her tail started wagging and she pranced to the edge of the bed.

"How's he doin', girl?" I whispered. "Did he give you any trouble?" I looked down at him. He slept with a frown on his face, as if he hurt. He was still very, very pale.

I took my wine and wandered into the bathroom. It was just too early to go to bed.

"A nice long bubble bath," I whispered to myself, and started the water. As it ran, I lit candles, dripped a little lavender oil into the water, and dug out a nightgown. I had to dig deep on account of being used to sleeping naked under my satin sheets most nights. But eventually I found a white cotton number with little satin ribbon ties. Tasteful. Chaste. A "company" nightgown that said, "Glad you're here, but don't go getting ideas." At least that's what I hoped it said.

I soaked until the water turned lukewarm and the wine was gone. Sleep was actually seeming like a possibility. I wandered into the dimly lit bedroom. Nailor was sleeping on "my side" and didn't move when I turned out the light and slipped gently under the comforter.

I lay there for a second, a foot away from a man who, under different circumstances, would have reduced me to a mass of trembling expectations. I moved a little closer and became aware that his breathing had changed, lightened. He moaned and rolled toward me, his arm falling gently around my waist. I was trapped.

"Thought you promised naked," he whispered.

My heart started racing and I felt my nipples harden as his hand brushed lightly against them.

"Didn't wanna take advantage of a wounded man," I said softly.

He nuzzled the back of my neck, another soft moan escaping his lips. He was in pain and still trying to go for the gold. That's a man for you.

"Go to sleep," I hissed. "I like my men healthy."

"I could take you with one arm tied behind my back." He chuckled softly.

"I doubt that, Nailor. And besides, I want both your hands in action. I won't settle for half your best."

He moved a little closer, his body molding to mine. "It's a deal," he said. "But once this arm's working, you'd better be ready, 'cause I'll be coming after you."

"I'm terrified," I whispered.

His fingers brushed my nipples again. "Yeah, I can tell."

I leaned back against him, a sigh escaping my lips. It was all I could do not to roll over and administer CPR, but I knew better. Instead I lay there, waiting for him to drift off to sleep. I listened to his regular, even breathing for hours before I joined him.

Twenty-nine

I woke up because I was on fire. Sun was streaming through the window of my bedroom. Coffee was brewing in the kitchen. And something was very wrong with Nailor. He was almost too hot too touch.

I sat up and looked at him. He was red and tossing restlessly in his sleep, moaning softly.

"Ma!" I ran to the door and yelled out for her. "Ma! There's something wrong!"

Ma came flying down the hallway. Raydean, her hair in yellow curlers, was right behind her.

"What is it?" Ma said, pushing past me and sitting down by John's side. "Oh Lord," she breathed. "He's burning up!"

John opened his eyes and looked at us. His eyes were bloodshot and watery.

"That does it," Ma said. "He has got to go to the hospital!" She pulled the bandage away from his arm and winced. "Look at that. It's infected." I leaned close and looked. The wound was an angry red, puffy and streaked.

"All right. I don't know what else to do. He's gonna die like this, isn't he, Ma?"

Al stood in the doorway, his face mirroring my concern. "We gotta take him," he said.

"I . . . can't . . . go!" Nailor said, every word an effort. "I . . . can't . . . risk . . . it! Too . . . dangerous."

Raydean stood at the foot of the bed, staring at John and nodding. She edged a little closer to Ma. Finally she pushed Ma away and slid down onto the bed in her place.

"Let me see, honey," she whispered, her gnarled fingers reaching for the dressing that covered his arm.

"Raydean . . ." I started, but let it drop. Stopping Raydean was always worse than letting her have her way.

With a gentle movement, Raydean pulled away the gauze and stared at the wound, biting down on her lower lip.

"Sepsis," she muttered. "Okay." She looked up at me, as if confirming her thoughts. "I'm callin' Arlen," she said, and reached for the phone.

"Whoa! Raydean, wait! What're you doing?"

"I can't treat him without antibiotics," she said, her voice clear and strong. This wasn't an alien watch, it was Raydean in for a landing, sane.

"Raydean," I said, "what do you mean treat him?"

"Lt. Raydean Charles, W.A.C, R.N., W.W. Two, at your service, sir!"

What I saw was a gray-haired old lady in curlers and bunny slippers, but in her eyes was something else. Hallucination or whatever, I was in no position not to ride with it.

"Who's Arlen?" I asked.

"My superior," she answered. "We did time together." She reached for the phone and started dialing.

"In the service?"

Raydean shook her head as if I was slow. "No, honey, in the Big House. State Hospital. Nineteen sixty-four." Someone answered on the other end and Raydean cupped her hand around the receiver. "Got a patient, sir," she said. Then: "My house." She leaned around to look at the clock on the bedside table. "Oh-nine-hundred hours, sir. Yes, sir!" There was a pause. "Oh, and, sir? Bring them horse-pill antibiotics you got. He's a sick'un!"

Raydean hung up and smiled down at Nailor. "Baby, you ain't got a care in the world. The best vet what ever birthed a cow is on his way! We'll have you crowing with the roosters by this time tomorrow."

In his sleep, Nailor smiled.

Al could stand it no longer. "I gotta tell you," he said, the words bursting from him like a balloon losing air, "this ain't working for me."

"Shut up, Al!" Me and Ma said in unison.

Raydean stood up, her cheeks pink, her hands flying to her head. "Mercy me," she sputtered. "I've gotta run. I cain't have Arlen seeing me like this!" She started shuffling toward the door. "He'll be here in less than fifteen minutes. I'll be back." She reached over and patted my arm. "Don't worry, sugar, I'll have him on his feet and ready to howl at the moon. Just make sure you have your track shoes on when I do. That boy'll give you a run for your money!"

I was dressing when I heard him call my name. I crossed the room and perched on the bed again.

"You called?"

He opened his eyes and for a moment he just stared. It scared me. I'd never seen anybody, let alone him, like this. I didn't know if he was dying. I certainly wasn't sure that we were all doing the right thing by keeping him here.

"Sierra," he said, "give me some water. My throat hurts."

I propped his head up and held the glass to his lips while he drank. He took two sips and leaned back. "That's better. Sierra, you have to do something. Dial a number for me." He slumped back against the pillow, exhausted with the effort it took to talk.

I picked up the phone and waited as he slowly called out

a long-distance number. Maybe it was the area code for Tallahassee? I held the receiver to his ear, waiting.

"Hey," he said, his voice a near whisper. The person on the other end obviously had questions because there was a long silence from John and then a sigh. "Wait. I can't . . . not now. Listen . . . the mouse . . . is on . . . the move! You hear me? Tonight." When the voice acknowledged the message, Nailor slumped back.

The person on the other end wasn't finished. I could hear a woman's voice yelling, "John! John! Answer me!"

John wasn't going to be doing any more talking, that much I could tell from looking at him.

"He can't talk anymore," I said into the receiver.

"Who's this?!" The woman's voice demanded.

"Sierra Lavotini. And who the hell are you?"

There was a pause, then, "Oh, my God! Not you! The stripper, right?"

The awful realization sank in. I knew exactly who the voice was on the other end of the phone. I'd heard it enough in person when my friend Denise had gotten in trouble over her dope-dealing husband. Carla Terrance, DEA agent and John Nailor's ex-wife.

"Ain't you sweet to remember?" I said.

"What happened to John?" she asked. She needed me. She needed what I knew.

"He's been shot."

There was a sharp intake of breath. "Is he all right?"

"Hell, no, he isn't all right, and he won't let me take him to a doctor or a hospital, either! That probably has something to do with you, doesn't it?"

"What do you need?" she asked. "He's right. No hospital. Just tell me what you need."

I looked over at John. "A doctor might be nice," I said. "I think he's infected. That's what Raydean thinks."

"That crazy woman that lives across from you and shoots at aliens?"

"Hey! She's got training and she's got a friend on his way over here with antibiotics. I'd say Raydean's doing all right."

Carla sighed. "Well, if you got a doctor coming, what do you need another one for?"

"The one on his way's a vet. I was thinking maybe you could do a little better, even though it's your ex."

"It may take me a little while," she said. "We may have to wait until after dark. I don't want to take any risks." But she didn't mean with John's life, I knew that much from the one time I'd had dealings with her. Carla had a one-track mind. She only wanted what was best for the DEA.

"Yeah, well, if he ain't alive, Carla, how's about I have him stuffed for you!"

She hung up on me. Just as well. If we'd chatted two seconds longer, I'd have gone through the phone and kicked her shapely little behind. Carla Terrance! I knew it all along. She was the only one who could yank him out of his department and make him dance like a puppet at the end of her little string.

I looked over at John. "She must've hurt you bad, big man. She must've tied Mr. Happy in a hell of a knot for you to be in this much of a mess!"

He moaned softly in his sleep.

"Yeah, well, when this mess is over, you can have her if that's what you want."

The phone rang again and I snatched it up, ready to tell her the rest of what I was thinking.

"What?" I yelled. "You haven't done enough?"

"Sierra, that you?" a male voice asked.

"Who wants to know?"

"Albert—uh, Meatloaf. Lord, honey, you'd better come quick. Roy Dell's got Frank and I think he's fixing to kill him!"

"Listen, Meatloaf, this isn't a good time."

From the background I could hear an ungodly scream.

"What was that?" I asked. The hair on the back of my neck jumped to attention. "Meatloaf! What's he doing?" But Meatloaf wasn't listening to me.

"Roy Dell! Roy Dell! Stop it! Are you nuts? Look at him! You done cut the circulation off!"

Roy Dell said something I couldn't make out. Then there was another long scream, this time ending with a shriek.

"I hate to do this," Meatloaf said into the phone, "but right now, you're the only one he'll listen to. Roy Dell!" Meatloaf yelled at him again. "The phone's for you!"

"What? Huh? The phone?" Roy Dell's voice sounded liquor-slurred. "Tell her I ain't talking!"

"It ain't Lulu. It's Ruby's friend, Sierra."

Oh, just dandy, I thought. Turn the psycho over to me! Thank you, Meatloaf! I could here two sets of shoes shuffling over to the phone.

"Here," said Meatloaf, apparently guiding Roy Dell's drunken progress.

"Hello, darlin'," said Roy Dell, pitching his voice to sound low and sexy. It sounded more like a sick animal, but I didn't let on.

"Roy Dell, what in the hell is going on?" I wasn't going to waste time on sympathy. He needed a mama.

"Ma'am?"

"Are you drinking?"

"Yes, ma'am," he answered, his voice a sheepish little boy's.

"And did you go against what I told you and go after Frank?"

"You're damn right I did," he roared. "And Meatloaf agreed with me, too!"

236

Uh-oh. Wrong question. "Well, you left me all alone," I said. "Where did you go?"

"Aw, now darlin', I didn't mean nothing by it. I was sittin' out in your car, with that blanket what Lulu and I inaugurated with our love, and I jest got to thinkin'. Then, before I knew it, I saw Mr. Rhodes go driving by, real slow. I needed to talk to him about something, so I took off, thinking maybe I could catch him."

"Then what?"

Roy Dell sighed, torn between talking to me and exacting revenge from Frank. "Well, he parked and said he had business to attend to and he couldn't talk just then. I told him I was done waiting for my money. It had been six weeks and I wanted some action." Roy Dell took a swig of something. "Summ'n a bitch told me to come up to his office later in the afternoon and he'd pay me. Then he walked off. And do you think he was anywhere to be found? No indeedy."

I could hear voices coming from the direction of my kitchen. Raydean was back and I was going to have to wrap this up quick.

"Roy Dell, did Mickey Rhodes go into Wannamaker Lewis's house?"

"Hell, honey, I don't know. He walked off in that direction, but you know, the place caught on fire right after that. Why would he go in there?"

So, Roy Dell stuck around long enough to know the house was on fire but was gone when the firemen arrived.

"Where are you, Roy Dell? I want to see you."

"No, ma'am! Whass about to happen here ain't fit viewin'," he said. "Frank done wrong and I got to let him know you don't dog Roy Dell Parks."

"Roy Dell! Did it never occur to you that I might have a few resentments toward Frank, too?"

Footsteps were moving down the hallway. John Nailor was

burning up. And I was stuck talking Roy Dell out of killing a man I agreed needed killing. There'd be an extra jewel in my crown for this. Maybe I'd have to say one less Hail Mary when the final reckoning came.

"All right, all right," he sighed. "If you want to wop him upside the head once before I finish him off, you can come on."

He dropped the phone and shuffled away. "Roy Dell! Roy Dell, where are you?" I could hear Meatloaf ask.

"We gotta wait to kill him," he said. "Women! Always wanting to direct the action."

The door to my room opened and Ma stepped in, followed by an entourage.

"Don't hang up!" I yelled into the receiver. In the far distance, I heard the unmistakable sound of a pneumatic lug-nut loosener. Then Frank screamed again.

"Sierra, you there?" Meatloaf sounded breathless.

"Where are you?"

"The garage."

"At the track?"

"Yeah, don't worry. Won't no po-lices ever find us here. Roy Dell's got an early warning system. Hurry now!"

"Don't let Roy Dell kill him till I get there!"

He hung up and I turned around to face the small crowd that had gathered in my room. There was a much larger crisis at hand than saving Frank's ass. Arlen the vet had arrived.

He stopped at the edge of the room, a short man with thinning white hair and twinkling blue eyes. Judging from the three-piece suit he wore, time had stopped for him in the late-thirties. I figured he had to be closing in on ninety. But Raydean was oblivious to this. She stood by his side, beaming, her Easter bonnet secured to her head with a huge hatpin, and white go-to-church-lady gloves on her hands.

"Sierra, this is Dr. Arlen Fellows," she said proudly, blushing. "Rear Admiral, U.S. Navy, Retired."

Yeah, retired many times over, I thought.

"Where is my patient?" he asked, peering myopically past me. Raydean motioned me aside and led Arlen up to John's side.

Arlen changed abruptly. "My bag, nurse," he said, brusquely.

Raydean stiffened, took the cracked leather bag Ma carried, and plopped it down on the bed next to Nailor.

"Yes, sir!" she answered.

Arlen reached forward and briefly touched Nailor's nose. "Dry," he said. "Not a good sign in a human."

Ma shook her head and looked at Al. She was thinking the same thing I was. The man was a lunatic.

Arlen took out a penlight and shone it in Nailor's eyes. "Hmmm," he murmured. "Nurse, horse pills it is! Let's start with a broad spectrum antibiotic, this ampicillin oughta get it. Acetamenophen and ibuprophen, alternating every two hours for the first eight. Oughta bring that fever down."

Nailor was struggling to be awake, trying to track Arlen with his eyes.

"You hurt just everywhere, don't you, boy?" Arlen said. "Not just your withers, but your flanks, too, I'd reckon. Well, you'll feel better soon."

Arlen turned to Raydean. "Nurse," he said, "Clean and dress that wound again. Give him his meds. Then let's play a hand or two of cards."

Raydean nodded and started hauling medicine bottles, gauze, and tape out of the black bag. As an afterthought, she reached in deep and pulled out a pack of playing cards, which she tossed to Al.

"Doc's orders," she barked. "Deal 'em out in the kitchen. Five-card draw! Boil water!"

"Boil water?" Al sputtered.

"You don't know how?" Raydean asked.

"Well, sure I know how," he said. "I just don't know why."

Raydean was calmly pulling on a pair of latex gloves. "Coffee, you young idiot!"

Ma laughed. "Come on, Dr. Fellows, I got some cinnamon buns with your name written all over them."

She led him away, leaving me and Raydean to change Nailor's bandage. We boosted him up in bed, with him moaning every time we touched him.

"It's the fever, Sierra," Raydean said. "He cain't stand our touch to his skin. I'm gonna get him a cool rag in a minute."

He choked on the pills, but we got them into him. He didn't say a word when Raydean cleaned his arm. He was out of it.

"Sierra," Raydean said, as we finished. "I want you to listen to me."

I stopped and looked at her, recognizing the clear, distinct tone of Raydean sane.

"You think Arlen's a kook. Don't bother denying it!" She held up her hand to stop my comment. "And in some respects he is. Just like me. But he's a good vet. We're taking good care of your man. You trust me, don't you?"

I looked right back at her. "Of course I do, Raydean."

"That fever'll be down some in thirty minutes," she said. "He's starting to mend. So if there was anyone whose life was hanging on yours . . . anyone you might've said 'don't kill him yet' to . . ."

"Oh! Oh, yeah!" I looked back at Nailor, lying on the bed, his face pale again.

"Honey," Raydean laid her hand on my arm. "Let me take care of him. He won't die. I promise you."

I hugged her and stepped over to the bedside. I sat down and ran my fingers lightly through his hair.

"I gotta go over to the racetrack for a little while," I whispered. "I'll be back soon."

His eyes flew open. "No!"

"It won't take but an hour, I promise."

"No! I told you. The . . . mouse. It's moving. Any second!"

"It's the fever, honey," I answered. "Carla knows about the mouse. You told her. It's all right."

He grabbed my arm with his good one. "No!"

"Okay, okay, then I won't go. I'll just hang around here." Panic was rising up, choking me. What if Roy Dell really did kill Frank? Then it would fall on my head because I could stop him if I left now.

Raydean stepped in then. "Sugar, go eat," she said, giving me a little shove. "Here, honey," she said soothingly to John, "I got a nice cool cloth for your head. Sierra's gonna go eat her lunch now. She'll be right back."

I felt like a heel. I wasn't going out into the kitchen to eat. I was going up to the racetrack and save a lowlife from death. Or so I thought.

Thirty

I didn't think I was in any danger of becoming a detective. That much I knew as I drove up to Wewahitchka and the Dead Lakes Motor Speedway. I couldn't make sense out of anything. Ruby was killed at the Speedway and Nailor was working undercover for the DEA at the Speedway. There were drugs in Wannamaker's house. Wannamaker Lewis was dead and so was his daughter. There were millions of dollars up for grabs and only one person in the world in line for all of that money. Ruby's biological brother.

"What does a cop do?" I asked no one in particular. "I'll tell you: They ask questions. They ask everybody questions. So that's what I'm gonna do. I'm gonna ask everybody questions, starting with Roy Dell and Mickey Rhodes and ending," I said as I turned into the track drive, "with that little brunette in the front office!"

I pulled the Camaro up to the gate. It was locked. There was no way to drive around it, so from this point on I was gonna have to hoof it.

"Bet cops don't walk," I muttered. "Cops would flash a search warrant and the gate would just automatically open!" I slammed the car door shut and started walking.

"It can't be Roy Dell," I said aloud. "He's Raydean's

nephew. He wasn't adopted. So who else do I have on the list? Who else was at both scenes?" I let my voice die off, because now I knew. I knew who had motive and opportunity. I only needed confirmation. My stomach tightened. I had to play this one real smart or I'd end up real dead. He'd loosened the lug nuts on my car. He tried running me off the road. He'd attacked me outside the club. He'd been there every time something bad had happened.

As I crossed the track and started down into the pit, the sound of revving engines got louder. Whatever Roy Dell's early warning system was, it didn't seem to be ringing any alarms at my appearance. In fact, aside from a stray catcall or two, I proceeded unnoticed to Roy Dell's garage.

The yellow Vega was resting on jacks, its rear wheels missing and its mouth wide open. There wasn't a soul in sight. I slipped around past the car and headed for the flimsy metal garage that served as Roy Dell's worksite. Something didn't seem right. This was just too easy.

The entrance to the garage, a sliding metal door, was almost completely shut, the interior darkened. No sound came from the inside. I looked over my shoulder, making sure no one saw me, and pushed the door open just wide enough to slip inside. Big mistake.

As I stood in the darkness, waiting for my eyes to adjust I realized I was not alone. Somewhere in the dimly lit garage someone else was breathing.

"Roy Dell?" No answer. I took a step farther into the building. "Roy Dell, is that you?" Nothing.

I was beginning to see things, shapes and lumps of machinery. I stepped back toward the door and pulled it open, just enough for a shaft of midafternoon sunlight to stream through. The light fell on two bodies sprawled out on the floor at the far end of the building. Naked.

My worst personal nightmare had come to reality. Roy

Dell Parks and his wife Lulu lay clumped together, their arms resting on significant body parts, smiling in their post-nookie slumber. A bottle of tequila lay empty at their sides.

"Oh, God!" I cried. I couldn't help myself.

Lulu roused herself enough to open one puffy eyelid and give me the once-over.

"Where's Frank?" I asked, keeping my voice low so Roy Dell wouldn't hear us.

Lulu appeared confused for a moment, then caught sight of her husband and started to smile.

"Roy Dell fought for my honor," she said, and a smug look crept over her features. "He applied his impact wrench to Frank's private jewels. It was all I could do to get him to turn loose of the boy." Lulu shook her head. "He oughta be able to use it again, once the swelling goes down, but they had to take him over to the hospital. He needed a little something for the pain."

Lulu leaned against Roy Dell and fell back to sleep, which in my opinion was a good thing, considering my last dealings with her were at the business end of a shotgun.

I walked back out into the sunlight, blinking and knowing the vision of the two of them would stay stuck with me for perhaps a lifetime.

"A cop would think logically at this juncture," I said to myself. "A cop would say, 'Don't think about all that nakedness. The world is a horrible place, full of horrible sights. Focus instead on the case at hand.'"

I stepped out into the pit lane and started checking out the other racing crews. It was long past lunchtime and the smell of grilled onions and frying meat filled the air as the snack shack catered to its carnivorous customers. I hadn't eaten all day, but the smell mingled with the memory of the last hamburger I'd eaten at that shack, the night Ruby was killed, and somehow my appetite faded.

"Just ask a few questions," I reminded myself. And I would've too, had I not looked back up toward the gate and seen an ominous sight. Detective Wheeling and five uniformed police officers dressed out in SWAT gear.

There was no way to run back and warn Roy Dell. And after seeing the look on Wheeling's face, I didn't think I wanted to see him, either. Instead I ducked around the side of the snack shack and remembered my other mission. A little chat with a certain brunette.

"I'm gonna enjoy this," I said to myself, and headed up the metal fire escape.

A blast of cold air hit me as I stepped into the tiny reception area. My feet sank down into the plush carpeting and the world of racing went from dirt track to high-dollar concrete.

"I don't give a shit," a man's voice yelled, coming from the brunette's office. "I'm telling you how it is and how it's gonna be. Do them the way I tell you." It sounded like the urbane Mickey Rhodes was losing his super-slick cool.

"All I'm telling you is, I'm certified in bookkeeping and it ain't right!" My quarry was defending her mental skills, not the first thing I would've expected from her. A moral stance. Go figure.

"I pay you to do as I say!" he yelled.

"You know," she said, her voice almost as loud as his, "if I hadn't just known for a fact that amount was wrong, your account would've shown even more of a loss than there really is! You'd think you'd be grateful I found the money!"

"It ain't found money," he screeched. "That figure's wrong!"

"One of us is dumber'n hell," she said, "and it ain't me! We've got creditors calling and people we ain't paid in months. Here I go and find money and you insist it ain't really there! Now what the hell kind of businessman are you?"

A money-laundering businessman, I thought. A hide-from-the-government businessman. Just the type John Nailor would take an interest in. I slipped a little farther down the hallway and into one of the offices. Mickey's office.

They were still arguing, the voices louder now that I was closer. I stood in Mickey's office, half listening and half curious about my surroundings. If Mickey was in money trouble, it didn't show here. Leather couch, cherry-wood desk, Oriental rug on the floor over of the thick carpeting. The man had taste, even if he did run a sleazeball dirt track.

"You are being insubordinate!" Mickey thundered.

The brunette wasn't fazed. "Well, I got a sister that works at the police department and she'll tell you that I could have you arrested for verbal assault right now!"

That brought him up short. "I ain't assaulting you! Now, look, this here's a misunderstanding. Let's just drop it. It's late and past time for you to go anyhow."

"Well, it'll be no different tomorrow," she huffed.

"Probably not," he admitted. "What's she do there?"

The voices were coming closer, as if they were out in the hallway. I looked around for a place to hide, my heart beating so loud it almost drowned out their voices. Louvered doors took up one entire side of the room.

"Please, God, be a giant closet," I whispered and ran to duck inside.

"She works patrol," I heard her say. "Third shift. She has to do it that way on account of nepotism."

"Nepotism?" Mickey's voice squeaked with anxiety.

"Yeah, our daddy's the assistant chief."

I heard a sigh, but the sigh was altogether too close to my left shoulder. It couldn't have been Mickey who sighed. A thick hand wrapped itself around my mouth, while another one grabbed my waist, pinning my arms and pulling me down.

"Don't move. Don't do anything but breathe or I'll have to hurt you," the voice whispered. Meatloaf. His breath smelled of fried onions. He pulled me back against the wall of the pitch-black closet, and we slowly slid down until we were sitting on a metal case.

I must've started as my thighs connected with the cold metal, or maybe it was just that I was scared shitless, but he took that as a bad sign. Instantly his fingers pinched my nose shut while the other fingers covered my mouth. I couldn't breathe.

"Struggle and you'll pass out quicker," he whispered. "Sit absolutely still and I'll let you breathe." I froze, my ears ringing, my lungs heaving for air. He took his fingers away from my nose and I sucked in stale closet air.

Mickey had walked into his office and from the sound of it was punching out numbers on the phone.

"Hey," he said, "it's me. No! No! I ain't got the money. We're going ahead anyway." He paused, listening. "I don't give a shit about that!" he said. "I'm on the verge of being wealthy. This is gonna be piss-ant chump change a month from now." More silence. The man who held me tightened his grip as he listened. "This is the last of it tonight, you hear me?" Mickey said. "I don't want to hear it! I got problems of my own. Just bring the shit and I'll take care of it. I'm good for the money, you can take that to the bank."

The phone slammed down and Mickey sighed. "Oh, God! 'The assistant chief is my daddy,'" he mimicked. "Man, just when you think it's your turn to ride, somebody goes and steals the pony!"

The closet was getting hotter by the second, as well as smelly with fried onions and the scent of dead ashes. I tried to hold it back, I really did. But between the tickle of the hand just under my nose and the smell, well, the sneeze came blowing out. It wasn't loud, just a tiny snarf, actually, but it was enough.

Mickey quit talking to himself and a drawer slid open. It

was impossible to hear him coming, but my captor knew it was happening. He pushed up, standing with me as a human shield. And when the closet door flung open, I was the Kevlar vest between Mickey's huge cannon of a gun and the man behind me.

"Aw, I hate this," Mickey said. He leveled the gun and pointed it straight at my heart.

I felt Meatloaf's strong arm shove me aside with a force that sent me reeling and heard a grenade explode in the space of air where my head had been. I went sliding sideways as a force of nature blew past me and out of the closet. Meatloaf and Mickey went down in a tangle of black satin and blue jeans, rolling around on the floor like a World Federation Wrestling match.

I couldn't tell what happened to Mickey's gun. From the way the two men were brawling, it could've been anywhere. Meatloaf's head was soaked in blood, and he seemed to be on the losing end of the battle, a surprise since he was a foot taller and probably eighty pounds heavier.

As I watched, the gun reemerged in Mickey's hand. He was going to kill Meatloaf.

"No! No! No!" I reached in my pants pocket and pulled out the Spyderco, flicking it open on the first try. Neither man heard me, but Mickey felt me as I jumped on his back, grabbing for a hunk of hair.

I was moving fast, so when Mickey's toupee came off in my hand, I had to wonder if maybe I'd scalped him by accident. Then I pressed the cold steel tip of the blade against his cheek and grabbed the collar of his racing jacket.

"Drop it or I cut your fucking jugular!" I screamed.

The gun fell to the ground beside him, only to have Meatloaf roll over and grab it.

"Don't start with me," I demanded, "or I'll cut this bastard and come after you!"

To add to the general pandemonium, there was a loud buzzing noise that filled the room and set the building to vibrating. The door to the front office slammed back against the wall of the reception room, and the hallway was filled with black-booted, camouflaged SWAT team members, with Detective Wheeling standing right in front. The buzzing noise was so loud now I could hardly hear him yell. "Freeze! Drop your weapons! Now!"

Meatloaf and I just stared at him. "You mean me?" we both said.

For a brief second, it was a standoff. The buzzing noise stopped, and from overhead a I could hear footsteps running across the roof.

"Did you call them?" Wheeling asked Meatloaf.

"No, did you?" he answered, dropping his arm to his side.

I still held my knife up to Mickey's throat. The pieces were in place for me. I glanced back at the closet for a second, just to make sure.

"Oh, shit," Wheeling said, sighing. "I bet Terrance did."

There was the clatter of more feet running down the hallway and a woman, dressed in dark navy-blue pants and a navy-blue windbreaker with a huge DEA logo, pushed her way into the room, a black gun in her hand and the same little sneer she always wore covering her face. Carla Terrance.

"I'll take over here," she said.

"The fuck you will," Wheeling answered, his gun still trained on Mickey Rhodes.

"Over my very dead ass," I added.

"My pleasure," she said.

Meatloaf was the only one who seemed not to have a vested interest in who got Mickey. He walked away, positioning himself next to Wheeling.

"DEA had jurisdiction over this loser," she said. "He's part of one of our operations. Drug dealing and money laundering."

Wheeling didn't say anything.

"Yeah, well, him and me," I said, nodding toward Wheeling, "want him for murder."

Wheeling's eyebrow went up slightly and his mustache twitched. The asshole thought I was being cute.

"See that burnt-up safe in the closet?" I said to Wheeling. "It's from Wannamaker Lewis's house, I guarantee. I bet his will's in it." Mickey moaned. "He killed Wannamaker and he killed Ruby. Ruby was his sister, wasn't she, asshole, or should we be calling you Michael?" That's when the knife slipped a little and nicked Mickey's neck. Nobody moved.

"Wannamaker was your father, huh?" I said, the knife caressing Mickey's cheek, leaving a thin red line of blood.

"Somebody stop her!" he screamed.

"I was thinking you might answer her question, smart ass," said Wheeling. "Then we might address your problem."

"Yes," he groaned. "I did it!"

There was a moment there where I knew what it felt like to decide to take a life, but my Catholic training took over. Sister Mary Magdaline would've been disappointed.

"You want me to cuff him, boss?" Meatloaf said.

Wheeling smiled. "Sure, bud."

"Wait," I cried, "you can't let him do that! How do you know he's not in with him? He's got a criminal record a mile long!"

Meatloaf and Wheeling exchanged a look, and Meatloaf chuckled.

"Ain't computers great?" he said.

"Sierra," Wheeling said softly, "he works for us, kind of part-time. He's a narc."

Meatloaf gingerly stepped up to where I stood with the

knife still clutched in my hand, still touching Mickey's cheek. He smiled at me. "Can I have him, Sierra?"

"Where're your cuffs?" I asked, not willing to give him up without security, even though Mickey would've had to go through over ten armed DEA and SWAT team members to leave.

Meatloaf dangled them in front of me. "Police auxiliary," he said. "Always prepared."

I took the knife away slowly, folded it, and put it in my pocket.

"Are you just going to let her do that?" Carla screeched.

"Absolutely," Wheeling smiled. "She's police auxiliary, too."

"No, she's not!" Carla wasn't having any of it, but then, neither was Wheeling.

"Try me," he said. "You may have my partner's balls in a sling, but you're nothing to me. I don't owe you a thing."

"I'll have him in my custody before the day's out," she huffed, watching one of Wheeling's men lead Mickey away.

"Maybe," he said. "Maybe not."

Then he looked over at me, the mustache twitching to beat the band, his face held as stiff as ever, but just barely.

"Let's go see about my partner," he said, crooking his elbow.

We left Carla sputtering and walked out onto the fire escape. Detective Wheeling looked over at me, his eyebrow raised speculatively.

"Okay," he said, "the DEA's been camped out on Rhodes's doorstep for months, watching his money-laundering operation. I've been here investigating a murder. How come you, a"—he struggled for a moment—"an amateur, could figure out that Rhodes killed your friend and her father?"

I leaned against the railing and watched the action on the ground below. Mickey was being searched, a small crowd of drivers and mechanics gathering to watch, incredulous looks on all their faces.

"I wasn't sure," I said. "But I knew that Ruby and Wannamaker were killed for a reason, and the only link was the missing brother, Michael. After Wannamaker was killed, I knew money was the motive. The killer had to be somebody who needed or wanted money badly enough to kill for it. I nosed around until I figured out who it was. Mickey was at both murder scenes. Looking back on it, he was at the club the night I got beat up." Wheeling looked surprised. "I didn't tell you about that one," I said. "Mickey owed everybody money. Hearing him say on the phone that he'd be coming into money confirmed it for me. Tripping over his safe, now, that was a giveaway."

Detective Wheeling's mustache jerked. He shook his head and led me down the steps.

"Mind if I catch a ride with you?" he asked. "It isn't everyday I ride with a good-looking detective. Most of the time, I gotta ride with ugly cusses, like your boyfriend."

We drove back toward Panama City. Ahead of us was the squad car carrying Michael, a.k.a, Mickey Rhodes. Behind my Camaro were five Panama City police cars, lights flashing and sirens wailing. Not because they needed them, but simply because they could. That's Panama City. We may be small, but we're living large.

Thirty-one

*W*e pulled up onto my parking pad and I cut the engine. The sun was beginning to set, and the early evening sky washed the silver trailers with color.

"I guess you got a lot to take up with him, huh?" I said. "But just so you know, he's not feeling too well."

Detective Wheeling looked over at me. "You don't have to worry. I think I know why he did it, and I'm not going to bust his chops about it."

"Why, then?"

Wheeling looked down at his lap, his hands twitching a little as he debated what to say.

"Sierra, I'm thinking you might be around for a while," he said. "I'm thinking you might be trustworthy with this, but God knows, I don't want this getting out." He took a deep breath and looked away. "Awhile back, I had an affair with a patrol officer. It's not something I'm proud of, but it happens. I could tell you it was the hours or the work, but that would just be crap. I had an affair. It almost cost me my family, and if anyone in the department had known, it would've cost me my job. Still could."

I reached over and put my hand on his arm, but I don't think he was even aware.

"When I saw her sister coming out of the racetrack office

a while back, I knew. John didn't want to risk me getting involved. And I hate to say it but I'm pretty sure Carla knew about it, too. The police department's a small place, and back when I was seeing Suzi, Carla was working third."

"You think she'd hold that over John's head?" The woman was lower than I thought.

"You don't know her," Wheeling said, "she's got a one-track mind for the job. She'd use whatever leverage she had to pull John into the investigation, even if it meant threatening his partner or forcing him to lie to his chief. Loyalty doesn't matter to her. She wanted to crack that money-laundering operation. It didn't matter what it took to do it. The job is everything. That's what broke her and John up." He looked at me. "So that's that, all right? Stays between you and me, okay?"

"Deal," I said. "Let's go see your partner."

The trailer was rocking when we stepped inside. Ma, Al, Arlen, Raydean, and Vincent Gambuzzo all sat around the kitchen table, the remains of lunch scattered across the countertops. A ferocious card game was in progress, and Pa's gallon jug of Chianti was almost empty. Even Al was smiling, a large pile of poker chips sitting next to his empty tumbler.

"Youse gonna ante up, or what?" he demanded of his tablemates.

Raydean threw in a red chip and cried, "Hit me, big man! One card!"

Arlen hooted and folded his cards. Ma sighed and threw in a blue chip.

"Give me four," she said.

It was gonna be a long night.

Raydean spotted me first, about the same time Fluffy came prancing in from the back.

"He must be better, huh?" I asked, hoping they hadn't forgotten their patient.

"Get out them track shoes, girlie," Raydean cried. "The fever broke and he's asking for food!"

"Yeah," Al said, "but these two loaded him up on the vino as an extra precaution. The guy's probably floating on the ceiling by now!"

I looked over at Fluff for a report. "He doing better?" I asked.

Fluffy yapped once and went over to the game. She hopped up in Al's lap, never one to go for the underdog, and appeared to be reading his cards.

"You go on," Wheeling said. "I'll wait."

I wanted to go, worse than anything, but he'd been right, he had the longer relationship, and right now that needed attention.

"At the end of the hall," I said, giving him a push. "You go. I'll wait."

"Thanks, Sierra." He walked off and I watched him for a moment, his back stiff, his hands at his side.

I stepped out onto the back stoop, the card players oblivious to my leaving, all except for Fluffy, who followed and curled up in my lap when I sat down on the top step.

"Hey," I said softly, looking up at the clouds, "I don't know if you can hear me, but if you can, I want you to know I made it square for you. I got him."

There was no answer, just a soft breeze blowing across the grass and the first firefly of the evening dancing above my gardenia bush.

Fluffy settled a little closer into my lap. "I don't know what it's like, dancing with the angels," I whispered, "but I gotta believe you're teaching 'em a trick or two." A tear slid down my cheek and I buried my face in Fluffy's soft hide.

The door creaked open and John Nailor stood framed in the doorway. Wheeling was supporting him, but not by much.

"Is the seat next to you taken?" he asked. He made his

way to the railing and slowly sank down beside me. Wheeling vanished back inside, the door closing softly but firmly behind him.

"Hey," he whispered. "You lied to me. You left for that track like I told you not to do."

I shrugged, tears running down my cheeks.

"Well, I had to call Wheeling to back you up. I figured you might get in over your head."

"I was doing all right," I muttered.

"Yeah, you and that knife." He laughed softly, then let his hand rest softly on my thigh. "You're thinking about Ruby, huh?"

I nodded, the tears closing off my throat.

"Come here." With his good arm he pulled me close, wrapping his arm around my shoulder. "Put your head down, right there."

We sat for a few minutes, with no sound but the crickets whining in the heat. Then he began to sing, very softly at first, and then loudly enough for me to recognize the tune and join in.

"I'll fly away, oh Glory, I'll fly away. When I die, Hallelujah, by and by. I'll fly away . . ."

We sat there singing, my head on his shoulder and his arm around me, tears sliding down my cheeks until the song was finished and the sky had turned to darkness. Then I heard his voice, speaking this time.

"I'll keep an eye on her down here," he said.

And then he pulled me toward him. "Let's go in there and show 'em what a couple of real card players can do," he said.

I took one last look up at the sky and saw the first star of the night pop out.

"Yeah," I said, "this oughta be something to see. You beating the house with one hand tied behind your back."

"Ah," he sighed, "but you haven't seen what that hand can do!"

The door opened, and the sound of laughter floated out into the night.

"All right, hot stuff," I said, "let's see the one-armed man produce."

He was looking over at me, smiling that smile I knew only too well.

"Oh, I'll produce, all right. Question is, can you handle it when I do?"

Right there, in front of Al and Ma and the entire table full of card players, John Nailor kissed me. It was long and slow and left no doubt that we had unfinished business. But that was all right, 'cause Sierra Lavotini, the Queen of Unfinished Business, was on the case. And if John Nailor was looking to start something, I was just the woman to finish it.